"Would you like to come in?"

"Very much," he answered.

"But you're not going to."

He shook his head.

"Why not?"

Because it was wrong—more so than the first time, not as much as the second, but still wrong. Because, in spite of her assurances, he wasn't sure what her expectations were. Hell, he wasn't sure what *his* expectations were. Because they were a great match for a one-night stand, but neither of them brought much hope to the success of anything more.

And because he liked her, honestly liked her, and though he didn't know what he wanted from her, he did know one thing for sure: he didn't want to hurt her. She'd gotten enough of that for a lifetime.

Dear Reader,

July is a sizzling month both outside *and* in, and once again we've rounded up six exciting titles to keep your temperature rising. It all starts with the latest addition to Marilyn Pappano's HEARTBREAK CANYON miniseries, *Lawman's Redemption,* in which a brooding man needs help connecting with the lonely young girl who just might be his daughter—and he finds it in the form of a woman with similar scars in her romantic past. Don't miss this emotional, suspenseful read.

Eileen Wilks provides the next installment in our twelve-book miniseries, ROMANCING THE CROWN, with *Her Lord Protector.* Fireworks ensue when a Montebellan lord has to investigate a beautiful commoner who may be a friend—or a foe!—of the royal family. This miniseries just gets more and more intriguing. And Kathleen Creighton finishes up her latest installment of her INTO THE HEARTLAND miniseries with *The Black Sheep's Baby.* A freewheeling photojournalist who left town years ago returns— with a little pink bundle strapped to his chest, and a beautiful attorney in hot pursuit. In Marilyn Tracy's *Cowboy Under Cover,* a grief-stricken widow who has set up a haven for children in need of rescue finds herself with that same need—and her rescuer is a handsome federal marshal posing as a cowboy. Nina Bruhns is back with *Sweet Revenge,* the story of a straitlaced woman posing as her wild identical twin—and now missing—sister to learn of her fate, who in the process hooks up with the seductive detective who is also searching for her. And in *Bachelor in Blue Jeans* by Lauren Nichols, during a bachelor auction, a woman inexplicably bids on the man who once spurned her, and wins—or does she? This reunion romance will break your heart.

So get a cold drink, sit down, put your feet up and enjoy them all— and don't forget to come back next month for more of the most exciting romance reading around…only in Silhouette Intimate Moments.

Yours,

Leslie J. Wainger
Executive Senior Editor

Please address questions and book requests to:
Silhouette Reader Service
U.S.: 3010 Walden Ave., P.O. Box 1325, Buffalo, NY 14269
Canadian: P.O. Box 609, Fort Erie, Ont. L2A 5X3

Lawman's Redemption

MARILYN PAPPANO

Silhouette®

INTIMATE MOMENTS™

Published by Silhouette Books

America's Publisher of Contemporary Romance

SILHOUETTE BOOKS

ISBN 0-373-27229-4

LAWMAN'S REDEMPTION

Copyright © 2002 by Marilyn Pappano

Books by Marilyn Pappano

Silhouette Intimate Moments

Within Reach #182
The Lights of Home #214
Guilt by Association #233
Cody Daniels' Return #258
Room at the Inn #268
Something of Heaven #294
Somebody's Baby #310
Not Without Honor #338
Safe Haven #363
A Dangerous Man #381
Probable Cause #405
Operation Homefront #424
Somebody's Lady #437
No Retreat #469
Memories of Laura #486
Sweet Annie's Pass #512
Finally a Father #542
*Michael's Gift #583

*Regarding Remy #609
*A Man Like Smith #626
Survive the Night #703
Discovered: Daddy #746
*Convincing Jamey #812
*The Taming of Reid Donovan #824
*Knight Errant #836
The Overnight Alibi #848
Murphy's Law #901
†Cattleman's Promise #925
†The Horseman's Bride #957
†Rogue's Reform #1003
Who Do You Love? #1033
  "A Little Bit Dangerous"
My Secret Valentine #1053
†The Sheriff's Surrender #1069
The Princess and the Mercenary #1130
†Lawman's Redemption #1159

Silhouette Special Edition

Older, Wiser...Pregnant #1200
The Truth About Tate #1425

*Southern Knights
†Heartbreak Canyon

Silhouette Books

Silhouette Christmas Stories 1989
"The Greatest Gift"

Silhouette Summer Sizzlers 1991
"Loving Abby"

36 Hours
You Must Remember This

MARILYN PAPPANO

brings impeccable credentials to her career—a lifelong habit of gazing out windows, not paying attention in class, daydreaming and spinning tales for her own entertainment. The sale of her first book proved that she wasn't crazy but creative. Since then she's sold more than forty books to various publishers and even a film production company.

In winter she stays inside with her husband and their four dogs, and in summer she spends her free time mowing the yard and daydreams about grass that never gets taller than two inches.

You can write to her at P.O. Box 643, Sapulpa, OK, 74067-0643.

Chapter 1

The first time Brady Marshall ever saw Hallie Madison, he picked her up in a bar, took her back to her motel and spent most of the night having amazing sex with her.

The second time was in church.

In a wedding.

Thank God, not as the bride.

He stood at the front of the First Baptist Church of Heartbreak, Oklahoma, with Jace Barnett, the best man, and Reese Barnett, the groom, on his right and Del, Reese's father, on his left. As the organist played a slow processional, he gazed out over a full church and watched the bride's attendants come up the aisle. First were Emma and Elly Harris, wearing matching dresses and scattering baskets of petals. A few yards behind them was the first bridesmaid—a petite china doll with silvery-brown hair cut as short as a boy's...though with those delicate features, no one would ever mistake her for one.

Bringing up the rear was the maid of honor. She was of average height, athletic looking, her also-short hair also silvery-brown. Despite her lack of curves, no one would ever mistake her for a boy, either—but neither would they figure her for a private investigator, which she was.

And in the middle was Hallie. His mystery woman from two nights ago. She hadn't offered her name or asked for his, and he'd been satisfied not knowing. He should have asked. Even if he'd known she was sister and soon-to-be sister-in-law to his best friends, he still might have gone to the motel with her…but he wouldn't risk money on it. Most likely, if he'd known, he would have high-tailed it out of that bar and spent the night regretting what he hadn't done.

Better than spending his time regretting what he had done.

Hallie was about five foot eight and slender, but with curves in all the right places. Her hair was silky and blond and past her shoulders, her eyes were hazel—he hadn't realized he knew that until just now—and her smile was bright and cheery, but anyone who looked closely could see the tension underlying it. For whatever reason, this wasn't a great time for her, but she was doing her best to hide it for her sisters' sake.

There they were—the Madison sisters. He'd heard a lot about them from their oldest sister, Neely. There was Kylie the pretty one, Hallie the popular one and Bailey the smart one. If Hallie made a habit of doing what she'd done with him two nights ago, he could understand why she was popular.

But he didn't think she did. Maybe his ego needed to think that he'd been special, though he knew too well that wasn't true. While Hallie might not routinely pick up sex partners in bars, he did, and he knew special had nothing to do with it. Being lonely did. And alone. Not interested in a relationship. Not able to connect with people except in the most superficial way.

The bridesmaids took their place opposite the groomsmen, and the organ music swelled as Neely appeared at the back of the church, putting the other women out of his mind. Her ivory gown was all lace and satin, sleeveless with a deep V, and a stream of lace was attached to a band of flowers worn in her hair. She was more beautiful than anyone he'd ever seen. She was the only woman he'd had any sort of relationship with in the past fourteen years, and he'd been half in love with her ever since they'd met. Not that he'd ever expected or even wanted anything to come of it. Neely belonged to Reese, heart and soul.

Lucky guy.

When she reached the front, the guests took their seats and the wedding party turned to face the minister. Brady's one and only wedding seventeen years ago had been nothing like this. He and Sandra had gone to the county courthouse one Friday afternoon and been married by a judge in a hurry to get to his golf game. He'd worn jeans and a white shirt, and Sandra had worn a flowery dress with a big white collar edged with crimson ribbon.

Funny that he could remember that, but couldn't quite recall her face. He could see the curly brown hair, he could even call up the memory of sliding a plain gold band on her finger, but he couldn't see her eighteen-year-old face.

Of course, he'd spent fourteen years trying to forget everything about her. He'd been a fool to marry her. The good times hadn't come close to balancing out the bad, and in the final months, there had been some really bad times.

Between all the people and the candles that flickered everywhere, the church was a little warm. The reception afterward wasn't bound to be much better, since it was going to be outside and Oklahoma in August wasn't hospitable. But for wedding cake, cold drinks and dancing, people would forget the heat.

For their friends, they would forget anything.

Finally the pastor came to the part they'd all been waiting for. "You may now kiss the bride," he announced, and Reese took him at his word. Amid laughter and clapping, he sealed the promises he'd just made with a kiss, then, prompted by the organ music, escorted his bride to the back of the church.

Too bad Brady had been called out last night and missed the rehearsal. If he'd made it, he would have been better prepared for walking down the aisle with Hallie Madison in front of every soul he knew in Oklahoma. Not that he really needed preparation. No one would get the slightest hint from him how intimately he knew her.

Jace hooked up with Bailey and followed the bride and groom, leaving Brady and Hallie facing each other. He wasn't sure when she'd recognized him—he hadn't caught her looking at him when she'd come down the aisle—but obviously at some point she had. There was no surprise in her eyes—just a sheepish, faintly embarrassed look.

They met in the center of the aisle and he offered his arm. When she slipped her hand through and rested it on his forearm, they started down the aisle.

"Fancy meeting you here," he murmured.

"I bet you thought you were never going to see me again," she whispered while keeping her smile in place. "Sorry to disappoint you."

"Who's disappointed?" He should have known it was bound to happen. For fourteen years he'd allowed himself nothing more than one-night stands with strangers. The odds that he could continue forever without running into one of those women again had been growing slimmer. Now he just had to make the best of it. It shouldn't be hard. Neely and Reese were leaving on their honeymoon after the reception that night, and all the Madisons would be going home the next day—Kylie back home to Texas, Bailey to Tennessee, their mother to Illinois and Hallie to…wherever.

How had he learned where home was for the rest of her family, but missed that bit about her?

"I-I'd appreciate it if you don't say anything to Neely about…"

He fixed a steady gaze on her. "Do I look like the sort of man who would share the details of his sex life with anyone?"

"No," she murmured.

They reached the back of the sanctuary, then moved down two steps into the foyer. As soon as Del and Kylie joined them, an usher closed the doors, Reese immediately kissed Neely again, and Hallie pulled away. She clasped her hands together and looked everywhere except at him. "I…uh…" An expression of great relief crossed her face when Neely joined them.

"So you two have met," Neely said, hugging her sister before rising onto her toes to brush a kiss to Brady's cheek. "Isn't he gorgeous?" she asked, beaming as she wiped the lipstick from his skin. "But don't get any ideas, Hallie. I've got plans for him and Kylie."

The warning created a panicked look in Hallie's eyes as she glanced from Neely to him to her younger sister. Brady wished he could tell her not to worry. Neely might intend to hook him up with Kylie, but he had no intention of letting her set the hook. He wasn't interested in the baby of the Madison family. He damn sure wasn't interested in anyone who lived in Texas.

"I've been fresh out of ideas of that nature for about six months now," Hallie said, fooling her sister with her careless manner but not Brady. He wondered what had happened six months ago that had turned her off romantic entanglements and most likely put that stress in her eyes. Obviously, she'd been hurt, and more than likely he'd heard something about it from Neely. Damned if he could remember, though.

"Oh, you'll get over it," Neely said, then thoughtlessly added, "You always do. Brady, come on and let me introduce you to Kylie. She is such a doll."

Brady let her pull him down the hall, where she left him while she went to retrieve Kylie from her conversation with Reese and Jace. "Such a doll" was about as accurate as a description could get. Even her voice had a little-girl quality to it. He wasn't sure how old she was—probably somewhere between twenty-five and thirty—but she looked about sixteen. There was no way he could even think about doing anything with her without feeling as if he were committing some statutory offense. But he talked to her, and then to Bailey—or, at least, he listened to them. Like Neely, neither of them appeared to be the least bit shy.

And what about Hallie? She was hugging the wall as if she'd rather be anyplace else. Shy? Or uncomfortable because of him? There had been nothing shy about the way she'd approached him in the bar Thursday night. But then, he knew better than most that the way people behaved in bars could be very different from their usual manner. He'd broken up more than his share of bar brawls started by some normally shy woman or unassuming man.

After a few minutes, the usher opened the doors to the sanctuary again. While they'd been waiting in the foyer, the guests had left the church through a side door and moved to the pavilion in the park across the street where the reception would be held. Now the sanctuary was empty for photographs.

It seemed the picture-taking took longer than the ceremony had, but finally they were finished. He was wondering what kind of luck he would have slipping out the door and heading home when Reese clapped him on the back. "Don't even think about it."

"About what?" Brady asked, keeping his expression bland.

"Going home. Not before Neely gets a dance with you."

"The thought never crossed my mind," Brady lied.

"Yeah, right. I know being social isn't your favorite thing. You'd rather be home alone watching TV with a pizza and a beer."

Brady shrugged, then quietly said, "Well, you did it."

Reese glanced at Neely, coming their way, and smiled a satisfied smile. "Yeah. I did. Who knows? Maybe you'll be next."

"No, thanks. Been there, done that."

And had the scars to prove it.

When Neely had told her they were having their reception outside, Hallie envisioned a setting similar to the parties she'd held back home in Beverly Hills—the pool sparkling in the night, the lush gardens perfuming the air, acres of emerald-green grass and uniformed servers attentive to the guests' every need.

The scene surrounding her was quite different. They were in a park that was basically one square block with a pavilion in the center. Lights had been strung from tree to tree and around the canopies circling the pavilion, and a band had set up on a stage nearby. The grass was parched from Oklahoma's typical hot summer with too little rain, and the only servers were keeping the occasional fly away from the cake and the small hands out of the grown-ups' punch.

But this party had something hers never had—a sense of joy. Real affection and friendship. A warm sense of home.

Her sister had landed herself in the midst of some very nice people. Hallie had gotten introductions to plenty of them after the cake was cut, and she thought she'd kept them pretty straight in her mind. Over the next few weeks she would have a chance to find out.

After taking a bottled water from a tub of ice near the punch table, she found a place to lean against the massive trunk of an oak tree and watched the dancing in the pavilion. A couple of friendly young men had asked her to dance, but she'd politely refused. Kylie and Bailey weren't refusing any offers. They hadn't missed one tune in the past half hour. They had each danced once with Brady Marshall, and so had Neely.

When Hallie had peeked around the hallway before the ceremony started and spotted him standing with Reese and his family, she had practically swallowed her tongue. She'd tried to sound casual and merely curious when she'd returned to the classroom they were using for a dressing room and asked Neely about him, but with her face flushed and her voice breathy like Kylie's, she wasn't sure she'd pulled it off.

Neely hadn't told her much—just his name, that he would be the acting sheriff while she and Reese were gone and that he was a good friend. At the time Hallie had thought she was too distracted to say much else. Now she knew her sister had been saving the good stuff for Kylie.

Frankly, Hallie couldn't see him with Kylie.

Not that she cared. She'd sworn off men for the rest of her life, except for occasional flings. She was never getting serious, never getting married and for darn sure never getting divorced again. She couldn't survive it. And since love came with no guarantees, she wasn't giving it another try.

Though it seemed that Neely had gotten her guarantee. The way Reese looked at her—as if she were the most important person in his life, as if he were the luckiest guy in the world to have her—was enough to make Hallie's heart hurt. Had any man ever looked at her like that? No, not even the three she'd married.

And they'd divorced her. One because she refused to use the drugs he couldn't live without, one because she was a drag, and Max because she wasn't young enough. For heaven's sake, she'd just turned thirty the very day he'd told her that!

She was certainly being a drag tonight. She was happy for

Neely, truly she was, but there was a part of her that just wanted to go back to her motel and hide.

"You having a good time, baby?"

The voice was her mother's, and Hallie had only a moment to paste on a bright smile before facing her. "Yes, Mama, I am. How about you?"

"I couldn't be happier. Neely finally married." Doris Irene smiled. "We've come to expect weddings from you, but I'd just about given up hope Neely would ever settle down."

The muscles in Hallie's jaw clenched. Her mother didn't mean anything by her remark, just as Neely's comment at the church—*You'll get over it. You always do*—hadn't been meant to hurt, but that did nothing to ease the ache in her chest. She'd always been the Madison family screwup, the one who could never do anything right. Her family joked about it and treated her failures lightly, and she smiled when they did and played along, but failing again hurt. She'd loved Max Parker with all her heart, and she'd believed he loved her, too…right up to the time she found him celebrating her birthday with the star of his most recent movie. He'd broken her heart, but because he hadn't been the first—or even the second—her family assumed it was no big deal.

"Well," she began when she was sure her voice would be steady, "she's settled now. She and Reese are very happy together."

"They sure do look it." Doris Irene grinned slyly. "Maybe you can take some pointers from them." Then she leaned over and kissed Hallie's cheek. "I think I'll go find William and see if I can get him to dance with me. I haven't kicked up my heels in far too long. See you, baby."

Though she tried her best not to swear, once her mother was out of sight, Hallie muttered, "Damn, damn, damn."

"Careful there." The words were delivered in a low, throaty, lazy drawl from behind her. "Oklahoma's got a law on the books against swearing in public. I'd hate to have to take you away from Neely and Reese's party in handcuffs."

She turned to find Brady Marshall leaning one shoulder against her tree trunk. Like the other groomsmen, he'd changed out of his tuxedo, and he looked even better in his jeans and a black shirt than he had in the bar the other night. When she'd seen him sitting there alone, she'd been speechless for a moment. He was quite possibly the most handsome man she'd ever seen. He stood six-four, was lean and hard-muscled, and everything about him that night, like tonight, had been dark—from his hair and skin to his shirt, jeans and cowboy hat, to the aura surrounding him. He'd been the epitome of tall, dark and handsome…to say nothing of dangerous.

She'd spent ten minutes at the bar, watching him, speculating about him. Why was he there, and why was he alone? Was there a Mrs. Tall, Dark and Handsome, and if so, why did she let him out of the house without her protection? Finally she'd found the courage to take him a bottle of beer, and she'd seen that not everything about him was dark. His eyes were as blue as the clearest spring sky.

He'd looked incapable of smiling, of any tender emotions at all, but later, at the motel, he'd touched her tenderly. He'd made her feel…. She tilted her head to one side, considering that sentence. No, there wasn't anything missing. That was all she wanted to say. He'd made her feel.

Shaking off the memories, she forced her attention back to his remark. "You're kidding, right?"

Under the neat black mustache his finely shaped mouth was unsmiling, but there was something she thought might be humor in his voice. "Well, I wouldn't exactly hate it, but I don't think seeing me arrest their bridesmaid is exactly the sort of memory Neely and Reese want to take away tonight."

She made a face. "I meant about the law."

"No, ma'am, I don't kid about such things. It's punishable by thirty days in jail and a fine of up to $500." After a moment, he gestured toward the dance floor. "Why aren't you out there with your sisters?"

"I'd rather enjoy it from back here."

"You don't look like you're enjoying it much."

Drat him. Her sisters and her mother hadn't noticed that she was putting on an act. How had this man who didn't know her at all guessed it? But rather than try to find a response, she turned the subject back on him. "Why aren't you out there?"

"I ran out of Madison sisters to dance with."

She lowered her gaze to hide the fact that she would enjoy dancing with him. She already knew, both from watching him with her sisters and from the hours she'd spent with him, that his movements were graceful, sensual and powerfully controlled. She would very much like to feel his arms around her one more time, to let the heat radiating from his body warm her, to close her eyes and breathe deeply of his purely male scent and sway slowly in time to the music.

Sure, and when the dance was over and he walked away from her, what would she want then? How would she feel?

She was tired of men walking away from her, tired of never being enough for them.

"I take it you're not fond of weddings," Brady remarked.

"Or too fond of them, according to my family."

"They've come to expect weddings from you?"

Realizing he'd overheard her conversation with her mother, she managed a quavery, embarrassed smile. "We weren't properly introduced, were we?" She stuck out her hand. "Hi, I'm Hallie Madison, Neely's younger sister and three-time loser at the game of marriage."

She'd meant it as a bad joke, but before she could withdraw her hand, he'd taken it, enveloping it in his. His hands had fascinated her Thursday night—large, powerful, his fingers long and narrow, capable of calming a small child, controlling a grown man or arousing a needy woman. She had wondered if his palms were callused, his caresses rough, and decided they were, then he'd proved it in her room. His touch had been enough to make a lonely woman weep.

"Three times, huh?" he murmured, still holding her hand. "At least you kept trying. I gave up after the first one."

A flicker of something shadowed his eyes after he'd spoken. Surprise? Uneasiness? Did he know he'd told her more than the simple fact that he'd been married and divorced—that now she knew he must have been brokenhearted over the end of his marriage? With the shortage of marriageable men, it was a fact of life that men as handsome as he, as amazingly sexy as he, didn't remain single long, not unless the scars from their failed relationships ran too deep to heal.

"You learned from your mistake. I didn't." Though she would be perfectly content to stand there all night with her hand in his, she caught the looks that said people were starting to notice. Gently she tugged, and after a moment's hesitation, he let go. "What did you think of Kylie?"

"Truthfully?" He waited for her nod before he went on. "She's not my type."

"Nope, sorry, wrong answer. If Neely thinks you two are right for each other, then you are. She's never wrong."

Ignoring her disagreement, he pushed away from the tree. "Come and dance with me."

A shiver skittered through Hallie, making her face warm, her palms damp and her hands unsteady. "I don't think that would be a good idea."

"I think it's an excellent idea." He pulled the bottle of water from her hand and set it on a nearby table, then clasped her hand in his and started for the pavilion.

The music was slow and romantic, and the lights cast flickering shadows back and forth as they swayed in the breeze. For one fearful moment, she wished she could break free and run off into the night. He was too tempting. She was too emotionally fragile. Neely honestly wasn't ever wrong.

But, as if he sensed her skittishness, he held her hand tightly as he led the way to the middle of the dance floor. There he stopped and pulled her slowly into his arms, closer than was proper, practically as close as they'd been Thursday night.

It was an incredible place to be.

Hallie held back as much as she could. Occasionally she made eye contact with one sister or another, and once Doris Irene and her husband, William, waltzed past, and Hallie was convinced they were all wondering what Brady was doing with her instead of Kylie. When she caught a glimpse of Neely and Reese both watching them, she lowered her gaze to the center of Brady's chest and wished once again that she was someplace else.

"Relax," he murmured in her ear. "Surely you're used to people looking at you."

"Why do you say that?"

"Because you're a beautiful woman, and people tend to look at beautiful women."

Tilting her head back, Hallie met his gaze. "Okay, I get it. Your job tonight—besides acting as a groomsman—is keeping the newly divorced bridesmaid from ruining everyone's fun with her mood, right?"

He gazed down at her a long time. His blue eyes revealed nothing, but she had the sense that her words offended or irritated him. When he spoke, though, his tone was no different than before. "Trust me, I would be the last person in the county anyone would choose to entertain, flatter or even talk to anyone else."

"And why is that?"

While he considered an answer, the music ended and so did the dance. He didn't release her right away, but held her and looked at her and made her feel incredibly warm and tingly, until finally Del Barnett's voice quieted the crowd.

"Reese wanted to sneak out of here, but Neely says she's got three single sisters and she's not going without throwing her bouquet. So all you unmarried ladies gather around up here, and all you single men be prepared to run."

It seemed to Hallie that everyone was moving someplace except her and Brady. He was still just looking at her, and darned if she couldn't pull her gaze away from his.

Abruptly he let her go. "Go on."

"I'm not single."

"You're not married."

"No, I'm divorced. There's a difference."

"Not enough to count. Go on, or your sisters will create a scene."

Already she was dimly aware of Kylie and Bailey calling her name in unison. She looked at Brady, and he looked away, breaking the spell that held her. Without a word, she walked away and joined the group of women on the grass.

With her back to them, Neely gave the flowers a great toss, and they tumbled, stem over bloom, through the air straight at Hallie. She didn't raise her hands, didn't move, didn't do a thing. When Kylie reached across and grabbed them before they hit the ground, Hallie looked back to where she'd left Brady.

He was gone.

He was a cold-hearted bastard.

Brady stood in the shadow of a clump of trees where no light could reach and watched as Neely and Reese said goodbye to their families. Neely hugged her mother, then her sisters, starting with Bailey and ending with Hallie. She was the only blonde in a family of brunettes, but it was more than her hair color that set her apart. She was lonely. Wounded.

And he wanted to take advantage of that.

Farewells said, Neely and Reese got into the waiting limousine, and the driver slowly pulled away. They were spending the night in Tulsa, then catching an early flight to the Caribbean. There they would be taken by boat to an isolated island where one of Reese's friends from his pro baseball days was letting them use his beachfront estate. They weren't planning to come back for three weeks—unless she decided just to stay forever, Neely had threatened.

As the limo disappeared from sight, the wedding guests began heading back to their dancing, visiting and celebrating. Hallie talked to her sisters for a few minutes and got hugs from both of them. Kylie tried to give her the bridal bouquet—probably with a joke about Hallie's multiple marriages. Her family didn't appear to have a clue how three divorces had affected her.

After refusing the flowers, Hallie left her sisters and headed toward the church. She passed within ten feet of where he stood, so close he could smell her fragrance on the warm night air. She spoke politely to guests going the other way, then crossed the street to her car, a flashy little blue convertible.

He waited until she'd driven away to move out of the shadows. His truck was parked down the block and around the corner, but he didn't hurry. There was only one main road from Heartbreak to Buffalo Plains, and he knew where she was staying.

Plus, he needed time to talk himself out of what he wanted.

He was almost at his truck when a voice called, "Hey, Brady."

He knew before he turned it was Jace Barnett. He was a couple of years older than Brady, Reese's cousin and a detective with the Kansas City Police Department, and after Reese and Neely, he was the closest thing to a friend Brady had. "Jace."

"You heading off this early? You know a few dozen of these folks will be here until the early hours of the morning—including me."

"I'm not much on parties."

"Reese says you'll be acting sheriff while he's gone."

"Yeah." He'd never officially held the position—Reese wasn't in the habit of taking vacations—but he'd been in charge every other weekend for the past two years. He could handle it for three weeks. It wasn't as if Canyon County was likely to develop a rash of crimes the minute the sheriff left the state.

"Watch out," Jace said good-naturedly as Brady reached his truck. "Don't let the paperwork get to you."

Something had already gotten to him, Brady thought as he climbed in, and it wasn't work. He waved goodbye to Jace, then headed for Main Street.

It took five miles, and passing a half dozen cars, to catch up to the convertible with California tags. He got only close enough to be sure it was Hallie's car, then dropped back a fair distance.

He wasn't going to follow her to the motel, and there were a dozen reasons or more why. She was his boss's sister-in-law, and anyone knew you didn't mess with a man's family. He'd be better off home alone. She'd been hurt before. He would just be using her, and she'd been used enough.

When they reached the Buffalo Plains town limits, she headed into downtown, where a right turn would take her to her motel on the east side of town. After a moment's hesitation, he took the first right, onto Cedar Street, and drove the block and a half to his house.

Until two weeks ago, he'd spent his entire six years in Buffalo Plains in a six-hundred-square-foot apartment on the west end of town and had been satisfied there—satisfaction being relative, of course. Then one day while on patrol, he'd seen an old man hammering a For Sale sign in the yard that fronted a small neat house. He'd stopped to ask him about it and had driven away a half hour later with the keys in his pocket and a sales contract pending.

It wasn't a great house. It was sixty years old, one story, painted white with dark green trim. There was a front porch wide enough for a swing and a back stoop barely big enough for a man to stand on. Inside was a living room, a dining room and kitchen, one bedroom and bathroom, and an additional room he planned someday to incorporate into the living room. The floors were wood, with cracked and peeling linoleum in the kitchen, and the walls needed painting, the bathroom updating, the roof reshingling. He'd paid cash for it, and could have done the same for a house ten times its price, but he hadn't wanted a bigger, nicer place.

After all, he hadn't been buying a house but a memory.

One of the few childhood memories he recalled with fondness.

He pulled into the gravel driveway and parked next to his sheriff's department SUV, then shut off the engine. Nights were quiet in this part of town. The lots were several acres, the houses distant from each other, and behind them was pasture. Forty acres of it had come with the house, but the old man had leased it to a neighboring rancher, and Brady had continued the lease.

Someday, though, he planned to put up a barn and buy a few horses from Easy Rafferty, one of Reese's friends over in Heart-break who raised damn fine paints.

He went inside the dark, empty house, turned on the TV and settled on the sofa with a beer. Welcome to his usual Saturday night.

Most of the time he didn't care how alone he was. Hell, he'd been that way so long it had come to feel natural. Growing up, he and his kid brother, Logan, had pretty much been each other's best—and only—friends. They'd known other kids at school, of course, but they'd kept to themselves. It had seemed safer that way.

Then Logan had disappeared without a trace nearly seventeen years ago. Brady had gone to bed one night and Logan was there in the next room, and he'd awakened the next morning and his brother was gone. He'd taken his clothes and left a note, one line that had just about killed Brady.

He didn't let himself think about Logan very often, but tonight it somehow seemed appropriate. Where was he? Had he even survived the last seventeen years? Had he managed to make himself over into someone who could live a normal life, have friends, laugh, be happy? Had he ever married, had kids? Did he ever think about looking up his older brother?

Probably no more often than Brady thought about trying to find him. He had run a nationwide driver's license check a few years ago and come up with a number of Logan Marshalls, but none whose birth date matched his brother's. He'd even considered hiring a private investigator, but had discarded the idea. Logan had had his reasons for taking off the way he did. The least Brady could do was respect them.

He flipped through the channels, watched the clock and told himself that, barring any emergencies, he was home for the night. Bored with television, he went in and took a shower, then went into the bedroom to get a pair of boxers. He wasn't getting dressed, he told himself, even as he took a clean pair of Levi's from the closet, and he repeated it as he pulled a T-shirt from the dresser drawer. He absolutely wasn't going anywhere, he insisted as he picked up his wallet, pager and keys from the dresser, then started toward the front door.

He wasn't going to the motel.

Wasn't parking beside her Mercedes in the back lot.

Wasn't climbing the stairs.

Wasn't standing in front of Room 22.

He stood there, trying desperately to talk himself out of knocking. But damn it, being accustomed to being alone didn't mean it didn't eat at him sometimes. Some days the need for somebody got under his skin and damn near drove him mad until he'd satisfied it. That was what had sent him to the bar Thursday night—what had made him come back to the motel with Hallie. Usually that one night would have been enough to fill the emptiness that sometimes consumed him and would enable him to go back to his life for a few more months.

But this time, God help him, he wanted more, and Hallie Madison was the perfect person to give it. They'd already filled each other's needs once. He liked her, and she... He didn't know whether she liked him, but at least she wasn't intimidated by him.

And most important of all—she was leaving town the next morning. He would probably see her again, but not until she came back to visit Neely, and that could be months—even years. By then she might not even remember his name.

Raising his hand, he hesitated, then rapped sharply on the door.

Seconds ticked past with no sound from inside the room. He wouldn't blame her if she refused to open the door—half wished she would do exactly that so he would have no choice but to go home. But after a minute, maybe two, there was a rustle inside, then the door swung open.

She'd obviously showered since the party. Her face was free of makeup and her hair, still damp, was slicked back from her face, and damned if she didn't look as pretty as she had all dressed up. She was wearing something thin and satiny held up by tiny straps and ending somewhere around midthigh, and she was naked underneath it. She looked sexy and innocent and vulnerable, and he knew if he touched her again, he would be damned to hell with no way to redeem himself.

Even knowing that, he reached out.

And he touched her.

Chapter 2

Hallie knew why he'd come.

It was in the hunger that made his blue gaze intense, in the tension that crackled around him and the heat where his fingers loosely held hers. She could send him away with no more than a shake of her head...or she could pull him inside and close the door.

Sending him away would be the smart choice, of course.

But in all her thirty years no one had ever described her as the smart sister.

Barely breathing, she watched him watch her. He hadn't taken so much as a step over the threshold, and she knew he wouldn't unless she gave him an invitation. Did she have the courage to offer that invitation?

Did she have the strength to hold it inside?

She didn't know how long they stood there—one minute or ten—but the sound of familiar voices in the parking lot below signaled that time had run out. Her sisters, mother and stepfather were back from the party, and while Doris Irene's room was on the ground floor, Bailey and Kylie were sharing a room down the hall and around the corner.

Send him away or let him stay?

She wanted to do the first. She needed the last.

Tightening her fingers around his, she took a step backward, then another. While her family said their good-nights downstairs, she drew Brady into the room and closed, then locked the door.

As he'd done the first time—what she'd thought would be the last time—he turned off the lights, then pulled her close. She thought of her smart, talented, capable sisters kissing their mother good-night, then coming arm-in-arm up the stairs, far too good and moral to indulge in anything so tawdry as a one- or two-night stand.

Then Brady kissed her as if she mattered, and she stopped thinking.

He aroused her expertly, stroked her, caressed her. Though she wore nothing but a simple satin shift, he took his sweet time removing it, exploring, touching, tormenting every inch of her. When she was naked and weak, when the need for him throbbed throughout her body, he clamped his mouth to hers and kissed her onto the bed before pulling away.

Her entire body was vibrating, thrumming with need. In the inky darkness, she heard his boots hit the floor, followed by the soft whoosh of his shirt falling and the rasp of his zipper. She raised up on one arm, but it was too dark to see. She could hear, though—harsh breathing, strong hands crinkling plastic as he tore open the condom wrapper. She could smell the clean, fresh scent of him as he came nearer, the faint hint of beer, the fainter essence of pure, base lust. She felt the mattress give under his weight, then the warm, satiny skin when she slid her hands to his shoulders.

Just as he'd done the other time, he grasped both of her hands in his, pinned them at her sides, then lowered his head to kiss her. Forgetting that she wanted to protest, she greedily welcomed his tongue, then, with a swallowed gasp, welcomed him into her body—every hot, silky, hard-as-rock inch of him.

For a moment he was content merely to be inside her, and she was content to feel him there again. He didn't move, but held himself rigid, letting her body adjust to his. She sighed deep in her throat at the pure simple pleasure of it. For this brief time, she felt connected. Wanted. Even needed.

And that was all she wanted—all she'd ever wanted. Tonight the feelings didn't even have to be real as long as she could believe in them for the moment.

"You're a beautiful woman, Hallie," he said, his voice little more than a growl that vibrated all the way through her. Then he began moving, slowly taking long, deep strokes, pulling out, filling her again. At the same time he lowered his head to nuzzle her breast.

She tried to free her hands, but his grip was too strong. "Please," she began, then caught her breath in a low groan as he sucked hard at her nipple. "I—I want…"

He increased his pace, thrusting into her faster, harder, deeper, and continued to kiss and torment her breasts. She was starting to see stars, quickly building toward a release that just might leave her shattered…then put her back together again. Every time his arousal rubbed against her, every time her body clenched his, every strong pull of his mouth on her nipple….

"Let me…Brady, I want…" To capture this feeling and make it last forever. To grab hold of him and never let go. To scream. Explode. Weep.

The pressure inside her kept building, increasing with every touch, every kiss, every breath. Her muscles were taut, her nerves quivering, her breathing ragged and shallow. He pushed her until she was sure she couldn't survive, and then he pushed her even farther, until her climax rocketed through her. She couldn't breathe, couldn't think, couldn't control the trembling that claimed her entire body. All she could do was feel and, sweet hell, she was feeling everything. She was drowning in incredible sensations, all hot and sweat-slick and shuddering and satisfied. Oh, yes, incredibly satisfied.

It wasn't until much, much later, after her second orgasm, when she lay quietly in Brady's arms, that she remembered what it was, in particular, that she'd wanted—to touch him. To run her hands over his body, to make him hot and achy, to feel his strength, to cradle his hardness in her palms. To tease, play with and arouse him, the way he'd teased, played with and aroused her.

She turned so that she faced him, even though she couldn't see. "Can I ask you something?"

His breathing was so slow and steady that she thought for a moment he'd fallen asleep. Then he exhaled loudly and asked, "What?"

"Is it everyone or just me that you don't want touching you?" She felt the tension in his body ratchet up a notch or two before he answered.

"It would be physically impossible to touch more than we are right now."

That was true. Her head rested on his arm, her breasts were pressed against his chest, her legs tangled with his. But that wasn't what she meant, and she suspected he knew it. "I'm talking about with my hands. You held my wrists so I couldn't touch you."

"Did I?" He asked it as if he hadn't noticed what he'd done, but she knew better than that. He was too observant, too self-aware, for that to wash.

She stared at him, a shadow among shadows. When he didn't say anything more, she laid her hand on his ribs. Soft, warm, dark skin—she couldn't see, but she could visualize—as smooth and silky as her own pampered skin. She slid her palm up a few inches, then down again, then he caught hold of her hand and lifted it to his mouth for a simple, sensual, toe-curling kiss.

Hallie had to catch her breath before she could speak. "See? You don't like it when I touch you."

With another heavy sigh, he released her and rolled onto his back, arms and legs open wide. "You want to touch me, go ahead."

She considered it a moment, then in a pouty voice said, "No."

"Come on, Hallie," he coaxed, reaching for her hand and pulling it to his chest.

"No."

"Okay. Then I'll touch you." He raised up and reached for her, then rolled back again, lifting her on top of him. She tried to wriggle away, which caused an immediate and intriguing re-action in him, so with a womanly smile, she did it again.

Since he was being so agreeable, she took him up on his offer and spent some time exploring his body. Having a man in her bed was one of the things she missed about being married—the different textures of his body, the contrasts to her own body, even the simple sound of his breathing. Even when there was no sex, there was still intimacy, and she missed that with all her heart.

By the time she'd satisfied her curiosity, she'd aroused him to the point that his breathing was rapid, his voice guttural. "No more play. Come here."

She thought about refusing, at least for a while, but knew she didn't have the willpower, because all that touching, kissing and caressing that had aroused him had had the same effect on her. She was hot and achy, and she needed him, please, just once more.

She knew the moment she took him inside her that neither of them were going to last long, and she was right. The duration was short, the intensity killing.

Long after it was over, she found the strength to lift herself away from him. She pressed a kiss to his jaw, then bonelessly sank down to lie beside him.

She wasn't sure exactly when she fell asleep—right away, she thought—but it seemed like mere minutes until he was shaking her awake. "Hallie?"

"Hmm." She blindly reached for him and realized he was dressed again. She forced her eyes open and saw that the lamp nearest the door was on and he was, indeed, dressed and ready to go. She felt a twinge of disappointment that he wasn't going to stick around to wake up, maybe get some breakfast, maybe make love again. Next time—

She cut off that thought the instant it formed. There wasn't likely to be a next time. She'd already gotten so much more than she'd expected when she approached him in the bar Thursday night. She should be grateful for it and not hoping for even more.

"I've got to get home."

"Oh." She raised up on one arm, then shoved her hair from her face. She imagined she looked pretty darn scary without makeup, her hair standing on end and after only a few hours sleep. "Okay."

At least he was telling her. She'd awakened Friday morning to cold sheets and nothing to suggest that he'd even been there besides her incredible sense of satisfaction.

As she scooted to sit up with the sheet tucked under her arms, he sat down next to her. Looking seriously intense, he threaded his fingers through her hair, tilted her head back and simply looked at her. When moments passed and he didn't say anything, she smiled awkwardly. "Thank you."

His mouth twitched as if he might smile, but he didn't. Instead, he leaned forward and gently kissed her. "It was my pleasure."

Releasing her, he stood up and crossed to the door in three strides. He glanced back at her and finally did smile, just a little.

And then he was gone.

Sunday was just like every other Sunday in Brady's life for the past fourteen years—long and empty. He worked his usual every-other-weekend shift, did his usual chores and still had plenty of time to brood. Every time he'd left the sheriff's department, it had taken all the determination he could muster to stop himself from driving through the motel parking lot to see if the California Mercedes was gone.

Too bad he hadn't had that much strength last night.

He'd never been proud of the women-and-sex aspect of his life, but this time he felt particularly despicable. If he could learn how to live without occasional sex, female companionship or human contact, he would. Hell, if he could learn to open up to a woman, he would do that, too. But life had taught him a few lessons too well ever to forget them, the first of which was that the safest way to live was alone.

Even if alone was sometimes pretty damn miserable.

So damn miserable this time that he was grateful to see Monday and what promised to be a long, busy work week roll around.

He hadn't had any experience in law enforcement when he'd walked into the department and applied for a deputy's job over six years ago. He'd been hired in part because the salary was so low most people couldn't afford to work there, but also because Reese had been willing to take a chance on him. He'd been surprised by how much he liked the job and by how good he was at it. He'd advanced quickly to undersheriff, and wouldn't likely go any higher. The only job left to aspire to was sheriff, and Reese wasn't going anywhere. But that was all right. Work was one aspect of his life that he wouldn't change if he could.

After a morning spent on the paperwork Jace had warned him about, he picked up his Stetson from the filing cabinet and stopped by the dispatcher's desk. "I'm going to lunch, Wilda."

She waved her hand idly without looking up from her magazine. She was a good dispatcher and was less likely to miss work than any other department employee besides him, but she wasn't the friendliest of people. Some of the deputies complained, but it suited him just fine.

He left the department, located on the first floor of the Canyon County Courthouse, and stood for a moment in the shade of an old oak. Buffalo Plains was a nice town—not big enough ever to get crowded, but large enough to provide everything a person needed. If there was something you absolutely couldn't find, Tulsa was only an hour to the east, Oklahoma City about the same distance to the southwest. In six years, he'd made fewer than a half dozen trips to Tulsa and none to OKC.

After crossing the park alongside the courthouse, he walked half a block east to the sandwich shop. Eating alone in a restaurant was one of the hardest things he'd had to learn to do after his marriage ended. Even now, it didn't come easily. Most days he went to the Dairy King for a burger and fries, and on really slow days he'd go home. Today, though, a quick sandwich seemed best.

He got a roast beef sandwich, a bag of chips and a soft drink, then headed for an empty table. Just as he set his tray down, he happened to glance at the woman sitting by herself at the next table, and for a moment he froze.

Hallie Madison gazed back at him. After a moment, she waggled her fingers in a wave.

"What are you doing here?" he asked brusquely.

"Having lunch."

"You were supposed to go home yesterday."

She shook her head. "My mother and my sisters left yesterday. I'm staying awhile."

"How long?"

Wariness slipped into her expression. "Do you want to have this conversation from over there, or would you like to join me?"

It was a toss-up, he admitted sourly. He damn sure didn't want the other diners to listen in, but he also didn't want to share her table, not when he wasn't sure he could look her in the eye. But he picked up the tray and moved it to her table, then slid onto the bench opposite her. First thing he did was bump her feet, then bang his knee on the table's center leg.

"How long?" he asked again once he was settled.

"At least three weeks. I'm overseeing the construction on Neely and Reese's house."

Three weeks. Damn. He never would have gone near her or her motel Saturday night if he'd known that. He'd thought she was leaving. He'd thought he wouldn't see her again. He'd thought...

His jaw tightened. He'd thought he would take what he wanted from her, then say goodbye and forget her.

"Why didn't you tell me that?" he asked as he unwrapped his sandwich.

"When did you ask?"

She had him there. He'd known the other Madisons were leaving Sunday, and he'd assumed she was, too. That was his mistake, not hers.

She finished the last of her chips and stuffed her trash into the bag, then set it aside and rested her arms on the tabletop. "Look, Brady, you're apparently concerned that I might expect something from you. I don't. What we did...that's all it was. Two nights. Nothing more. I imagine in a town like this, it will be impossible to avoid each other entirely, but we can try. If we fail and you do run into me, don't feel you have to acknowledge me. I don't expect that, either."

She looked so cool, but her hazel eyes were a little too bright, the muscle in her jaw clenched a little too tight. Picking up her purse, she slid across the seat to leave, but he extended his leg, blocking her way.

"Don't go. I didn't mean— I just thought—"

When he didn't go on, she finished for him. "That you would never have to see me again. I'm not yet as experienced at one-night stands as you are, but I do understand how they work. No strings, no commitment, no nothing once the night is over."

It was illogical as hell, but he took offense at her assumption that he had some vast experience at sleeping with strangers, and he took even more offense at her use of the word *yet*. She was implying that one day she *would* be as experienced as he was— an idea that made his gut tighten. As if it were any of his business.

"It's just that seeing you took me by surprise." And he didn't like surprises—never had. Most of his security came from controlling as much of his life as possible, probably because he hadn't had *any* control to speak of until after his divorce. His job wasn't predictable, but everything else in his life was, and he liked it that way.

Hallie was still poised to leave, stopped only by his size-twelve boot blocking her exit. He wished she would relax and stop looking at him as if he were the last person she wanted to see—which was only fair, since he'd made her feel as if she were the last person *he* wanted to see. "Sit with me while I eat," he said, trying to sound friendly but doubtful he succeeded. "Please."

After a moment, she moved back to the center of the bench and laid her purse aside. She sipped from her drink, then folded her arms across her chest. "Are you aware everyone in here is watching us?"

He didn't bother to look. He could feel the curious stares. "I imagine they're surprised."

"By what?"

"The fact that you're sitting here and we're talking." He scraped a pile of lettuce from his sandwich, then took a bite.

"People don't sit with you?"

"Generally not. I don't exactly invite friendly overtures."

"Oh, gee, now there's a surprise," she said with a delicate little sniff, and then she simply watched him. Figuring turnabout was fair play, he fixed his own gaze on her. Her blond hair was pulled back in a fancy braid, and she wore a sleeveless yellow sweater with white shorts and sandals. Even so casually dressed, she looked like money, and a lot of it. Her nails were manicured and painted a deep rose, and her only jewelry was a wristwatch and earrings…and a stud nestled in her navel. He hadn't seen it—had only felt it in the dark—so he didn't know exactly what it was.

Besides sexy.

How many other men knew that about her?

An ex-husband or two. Probably a few others. She hadn't said he was her only one-night stand.

"Tell me about your divorce," he said as he picked up the second half of his sandwich.

"I got the house, the Mercedes and a nice cash settlement. He kept his fabulous career and got the girlfriend and all the friends."

What girlfriend? he wanted to ask. At the moment he couldn't imagine the woman a man would pick over her. "I guess I made the wrong request. Tell me about the marriage."

"Which one?"

I'm a three-time loser, she'd said at the reception Saturday night, with more than a little bitter mocking. "The most recent one."

After a moment's silence, she shrugged. "His name was Max Parker. He's a film producer. We were married four years and were—I thought—happily in love. But at my birthday party last winter, I went looking for him and found him boffing the star of his last movie. He needed someone who could arouse his passion, he said—someone who was…oh, gee, how did he put it?" She pretended to think, then scowled. "Oh, yeah. Someone who wasn't as *old* as me."

He thought about the things he could say. *I'm sorry. That must have hurt. The guy's a bastard. You're better off without him.* He settled for something a little less sympathetic. "You look pretty damn good for an old broad."

For a moment she simply looked at him, her hazel eyes opened wide. Then slowly a smile curved the corners of her mouth, and he felt the first real warmth from her since he'd left her bed before dawn Sunday. "Thank you," she said. Uncrossing her arms from her chest, she settled more comfortably on the bench. "What about yours?"

Now that she'd relaxed, Brady grew stiff, stilled in the act of gathering the sandwich wrapper and lettuce shreds. Turnabout was fair play, remember? But weren't there limits to how many old habits a man could be expected to break all at once? He'd been in Reese's wedding, had attended the party afterward, had turned his one night with Hallie into two and was sitting with her now in full view of anyone who cared to look. Every one of those things was new for him.

And keeping his past in the past—and private—was old. The oldest habit he had.

But she was waiting quietly, patiently, and for some unfathomable reason, he didn't want to disappoint her.

"That's a deep, dark secret around here," he said at last.

"How deep? How dark?"

As she'd done, he pretended to need a moment to think about it. "Well, you're the only person in Oklahoma who even knows I was married."

"Of course, Neely and Reese aren't in Oklahoma right—" She broke off when he shook his head. "They don't know?"

He shook his head again.

"Then why did you tell me?"

"That's a good question." She'd been looking a little blue, her mother and Neely had trampled on her feelings, and she'd looked so wounded. He'd wanted… To let her know she wasn't the only one who'd failed? That he understood at least something of what she felt?

"What happened?"

He had never discussed his marriage or his divorce with anyone—not once in fourteen years. There had been one oblique conversation with Reese a while back, but he hadn't said enough to give away any of the facts. There was no reason why he should break his silence now, and no reason at all why he should break it with this woman.

But when he opened his mouth to say so, the wrong words came out. "Her name was Sandra. We were married three years, until I found out she was—" How had Hallie put it? "—*boffing* half the guys in town."

"So we both married people with exquisitely bad taste," she remarked.

"Looks like." He glanced at his watch. He got an hour for lunch, but he usually took less than half that. Today, for the first time he could recall, he wasn't anxious to get back to work. "Will you be staying at Neely's apartment while they're gone?"

"She offered, but I'd rather not. It would feel intrusive." She fiddled with her drinking straw for a moment, then gave him a direct look. "I understand you were there the night Reese's house got shot up."

He nodded.

"Neely says you saved her life."

"She's got it backward. She and Reese saved *my* life."

Hallie knew better. Neely didn't get things turned around. She was the best darn lawyer in this part of the country, and she *always* had her facts straight. She hadn't offered a lot of details about that night in June—being the oldest sister and mother hen, she felt it was her responsibility to protect the younger ones from anything that might worry them—but she'd told them enough to know it was terrifying.

Eddie Forbes, a criminal Neely had sent to prison when she was working as a prosecutor in Kansas City, had sworn revenge on her, and when he got out, he put out a contract on her life. One of the men trying to cash in on it had shot Reese, and a whole gang of them, including Forbes himself, had tracked them to Reese's house in Heartbreak.

It was at that point Neely's details had gotten a little fuzzy. All Hallie knew for sure was that Brady had gone to the house to help them, that he'd been willing to die to save Neely and that the house had been shot all to hell. Seven of the bad guys had died that night, including Forbes, shot by Neely herself.

Even weeks later in the middle of a hot, sunny day, the mere thought sent a shudder of revulsion through Hallie. God forbid, if she ever found herself in a similar situation, she hoped she would be as courageous as her sister.

"However it went," she said, "you have the undying gratitude of the Madison family."

A faint blush turned his cheeks crimson, and he shrugged awkwardly. "I was just doing my job."

Right. And if she believed that, no doubt he'd have some fine swampland to offer, too.

Casting about for something to keep the conversation going, she seized one of the more mundane questions new acquaintances always asked. "Where are you from? Or is that another of your deep, dark secrets?"

"Not so deep or so dark, but…yeah. Only Reese knows that one." He looked as if he wanted to drop it there, then took a breath and answered. "A dusty little town west of Dallas."

"A Texan. Well, that explains a lot." She softened the words with a smile. "Contrary to the opinions of every Texan I've ever met, being from Texas isn't such a big deal."

"You won't get any argument from me. I left when I could, and I've never been back."

"After the divorce?"

He nodded.

"So I take it you didn't have any kids."

A bitter look came across his face, and underneath the black mustache, his mouth thinned in a flat line. "No."

"Me, neither." That had been one of the issues in both her second and last marriages. She wanted kids—sometimes wanted them so badly her heart ached with it—and neither husband had been willing. Oh, Max had told her before the wedding sure, they would have all the babies she wanted, but after…. The time had never been right. Their lives were too busy. A baby wouldn't fit into their lifestyle. He didn't want the bother. Finally he'd quit making excuses and had told her straight out—no kids, not while she was married to him.

Which side of the question had Brady come down on? Had he wanted a little boy to play football with or a delicate little girl to pamper and protect? Or did he consider children a nuisance that would interfere with his own pleasures?

"What are your plans for this afternoon?" he asked.

"I'm driving over to Heartbreak to meet the contractor at the house. His name's Dane Watson. Do you know him?"

"I know who he is. He's a good builder. Honest. And single."

She gave him a dry look. The only man in the entire state of Oklahoma—heck, in the entire world—whose marital status mattered to her was sitting across from her. It didn't matter how desperate she was or how handsome and sexy he was, she would not sleep with a married man.

He checked his watch again, and Hallie politely asked, "Am I keeping you from something?"

"Nope."

"Well…" She hoped her sigh didn't sound as regretful to him as it did to her. "I should probably go. It's a bit of a drive to Heartbreak."

"Yeah, and the penalty for speeding around here can be pretty stiff."

It was a simple observation, and she was in a sorry state when the first interpretation to pop into her mind was lascivious, if not downright dirty. Now it was her own cheeks turning pink as she stood up, then slung her purse strap over one shoulder. She reached for her trash, but he picked it up first, threw it away, then followed her out the door.

"Where are you parked?" he asked as they stood on the sidewalk under the blistering sun.

"Across from the courthouse. Where are you headed?"

"Same direction."

She looked in store windows as they walked, but more often than not, her attention was on Brady's reflection rather than the merchandise. "I can't wait for the chance to go prowling through all these antique stores. I love neat old stuff."

"Some of these places would be better labeled junk stores," he warned.

She smiled up at him. "That's the best kind."

At the end of the block, they turned the corner, then stopped beside her car in the first parking space. She opened the door to let the heat radiate out, bent inside to start the engine and turn the air conditioner on high, then faced him again. "Can I say I enjoyed talking to you without scaring you into thinking I want something?"

"I don't scare easily."

"There's not a man alive who can't be flat-out terrified by the right woman." Feeling cooler air coming out of her car, she tossed her purse into the passenger seat, then looked back at him. "Anyway, I did enjoy it, and that's a reference only to the conversation we had today, nothing more. Like I said earlier, I don't have any expectations."

He studied her a moment before adjusting the cowboy hat lower over his eyes. "Maybe you should," he said in a gravelly voice, then started off. At the edge of the street, he glanced back. "See you around."

She watched until he'd disappeared inside the courthouse, then gave a shake of her head. She didn't understand men, not for one minute, and she swore she was going to learn to live without them—except, of course, for the occasional temporary lover. But every feminine instinct she possessed suggested that was going to be a much harder proposition here in Buffalo Plains than it would have been in Beverly Hills.

And for that, she could thank Brady Marshall.

Climbing into her car, she backed out of the space, circled halfway around the block and headed south to Heartbreak. It was twenty miles of rolling hills and heavily wooded areas interspersed with pastures that didn't appear to have anything left to feed the cattle and horses they held. She passed neat farmhouses, occasional trailers, more than a few shabby little places and one particularly ostentatious house just outside Heartbreak.

Heartbreak was *not* the town she imagined Neely spending the rest of her life in. It lacked the charm of Buffalo Plains, as well as most of the amenities. Downtown filled all of three blocks, and it was all shabby. She passed the Heartbreak Café— Café Shay, Neely called it, after its owner, Shay Rafferty. That was the place you went to find out what was going on in the town, the state and the world. Neely had also told Hallie about the doctor's office across the street, where Heartbreak's midwife practiced, who would someday deliver Neely's babies, and she'd mentioned the hardware store up ahead, owned by Grace James and her husband, Ethan.

Truth was, Neely talked about the place as if she loved it and couldn't imagine living anywhere else.

Hallie had never *loved* any of the cities where she'd lived. In fact, at the moment, she had no clue where she was going to live when she left Oklahoma. She hadn't realized how desperately she wanted out of California until last week, when she'd driven across the state line into Arizona. The terrain hadn't changed one bit—desert was desert no matter which state it belonged to—but her outlook had. In a matter of seconds, the tension knotting her shoulders had eased, and so had the tight, panicky feeling that had settled in her chest six months earlier and never gone away. Her fingers had loosened their grip on the steering wheel, and she'd sunk a little more easily into the seat.

She'd thought then that she might never go back, not even to pack the rest of her things and sell her house.

She just didn't have a clue where she would go.

Following the directions Neely had given her, she soon came to a mailbox marked Barnett. She turned into the gravel drive, passed through a heavy stand of blackjack oaks, then pulled into a clearing that wasn't particularly clear.

A fresh, raw area on the right side of the drive showed where Reese's house had stood. For the first few weeks after the assault, he and Neely had intended simply to repair, replace and clean up, then move back into the house. When they realized they kept putting off the simple jobs that would make that possible, they decided to raze it and start over from scratch.

Hallie didn't blame them as she pulled onto the grass beside a half-dozen pickups. All the clean-ups in the world couldn't make a person forget that people had died there. It would be too creepy to share the house with those memories.

On both sides of the house was pasture, and out back was a huge old barn. Next time she came out, she would have to bring her camera and get some shots of both the barn and the horses outside it.

Across the driveway from the old house site was the new house. Work was progressing rapidly—a good thing, since Neely had already issued invitations to everyone in both the Madison and the Barnett families for Thanksgiving dinner. Hallie found her way inside, got a wolf whistle from a carpenter and another from an electrician—*so there, Max*—and found Dane Watson in the master bedroom.

Good, honest and single, Brady had said. He'd forgotten to mention tall, muscular and handsome, with surfer-boy blond hair, blue eyes and the biggest dimples Hallie had seen. He looked her over with obvious appreciation, and when they shook hands, he held her hand far longer than he should have…and Hallie didn't feel a thing. He was gorgeous, funny, charming, and made her feel like the best part of his day, and all she could think was that she liked him, but that was the extent of it.

She felt a tremendous sense of relief when she left the site two hours later. Maybe she really was building up an immunity to men. Maybe, before long, she wouldn't pay them any more notice than she would the lovely purple-blooming crape myrtle over in the side yard or the Irish setter, gleaming deep mahogany, in the shade of a tree across the street. Pretty objects to be appreciated, then forgotten.

Unbidden, the image of Brady Marshall popped into her mind and burst her bubble. When he'd walked into the sandwich shop, she had gotten the oddest quivery sensation all through her torso—not just butterflies, but butterflies doing acrobatics. Her palms had gotten damp, and she hadn't been able to decide between sliding onto the floor under the table or making a quick dash for the door while he was facing the counter.

Maybe she *was* building up an immunity to men.

But apparently Brady Marshall was the exception to the rule. She was afraid she would have to be dead to be immune to *him*.

Chapter 3

By the time Brady left the courthouse Monday evening, the sun hung low in the western sky. There was little traffic and no activity as he walked to his department SUV in the lot out back. All the shops and businesses downtown were closed by six o'clock, except on Thursdays, when most stores stayed open an extra two hours. The rest of the week, any money spent in Buffalo Plains at night was spent on food, alcohol, gasoline or at the small Wal-Mart on the edge of town.

Before heading home, he drove by the county maintenance facility in the north part of town and filled up his gas tank. It wouldn't do to get called out on an emergency in the middle of the night and find out the gas tank was empty.

That done, he started home…and made it as far as the stoplight in front of the courthouse. It was red, and he stopped, wondering idly what he could fix for dinner that wouldn't take long, paying little attention to the music on the radio, when something—he couldn't even say what—caught his attention and made him look to his left.

There in front of the First National Bank of Buffalo Plains, fiddling with a camera and a tripod, was Hallie Madison. *I imag-*

ine in a town like this, it will be impossible to avoid each other entirely, she'd said at lunch. No kidding. He wondered why that was. In spite of the town's size, he rarely had any problem avoiding people, so why was she any different?

Maybe because she'd been on his mind ever since he'd seen her at the wedding.

Checking the rearview mirror and finding the street clear, he backed up far enough to pull into a parking space, then climbed out. When he crossed the street, Hallie was bent slightly, making adjustments to the camera. He kept his distance and remained silent until she straightened and took a step back.

"What are you doing?"

She automatically smiled when she saw him. "Taking a picture of the courthouse in the setting sun. You're a master at asking the obvious, aren't you?"

"That's what I get paid the big bucks for," he said dryly.

"Oh, so is this an official interrogation?" She stood straighter and raised her hands in the air. "I'm not doing anything wrong... What's your official title?"

"Undersheriff."

She wrinkled her nose. "Gee, I believe I'll stick with deputy. I swear, Deputy Marshall— Isn't that cute? Did you ever notice—"

"Yes."

"Okay, I'll get it right this time. I swear, Deputy Marshall, I'm not doing anything wrong, and I don't have any weapons, drugs or contraband. You can search me if you like."

One innocent, playacting sentence, and it changed the whole tenor of the evening. It was still hot and muggy, but now the air seemed to crackle all around them. Brady felt the strong pull of desire deep in his belly, as if he hadn't just spent practically two entire nights with this woman. He was finding it difficult to breathe, or think, or to find words to give voice to—especially when the only words he wanted to say were, yes, I like.

Slowly, her gaze locked with his, she lowered her arms, then laced her fingers together. "I—I didn't mean—"

"Damn," he murmured. "And here you got my hopes up." And that wasn't all.

For a moment she looked uncertain, as if she wasn't entirely sure he was teasing—fair enough, since he wasn't either. Then she started fussing with the camera again. "If you work this late every day, you need a raise," she remarked, her tone a shade too cheerful.

"Every deputy in the state of Oklahoma needs a raise."

"Not a job you'll get rich doing, huh?"

"Not if you're honest."

"And you are." She said it matter-of-factly, as if there could be no doubt.

"As the day is long." Coming a few feet closer, he gestured toward the camera. "Isn't it too dark to be taking pictures?"

"Not if you know what you're doing. For a time I worked as a photographer—did portraits, weddings, publicity photos. That's how I met Max. I did a portrait of his sister's kids, and we became friends—sort of—and she introduced us."

It appeared most of her friends in California had been sort-of friends, since at lunch, she said Max had gotten them all in the divorce. That couldn't have been fun. "Then you married the big Hollywood producer and…took up a life of leisure?"

"And photography became a hobby that interfered with my obligations as Mrs. Max Parker." She leaned back against the bank building and gazed at the courthouse. "It's impressive, isn't it? Looks as if it's been there forever."

He moved to stand a few feet from her and studied the building where he worked. It was built of native stone and stood three stories tall, with arched windows spaced equidistantly on all four sides. Carved into the stone above the main entrance was the date it was built. Eighty-two years old, he calculated, and still looking as solid as when it was new.

"What brought you to Buffalo Plains?"

With the heat seeping from the bank's stone facade into his back, Brady slowly turned his head to look at her. "How is it Neely's the lawyer when you're the one full of questions?"

She laughed. "Neely's the lawyer because she's the smart one."

"Uh-huh." He'd heard that before. "And what are you?"

For a long time she continued to gaze at the courthouse, but he was pretty sure she wasn't seeing the building. After a while, she shook her head, making her braid swing, then laughed again, though far less convincingly this time. "I'm the screwup. The dumb one, the ditzy one, the one who doesn't know the meaning of the word *commitment.*"

His jaw tightening, Brady looked away. His impulse was to disagree with her, to insist that her family didn't see her in those terms, but he wasn't sure he would be telling the truth.

Her eyes too bright, she bumped his arm with her shoulder. "Made you uncomfortable, didn't I?"

"No. I was just thinking that a better label for you is probably the misunderstood one." And he knew how it felt to be misunderstood.

Without giving her time to respond, he went on. "After the divorce, I wanted to be anywhere but Texas. First I headed out to New Mexico, then into Colorado, and about six years ago I wound up in Buffalo Plains. I got a job, I liked it and was good at it, and I stayed. It only took me eight years to find a place I could stay."

"Sheesh, I hope I have better luck."

"What do you mean?"

"I'm not staying in Beverly Hills. I'm going to sell the house and find someplace where I can belong. What do I need with ten acres of lawn and gardens, seven bedrooms, a dining room that seats thirty, a screening room that seats fifty and two guest houses?"

"That's not a house. It's a mansion."

She shrugged as if it didn't matter. "I never liked it anyway. Max picked it out, and his interior designer decorated it. All I got to do was live in it."

"If you didn't like it, why didn't you let him have it in the divorce?" He'd been more than happy to walk away from the house he'd built for Sandra. If he'd kept it after the divorce, he would have burned it to the ground, then left the rubble there so he would never forget.

By then the sun had set enough that the streetlights were on. In their artificial glow, he could make out the sheepish expression on her face. "The bimbo wanted it, and I— She'd already taken my husband. There was no way I was going to let her have my house, too.''

''Does the bimbo have a name?'' He hadn't set foot in a movie theater in longer than he could remember, but his satellite system delivered more channels of movies than a reasonable person could watch. Since he spent the bulk of his free time alone, he watched a lot.

''Lilah Grant.''

He gave a low whistle.

''I see you're familiar with her,'' Hallie said, her voice so dry it could suck the humidity out of the air. ''She wears a size two—which also happens to be her IQ, by the way—and she's got less acting talent than that post over there, but she never met a nude scene she didn't love. And, no, they're not real. Those are the best triple-D breasts money can buy.''

Earlier he hadn't been able to imagine the woman a man would pick over Hallie. Even knowing, he couldn't see it. The starving waif look had never appealed to him, not even with the big boobs. He liked women who looked like women, who had curves where they should, who had a little softness to them.

''So did you know when you married him that he was an idiot, or did you find that out later?''

Pushing away from the wall, she disconnected the camera from the tripod, returned it to its bag, then expertly folded the tripod and slid it through a loop on the bag. When she was done, she faced him. ''You're a nice man, Brady.''

Her words struck that place deep inside him that was always frozen and hard, and made his muscles clench and tighten. ''No, Hallie,'' he said quietly. ''I'm not.''

She shrugged as if his disagreement meant nothing. ''You see yourself your way, and I'll see you my way.'' Then... ''I guess I'll head back to the motel.''

She'd gone a few yards before he could bring himself to move. ''Hey, where's your car?''

''Back at the motel. I walked.''

''Let me give you a ride.''

She turned around, her head tilted to one side. ''I understand Buffalo Plains is about as safe as a town can get.''

"It is, but there's no reason to tempt fate." Which was exactly what he was doing. If he took her back to the motel, would he insist on seeing her to her door? Would he stop there?

He honestly didn't know.

After a moment's consideration, she nodded and returned to him. He automatically reached for the camera bag and was surprised by its weight. "What have you got in here?"

"Just the essentials. I'd be happy to take it back if you can't handle it."

He scowled at her. "Don't forget—I'm the one with the gun and the handcuffs."

"Yeah, and I'm the one whose favorite sister is married to your boss."

And he kept managing to forget that.

He directed her to his truck around the corner, then put her bag in the back seat. "Have you had dinner?" he asked when he settled in the driver's seat.

"I had a chili dog at the drive-in across the street from the motel."

"You like to live dangerously, don't you?"

"I've been doing that ever since I set foot in this town," she said quietly.

They drove the nine blocks to the motel in silence. How many times had he gone to a motel with a woman he hardly knew? And yet it felt strange this time. Maybe because he already knew to pull around back and park next to the Mercedes.

Or maybe because this time he wanted like hell to go inside with her…but not as much as he wanted to say good-night in the parking lot.

He shut off the engine, and for the space of a few heartbeats, they both sat there. Brady was looking at the window of the room in front of them, and he could tell by nothing more than feeling that she was looking elsewhere, too.

As the cool air inside the SUV was replaced with warmer, damper air, she opened the door. He did the same. She led the way up the stairs, and he followed…but only as far as the top landing. She had covered half the twenty-foot distance to her room before realizing that he'd stopped. Turning back, she smiled uneasily. "Would you like to come in?"

"Very much."

"But you're not going to."

He shook his head.

"Why not?"

Because it would be wrong—more so than the first time, not as much as the second, but still wrong. Because, in spite of her assurances, he wasn't sure what her expectations were. Hell, he wasn't sure what *his* expectations were. Because they were a great match for a one-night stand, but neither of them brought much hope to the success of anything more.

And because he liked her, honestly liked her, and though he didn't know what he wanted from her, he did know one thing for sure—he didn't want to hurt her. She'd gotten enough of that for a lifetime.

She smiled faintly. "It's okay. You don't have to answer that. I've got plenty of answers to choose from." Coming back, she held out her hand, and he gave her the camera bag. "Thank you for the ride home."

He nodded, then watched until she'd unlocked her room. "Hallie?"

She glanced at him.

"I'd like to see your pictures sometime."

"Sure." Once again she started to go inside, and once again he stopped her.

"You want to have lunch tomorrow?"

"Sure. Should I meet you at the courthouse?"

"That would be good. Around noon?"

"Okay. Good night." She went inside and closed the door. Even from that distance, he heard the lock click.

As he started down the stairs, he swore silently. He couldn't believe he'd found himself twenty-five feet from a bed and a beautiful and willing woman, and he was walking away. Sure, it was the safe choice, but how much was he going to hate himself a few hours from now, when he was alone in bed and unable to sleep?

Not as much as if he'd taken advantage of her again.

Hallie Madison was the most wrong person for him in all of Oklahoma. She was vulnerable and lonely and needed more than he'd ever been able to give.

But he wasn't going to hurt her. He swore to God he wouldn't.

He just wished he could be as sure that *he* wasn't going to get hurt, either.

Hallie loved old furniture—not antiques, necessarily. Just old. Pieces that people had lived with, that showed the marks and scars of use. Anticipating lunch with Brady far more than was safe, she went downtown more than an hour early on Tuesday and spent the time wandering through antique stores on the block across from the courthouse. She'd bought a couple of pitchers in the first store—one glazed green and brown, the other beige and brown. Oklahoma-made, the elderly woman behind the counter had declared, at Frankoma Pottery over to Sapulpa.

Hallie didn't care where they came from. She liked the lines, the colors, the weight in her hand.

Now, in the third store, she was eyeing an oak dining table. It was wide and long, big enough for six without the leaves, eight or ten with. It looked as solid in its own way as the courthouse did, as if it had already seated generations of hungry farmers and would continue to do so for generations to come. It could become her very own heirloom, passed down through the family for years to come.

Of course, first she would have to *have* a family, and the odds of that were somewhere between slim and none.

Still, it was a lovely piece, and came with eight equally sturdy ladder-back chairs, and it was such a tremendous change from the elegant and huge table in her dining room at home.

With a sigh, she drummed her fingers on the tabletop.

"Having trouble deciding?" The clerk slid into a chair opposite her. "What's the drawback? The price? The size? Afraid it won't fit in your dining room?"

"I don't actually have a dining room yet. Well, I do, but I'm getting ready to sell that house and everything in it."

"Someplace around here?"

Hallie shook her head. "In California. Beverly Hills."

"Oh." The woman gave her an appraising look, then laughed. "Don't worry. The price is the same no matter where you come from—well, except maybe Texas. Then we might have to add a surcharge to cover your ego."

With a laugh, Hallie extended her hand. "I'm Hallie Madison."

"Stella Clark." The woman leaned across to shake hands, then sat back again. "Are you just passing through?"

"Not exactly. I'll be here a few weeks—until my sister comes back from her honeymoon."

"Oh, you're Reese's new sister-in-law. We're all so happy to see him married. You know, his daddy and mama just got married themselves the week before his wedding."

"Yes, Neely mentioned that." Reese's mother had been the love of Del Barnett's life, but she'd never stayed around long, and every time she left him, she'd left their son behind, too. Initially, Reese had been disinclined to welcome her into the family—and considering the way she'd abandoned him, who could blame him? But he'd come around before the wedding. Almost getting killed could make a person rethink the grudges he was holding.

"So," Stella said. "No ring on your finger. Does that mean you're single, or are you just too liberated to wear one?"

"I'm...single." Hallie smiled to cover her guilt. It wasn't exactly a lie. As Brady had pointed out Saturday night, the difference between single and divorced wasn't enough to count—at least, not always.

"Well, now, we have a fair number of single men in town—some really fine-looking ones. Let me think..."

"I appreciate it," Hallie said quickly, "but I'm not going to be here long, and I'm really not interested in a relationship." Except for the one she had going with Brady...sort of.

Rubbing her finger along the grain of the table, she asked, "I don't suppose you know of any houses for rent around here, do you? Just for a month or two?"

"You staying at your sister's apartment?"

"No, the motel. I didn't want..." She shrugged.

Stella grinned. "After my husband died, I lived with my daughter and her husband for a while. Believe me, I understand. A body's got to have her own space sometimes, and the right to change it even if she doesn't. Let me see." Pursing her lips, she tapped one finger against them for a moment. "Of course, there's the apartments where your sister lives—"

"No vacancies." Hallie had called that morning, when she'd decided she didn't want to spend three weeks in a room where she couldn't walk barefooted for fear of sticking to the carpet.

"Yeah, there usually aren't. You know, Marlene Tucker's mother-in-law passed on a few weeks ago. Doctor said she died of heart failure. Well, of course she did! She was a hundred and one years old! Her poor old heart just wore out. Let me call Marlene and see what they're planning to do with her house."

While she went to the desk in the back of the shop, Hallie began wandering around. She was looking at some serving platters that matched the pitchers she'd bought when a Greyhound bus pulled to a stop in front of the store and opened its door.

The driver got off first, followed by a passenger. Scowling as if angry with the world, the teenage girl stepped up onto the sidewalk and waited while the driver retrieved her bag from the luggage compartment—one dirty army surplus duffel bag. With a battered backpack slung over one shoulder and the duffel bag leaning against her, she took a long look around.

When she noticed Hallie in the shop window looking at her, she made an obscene gesture. Hallie was tempted to stick out her tongue, poke her thumbs in her ears and waggle her fingers at the girl, but she restrained herself. Barely.

"Lord, would you look at that?" Stella made a clucking sound.

"What about her?"

"That hair. Those clothes. All them earrings." Then she chuckled. "I forgot I'm talking to Miss Beverly Hills. I bet you see weirdos like that all the time out there in California, don't you?"

"There are some strange people out there." She glanced again at the girl, who was walking away. Purple-haired, clothes that were one breath away from indecent, combat boots with a mini-skirt—that was nothing in Los Angeles.

It stood out in Buffalo Plains.

"I talked to Marlene, and she said they haven't decided what to do with the house yet, but you'd be welcome to rent it for a while. Here's her number. Give her a call anytime you want to go look at it."

"Thanks, Stella. Do you happen to know where it is?"

"Oh, it's easy to find. When you go out of town south on Main, the last street you'll come to is Cedar, and the Tucker place is the first house on the left after that. It's white, neat as a button—and, of course, the mailbox out front says Tucker." With another grin, Stella planted her hands on her hips. "So…what did you decide about that oak table?"

"Can you hold it for me?"

"Sure can."

"Then I'll take it. And these, too." She picked up several platters, then followed Stella to the checkout counter. A few minutes later, she was walking out the door, her platters in a bag and a Sold sign planted in the middle of her table.

She took the bag to her car and locked it in the trunk, then checked her watch. She still had a few minutes before she was supposed to meet Brady. Time enough for a quick walk through one more store.

Then lunch. With Brady. A part of her felt almost as giddy as a teenager going on her first date, but this wasn't a date. A date would have been dinner, picking her up at the motel, taking her back there—or to his house—when it was over.

This was just lunch. Between friends. Innocent.

Exactly what she wanted, she assured herself.

The little voice inside her head didn't agree, whispering a childhood taunt.

Liar, liar, pants on fire….

After a morning on patrol, Brady parked in his reserved space behind the courthouse, entered through the back door, then went into the sheriff's department and headed for his office. He was almost there when the dispatcher stopped him.

"Someone to see you, Brady."

He glanced at the cramped space set aside for a lobby, where the dispatcher gestured, expecting to see Hallie, a few minutes early for their lunch. The only one there, though, was a teenage girl. Though there was something vaguely familiar about her, he was sure they'd never met. Purple hair was hard to forget.

So were enough holes in her ears to make the wind whistle through. There was a gold bar and chain through her right eyebrow, a stud through her nostril and another in her navel, around which a circle in what appeared to be a Celtic design was tattooed. He didn't even want to think about where else she might be mutilated.

He backtracked a few steps in her direction. "Can I help you?" he asked brusquely.

She was sprawled on one of the molded plastic chairs, her long legs stretching halfway across the room. Her boots were clunky, black and scuffed, her skirt was too short and rode low on her hips, and her lace top had been too small a year ago. A pair of headphones dangled around her neck, she wore way too much makeup, and her expression was 100-percent whiny adolescent pout.

Her insolent gaze started at his feet and moved up. By the time it reached his face, she'd curled one lip in complete disdain. "You Brady Marshall?"

"Yes."

"A cop. Jeez, what a loser." She stood up, her thin body looking like a stick figure unfolding. She was about five foot ten—not a bad height for a young woman. Not a great one for a barely-a-teenager girl. "Well, there's my stuff." With a hand that bore rings on every finger, she pointed in the direction of a duffel bag. "Let's get out of here."

Clomping on the wood floor, she got as far as the door before realizing that he wasn't following. "We-ell?"

"Who are you?"

She clomped back to stand in front of him and sneered. "Don't you recognize me? Why, I'm your own little girl, and I've come to stay with you."

Behind the counter, a clipboard clattered to the floor, and over by the coffeemaker, someone muttered, "What the—" Brady didn't look at either eavesdropper. He didn't take his gaze from the girl.

He never thought of himself as a father, not even as having been a father for a few short months. Even though he'd paid child support without fail for the past fourteen years, it was testament only to how desperately he'd wanted out of the marriage. Sandra had wanted money, and he'd agreed to give it in exchange for a quick divorce and escape to go off and lick his wounds.

Even after she'd admitted to sleeping with any man who was willing.

Even after she'd taunted him with the fact that he wasn't the father of her little girl.

Even after she'd stripped him of even the slightest hope that the baby whose birth he'd been awaiting so anxiously could possibly be his.

He studied her, trying to reconcile this tall, skinny, odd-looking child with the tiny, cuddly baby he'd fed, rocked to sleep and changed diapers for. That baby had smiled sweetly and cooed whenever she saw him, and she'd clung to his finger every time he'd held her.

This one...

This one was waiting for some sort of response from him. So was everyone else in the squad room.

He moved a few steps closer to her. "What's your name?"

"Les Marshall." Then she rolled her eyes as if he were making unreasonable demands. "Alessandra Leigh Marshall. Can we go now?"

See? Sandra had explained, still woozy from giving birth. Sandra, Alessandra. Her pretty little girl could be named after her and yet still have her own name. Wasn't she clever?

Cleverer than he'd been.

He glanced around at the curious faces in the squad room. No one even tried to pretend that they weren't openly listening, and he couldn't blame them. He hadn't been kidding when he'd told Hallie he had deep, dark secrets. He'd worked with these people for more than six years, and this was the first any of them had heard of a marriage, a divorce or Texas.

Or a daughter.

"Tell me something," he said, gesturing from her spiked purple hair all the way down to her combat boots. "Are you making a fashion statement, or do you just enjoy making your mother squirm?"

The question took her by surprise. She blinked, then sneered, "That's none of your business."

Which meant she was making her mother squirm. Brady couldn't begin to imagine how intensely Sandra hated her daughter's look. She was the vainest, trendiest, most appearance-conscious woman he'd ever known, and it must have killed her every time Les walked into her line of sight.

Aware that everyone was still watching, he gestured toward the door. "Let's discuss this outside."

He hustled her out the door into the courthouse lobby, then outside. On the east side of the building, the lawn stretched across half a block, with sidewalks leading to park benches and war memorials. In cooler weather, retired old men and other folks with time on their hands often filled the benches, but thanks to the day's heat, they were the only ones there.

He stopped in the dappled shade of a large oak. There was a breeze blowing, but all it did was rustle the leaves. It didn't provide any cooling. "So you're Sandra Whitfield's daughter."

With a put-upon sigh, she ticked off names on her fingers. "Actually, Sandra Whitfield Marshall Davis Thompson Valdez Napier. For the moment."

So Sandra had five marriages and four divorces behind her. Of course, she wasn't looking for a husband, a family or any of the usual stuff. She wanted money, security, an easy life. She was a beautiful woman and thought nothing of trading on her beauty to fulfill her goals. Even if it did make her little more than a very-high-priced hooker.

"And you're my father," Les went on. "Like it or not."

She sounded pretty sure of herself—almost as sure as Sandra had been that he wasn't. She'd had no doubts, and she'd left none for him.

Obviously, Sandra had lied—either to him or to Les. The question was, which one?

"Where is your mother?"

Shoving her hands into her pockets, she shrugged and leaned back against the tree. "Right after she put me on the bus to come here, she headed south of the border for her annual summer spa treatment. She won't be back for a week…or two or three—though she promised she'd get home before school starts again. Until then, you're stuck with me."

Brady gazed across the park to a familiar little silver-blue convertible. For fourteen years his life had gone exactly the way he wanted it—no trouble, no entanglements, no complications—and he'd been perfectly…well, not happy, but satisfied with it. Then Hallie Madison had sat down at his table in the bar, and all his quiet loneliness and satisfaction had been shot to hell. And now this. Which gods had he pissed off lately?

"What about your stepfather?"

"Which one?"

"The current one." His voice sounded testy, and he made a conscious effort to control it. "Is he home?"

"Yeah…but you can't send me back there to him. Adam never lets me stay when Sandra's out of town. He married her in spite of my presence in her life."

"What about your grandparents?"

"You mean Jim and Rita? Your parents? You'd send me to stay with *those* grandparents?"

Brady's jaw tightened until his teeth hurt. He wouldn't let Jim and Rita Marshall have temporary custody of an angry copperhead. A copperhead's venom had nothing on theirs.

"Then your mother's parents."

"He died years ago, and we don't see Sandra's mother. She's poor, you know."

Sandra had been, too, dirt poor, until she'd seduced her way into some money. And he'd made it so easy for her. She'd smiled at him, touched him, and he'd been a goner. Even when she'd told him the truth—about the baby, her affairs, her only reason for marrying him—he hadn't wanted to believe her. He'd told himself she was lying, just trying to hurt him.

She'd succeeded, with her truths as well as her lies.

And if it turned out that her insistence that he wasn't her baby's father had been just one more of her lies, if she'd deliberately kept him away from his daughter for fourteen years, he swore he would make her so damn sorry she would never get over it.

"Listen—"

Les interrupted. "Sandra said you always made excuses for not ever wanting me to visit, but this time it ain't gonna work. She's gone, I'm here, and for a couple weeks, at least, there's nothing you can do about it." Her grin was mocking. "You can't even turn me over to the cops because you *are* the cops."

"I don't even have an extra bedroom."

"Well, I'm not sleeping on the floor. Better make some arrangements."

Was he actually considering taking her into his home? he wondered, more than a little panicked, then answered himself immediately. What choice did he have? He was the only person in the entire state of Oklahoma with any sort of ties to her. It would only be until he could get hold of her mother or her stepfather and make arrangements to return her to Texas. Besides, if she was his daughter....

That muscle in his jaw clenched again. "How can I get in touch with Sandra?"

"You can't. I told you, she's on her annual keep-me-beautiful spa retreat."

"Spas have telephones."

She smiled her mother's smug smile. "Not this one. No telephones, no televisions, no e-mail or faxes. Just days of pampering." She shoved her hands into her pockets. "Look, it's hot, I'm hungry, and I'd like to get cleaned up. Traveling by bus sucks big time. Let's get outta here."

He removed his hat and dragged his fingers through his hair, then glanced at the courthouse. Four faces hastily ducked out of sight at the sheriff's department windows. He couldn't even get angry with them for being curious. "I'm meeting someone for lunch. After we eat, I'll...uh..."

He didn't want to leave her alone for the afternoon in his

house. He didn't have much that was really private there, and the most important of those items was locked up in the gun cabinet in his bedroom. Still, he didn't know this kid. He didn't have a clue how much of a problem child she really was. He could come home and find the place cleaned out, trashed or burned to the ground.

The answer to this problem—possibly—came out of A Moment in Thyme across the street, stopped at the Mercedes, then crossed into the park. She smiled when she saw him, then the smile slowly faded as she noticed Les.

"Hi, Brady," she greeted him when she reached them. "Am I interrupting something?"

"No, not at all. Hallie Madison, this is Les…Marshall."

Les gave Hallie a bored look, then grunted a greeting. Hallie looked at her, then back at him. "And Les is your…?"

He figured she was hoping he would say sister, niece or cousin. He wished he could, but truth was, he couldn't say anything.

After a moment of awkward silence, Les sarcastically said, "He has trouble saying the word—which isn't surprising since he hasn't been around for *fourteen years* to practice. I'm his daughter, and I've come for a visit."

That surprised Hallie. Her hazel eyes widened, and her delicately arched brows arched even higher. Brady had no doubt she was remembering that just twenty-four hours ago, he'd told her he didn't have any kids. And now here one stood, in the all-too-bizarre flesh.

But almost immediately Hallie smiled, a bright practiced smile that could have fooled any one of her sisters but not him, and she offered her hand. "It's nice to meet you, Les."

Grudgingly, the kid shook her hand, then pulled back right away.

"This is quite a surprise," Hallie went on. "If you need to cancel lunch, Brady, I understand—"

"No. Les is hungry, too. There's a place a block away called the SteakOut. We can go there."

"A cop eating at a place called the SteakOut?" Les rolled her eyes dramatically. "How…small-town."

Brady scowled at her, then pointed north. "It's that way, if you don't mind walking."

As they started toward the intersection, he glanced at the department windows again, and saw even more faces pressed up against them. First they found out he apparently had a daughter no one knew about from a marriage no one knew about, and now he was meeting the sheriff's new sister-in-law for lunch. He was going to be the subject of gossip so intense it would probably get back to Reese and Neely all the way down in the Caribbean.

He really did have the damnedest luck.

Chapter 4

The SteakOut was the perfect ranch-country steakhouse, Hallie thought as they followed the hostess to a table. The walls were paneled with what looked like old barn siding, and the chandeliers were made from wagon wheels. Various brands hung on the walls, along with other cowboy stuff—lassos, horseshoes and blankets, a few rodeo champion belt buckles. The food smelled wonderful, making her realize how hungry she was, but apparently it wasn't enough to distract the other diners from them.

"Damn, all these hicks look like they've never seen a kid before," Les muttered.

"More likely, they've never seen a kid with him—" Hallie nodded toward Brady, who looked as if he'd rather be staked to an anthill under the desert sun "—who wasn't in handcuffs."

And they probably hadn't seen him in here with a woman before, either. In fact, she wouldn't be surprised if this was the first time he'd been in the place.

"Yeah, well, if they don't quit staring, I'm gonna—"

"What?" Hallie asked. "Give 'em something to stare at?"

Les looked at her belligerently for a time before letting a smile slowly form. "This isn't the worst I can get, you know."

"I know. I was your age once, too."

"Yeah, but that was a long time ago."

Hallie returned the smile. "Not so long that I couldn't wrestle you to the ground and tickle you till you pee your pants."

On her left, sitting at the head of the table, Brady cleared his throat but didn't say anything. Hallie exchanged looks with Les, then said, "I believe your father wants us to be quiet."

"You be quiet. I gotta go to the bathroom." Les pushed her chair back, then headed back toward the entrance.

As soon as she was gone, Hallie's smile faded. Now that the surprise was wearing off, she knew it was silly, but she felt betrayed. She'd thought she and Brady were building some sort of friendship—thought they had some kind of connection that they lacked with most other people. He'd shared his secrets with her, for heaven's sake.

They probably hadn't been secrets at all. Probably everyone in town knew everything about him, and he'd just lied to her.

Lied.

The man who'd told her he was as honest as the day was long, and she'd believed him.

"Listen, Hallie…"

Jaw clamped shut, she glanced at him. She wouldn't make it easy for him by asking questions or responding in any way. Let him get the explanation out all on his own.

"This is as big a surprise to me as anyone else."

Her resolution to stay quiet did a quick *poof!* into thin air. "You just happened to forget that your marriage to your ex-wife produced a daughter?"

His mouth thinned. "No, of course not. But…she's not *my* daughter. At least, that's what I always believed."

"And why would you believe that? Because it was easier than being a part of her life? Because then you could go off to New Mexico and Colorado and Oklahoma and do what you wanted and never have to deal with her?"

His eyes turned cold and hard, as if they'd been chipped from a chunk of frozen sky. "I believed it because her mother swore it was true. I told you Sandra had a lot of affairs. She was convinced that one of her boyfriends was Les's father, not me. That's when I ended the marriage."

"But Les uses your name. She believes you're her father."

"I know. Apparently, Sandra lied to one of us." A scowl settled over his features. "I don't think Les knows why I haven't been around for fourteen years, and if she doesn't, I'd rather not tell her."

Of course not. What would it do to the mother-daughter relationship if he said, Hey, kid, you haven't had a father in your life because your mother drove him away? Though judging from the way Les looked, Hallie wasn't sure there was much of a mother-daughter relationship to damage.

"I didn't lie to you, Hallie. When you asked me if I had any kids, I honestly thought the answer was no." He reached back to rub his neck as if it ached. "Even now I don't know…"

"But you're going to let her stay."

"For a while. What else can I do?"

He could put her on a southbound bus, or drag her onto an airplane, or simply call her mother and demand that she come and get her. He could even turn her over to social services. After all, a man had no obligations to his ex-wife's child.

But if she was his child, too…

"I, uh…I can't get off early today," he went on, his gaze fixed somewhere around her hands, resting on the tabletop. "Reese is gone, and one of the deputies called in sick today, so we're shorthanded. I was wondering…if maybe you could…" He drew a deep breath, then met her gaze. "You're going to make me say it, aren't you?"

She smiled a bit. "There's no shame in asking favors. Everyone needs help from time to time."

"Not me."

"Ha. You need help right now, and the reason is on her way back here." She didn't need to look to know that Les was returning from the bathroom. The central focus of virtually every diner's attention was enough to tell her.

In a rush, Brady blurted out, "Will you keep an eye on her this afternoon?"

"See? That wasn't so bad." She watched as Les circled the next table, then pulled out her chair. "I'd be happy to."

"Redneck goobers," Les said as she sat down. "They should keep their looks to theirselves."

"Aw, come on, Les," Hallie gently chided. "If you didn't want people to look at you, you wouldn't dress in a manner guaranteed to make them look."

The kid gave her a scornful look, then scanned the menu. "Jeez, did I forget to mention that I'm a vegetarian? And you bring me to a freakin' steakhouse? Don't you know what red meat does to your body? To say nothing of the fact that consuming animal flesh goes against the laws of nature."

"Animals eat animals in the wild," Brady muttered.

"Some of them even eat their young," Hallie said with a teasing smile. "What kind of vegetarian are you? Vegan? Ovo, lacto or lacto-ovo?"

Les's expression turned suspicious. "What do you know about vegetarians?"

"Honey, I live in California, where I used to give parties for hundreds of people with menus that allowed for every dietary restriction you could possibly think of."

"I'm lacto-ovo. I eat ice cream. And cheese. And ranch dressing."

"So you could have a salad, a baked potato, some veggies and dessert."

"Yeah, I could." Les looked from her to Brady. "Is she your girlfriend?"

Hallie looked at him, too, curious about the answer he would give.

His cheeks flushed just a little under his dark skin, and he answered with a frown, "We're...friends."

"Are you sleeping with her?"

His flush turned to a deep crimson blush, and he opened his mouth twice without getting any words out.

"If he is," Hallie said, "it's none of your business. In fact, if he isn't, it's none of your business."

"I bet he isn't. Sandra says he's dreadfully lacking in social skills. She says he never had a clue how to make a woman happy."

And Sandra was a deceitful, scheming, lying witch, Hallie thought snidely.

The waitress took their orders while dividing her surreptitious looks between the three of them, then returned almost immediately with drinks and salads. When the silence had dragged on interminably, Hallie nudged Brady under the table, then nodded slightly toward Les.

He raised his brows, then gave a little shrug. "So…what grade are you in, Les?"

"Tenth."

"Do you like school?"

"Jeez, what kind of moron would I be if I said yes to that?"

This time Hallie nudged *her* under the table. Les scowled in response, then grudgingly said, "No, I don't *like* it, but I'm good at it."

After another awkward moment, Brady asked, "Do you still live in the same town?"

"The only moving we do is from one man's house to another. You think Sandra would consider moving away from Marshall City when she's got the only Marshall grandchild in existence?" To Hallie, Les added, "The whole damn town's named after his family. His parents practically, like, *own* the place. Can you believe it?"

Interesting. And yet he hated the entire state of Texas, where this town was located, and seemed more alone than anyone she'd ever met. Apparently, Sandra wasn't the only one who'd broken his heart.

"Do you ever see them?" he asked stiffly, his gaze gone cold and hard again.

"Sometimes," Les replied with a careless shrug. "But not without Sandra."

"Good." Brady breathed the word so softly that Hallie barely caught it, but she couldn't miss the muscle twitching in his jaw or the way his fingers gripped his fork as if he might grind the stainless steel to dust.

Very interesting.

The rest of the meal passed in similar fashion. When they left the restaurant, Hallie gave a soft sigh of relief. She liked Les, and obviously she liked Brady, but the tension radiating from him after that mention of his parents had been unnerving, as had being the center of attention for everyone else in the restaurant.

They walked back to the courthouse in silence, then stopped out front. "I have to go back to work," Brady said, avoiding looking at either of them as he spoke. "Hallie's offered to keep an eye on you until I get off."

"I don't need a baby-sitter," Les protested.

"Aw, come on," Hallie said. "A few people have been known to actually find me pleasant company."

A half frown, half pout settled on the girl's features, pulling the bar through her eyebrow askew. "Sandra *said* you'd dump me on someone else the first chance you got."

Hallie slid her arm through Les's. "Let me guess. Sandra doesn't work, and she devotes every waking moment to taking care of you."

"Well, you're right about the not working part."

Hallie started walking toward her car and gave the kid no choice but to come along. "Brady, I've got Neely's cell phone," she called over her shoulder. "Give us a call when you get off."

"Hallie."

She glanced back, then disentangled herself from Les. "My car's the blue Mercedes. Want to wait over there? I'll just be a minute." She strolled back to Brady, who hadn't moved a step.

"Thank you."

"Not a problem. What are…friends for?"

Again his cheeks turned pink. "I really appreciate this."

"I know." She smiled ruefully. "You haven't even begun to scratch the surface of your deep, dark secrets, have you?"

The look that came into his eyes was bleak and made her regret the question. "No. I don't guess I have." After a moment, he shook his head as if to clear it. "I'll call you."

"I'll be around." Impulsively she squeezed his hand, then walked away. When she reached her car, Les was leaning against it.

"Nice car," she said. "Adam has one just like it."

"Who's Adam?"

"Sandra's current husband." Then her features shifted fluidly into a scowl. "She was right. He doesn't want me around. But that's okay. I don't give a damn."

"That's not fair." Hallie unlocked the car doors, then slid behind the wheel. "You dropped in out of the blue. Any man would need an adjustment period, but especially one as private as your father."

"How long have you known him?"

"Not long." But she'd wager she knew him better than anyone else in town, if not anyone else, period.

"You know he's got money?"

Hallie backed out of the parking space and into the street, then turned onto Main. "Truthfully, I hadn't given it much thought." If she had, she probably would have guessed he had some income other than his undersheriff's salary. He'd commented on how little deputies were paid, and yet he drove a late-model pickup truck that probably cost more than most houses in town.

"If you're not after his money, then what?"

Hallie took advantage of a red light to study the girl, then gave a shake of her head as she drove on. Her mother had had way too much influence on this child. She hoped Brady let her stay around long enough to counteract some of it.

Following Stella's directions, she drove to the Tucker house, pulled into the driveway five minutes before her appointment with Marlene Tucker and shut off the engine.

"Is this where you live?" Les asked as they got out.

"Not at the moment. But I might rent the place."

"It's kind of shabby."

"Of course you would think so, being part of the family your whole town is named after."

"Don't make fun of me."

"Don't be such a snob." Hallie climbed the steps to the porch and took a seat on the swing. When she patted the space beside her, Les grudgingly followed her up, but sat in a nearby rocker instead.

"You ever take those things off?" Hallie asked, gesturing toward the headphones around the girl's neck.

"When I take a shower and when I sleep," she replied with a touch of sarcasm. "Other than that, no. This way I'm always ready when adults decide to talk to me." She slid her hand in the outside pocket of her backpack, and a moment later music blared from the headphones. With a smug smile, she turned it off again. "So…what're you after with Brady?"

"I'm not 'after' anything," Hallie said. "We're friends. I like him. I think he's a good, honorable, decent man—" she grinned wickedly "—who just happens to be drop-dead gorgeous."

"Huh. If you say so."

"What does your mother tell you about your father?"

"She only talks about him when she's between husbands or mad at me. Sometimes she says she never should have married him, and sometimes she says she never should have let him get away. He was her first husband, and she was real poor until she married him. She *hated* being poor."

"There are worse things in the world, like being unhappy. Being sick. Having no friends or morals or decency."

Clearly the conversation bored the child. "Where do you live in California?"

"Beverly Hills."

"Do you, like, know any movie stars?"

"A few."

"How do you know them? Are you rich?"

Hallie stood up as a station wagon turned off the highway and parked behind her car. "My ex-husband is a producer. He's rich."

"Well, hell, it's real easy to talk like being poor don't matter when you have money," Les scoffed before Hallie shushed her.

Marlene Tucker was in her seventies, Hallie estimated— white-haired, pink-cheeked and polite enough to hide any dismay she might have felt on meeting Les. Squinting through her glasses, she studied Les's hair after the introductions were finished. "The style doesn't do much for me, but I like the color. What's that called?"

Les looked far more accustomed to negative reactions to her

appearance than positive. She self-consciously touched her hair, then shrugged. "Royal Passion."

"Don't you know that would open my husband's eyes wide, if he came home and found me sporting a new Royal Passion 'do?" With a great laugh, Mrs. Tucker unlocked the door, then led them inside.

Contrary to Les's pronouncement, the house wasn't at all shabby. It was simple and cozy and had wood floors, a stone fireplace and a kitchen straight out of the fifties. The floor plan was straightforward—living room across the front, dining room and kitchen on one side, two bedrooms on the other and a bathroom in the middle. It was maybe one-tenth the size of her house in California, and she thought it was great. Without hesitation, she traded Mrs. Tucker two months' rent for the house keys, then stood on the porch and waved goodbye as the old lady drove away.

Feeling a wonderful sense of satisfaction, she turned to Les. "You want to help me pick out some furniture?"

The girl put on a scowl as fierce as any her father managed. "I hate it when grown-ups ask if I want to do something when it's clear I don't have a choice."

"No, you don't, sweetie," Hallie said, patting her cheek. "So put a smile on and bear it."

Brady might as well have taken the afternoon off, for all the work he'd accomplished. It was hard to concentrate on anything when he kept wondering which one of Sandra's stories was a lie. *Was* Les his daughter? If she wasn't, exactly what were his obligations to her? If she was, what kind of changes would that make in his life?

And what did Hallie think of the whole mess?

Not that it mattered. She was only in Buffalo Plains for a few weeks. Even if she were sticking around, Les was only in town for a few weeks, too. And even if Hallie were sticking around, it wouldn't be with him. He didn't want a relationship, and she didn't either, and...

Hell.

Reaching for the phone on his desk, he dialed Neely's cell phone number. Hallie answered on the second ring.

"Hey, this is Brady. Are you ready for me to pick up Les?"

"Anytime's okay. We've had a pretty good afternoon. I didn't have to beat her once."

"What?" he asked sharply.

There was a moment's silence, then she said, "That's a joke, Brady. We're at Yesteryear. Do you want me to bring her by the courthouse? Or I can take her to your house, unless you don't want me knowing where you live."

"I live on Cedar Street."

"Hmm. I still don't know. So what's the plan?"

There was a rustle of noise in the background, then he heard Les's voice. "Tell him I invited you to dinner."

"You did not," Hallie murmured.

"Hey, you want to, like, have dinner with us?" Les asked. "There. See, I did, too."

"Anyone want to talk to me?" Brady asked dryly.

"I'm just awaiting your instructions," Hallie replied.

He liked the sound of her voice, and he was grateful to her for taking care of Les all afternoon, and he hadn't spent more than five minutes alone with her at lunch. Maybe an invitation to dinner *was* in order—especially since it would delay his being alone with Les. "Why don't you take her to the house? Then— here's a great idea—you can stay and have dinner with us."

There was another brief silence before she answered. "You don't have to provide me with food. I can drop her off and go back to the motel."

"I know I don't have to. I want to."

"Well…"

"Of course she'll stay and eat," Les said loudly.

"The address is 128 East Cedar. It's the last street when you're headed south out of town, on the east side of the highway."

"Okay. We'll be there in a little bit."

He said goodbye and hung up, then leaned back in his chair. In the center of his desk mat was a yellow sticky note with an area code and phone number. It was Sandra's number, but he hadn't found the nerve to call it yet. If she really was in Mexico, as Les had said, calling would be a waste of time. Even if she wasn't in Mexico, she'd lied to him so many times in so many ways that he wouldn't believe her if she told him the sky was blue.

So either way, calling Sandra was pointless. There was only one way to find out beyond a doubt if Les was his daughter—DNA testing—and for that he needed her mother's consent or a court order, since he doubted Sandra would give her consent.

Maybe if he paid her enough.

And if the DNA proved he wasn't her father, how would that affect Les? And if it proved he was, how would she feel, knowing he'd required proof before he could want her? No matter what the outcome, she was the one with the most to lose.

He didn't know if he could be the one to take it away from her.

He stared at the phone number a moment longer, then picked up the note and stuck it in his wallet. Then he grabbed his Stetson, cell phone and pager and left.

He made a stop at the grocery store, where he kept telling himself people weren't paying any more attention to him than usual. But when he pushed his cart up to the cash register, and the checker and the bagger both clammed up and turned shades of pink, it was hard to believe their whispers hadn't been about him.

Great. So he got stared at when Hallie or Les was with him, and now he was going to get stared at when they weren't.

When he pulled into his driveway, the causes of his sudden notoriety were sitting on the porch and laughing. It was an amazing sound in a place that never heard laughter or soft, feminine voices.

"Ah, there's something satisfying about a man who knows his way around a grocery store," Hallie said, rising from the rocker to take one of the bags so he could unlock the door.

"I take it Max didn't?" He pushed the door open, then stepped back, holding the screen door, so she and Les could enter first.

"Max didn't even know regular people were allowed in grocery stores,'' Hallie said as she passed him. ''He thought only housekeepers and cooks could walk through those doors.''

''Les?'' Brady prompted.

Looking sullen, she got up and clomped across the porch and inside. She stopped in the middle of the living room, looked around, then muttered, ''I hate your house.''

''Of course you do.''

Eyes sparking, she whirled around to face him. ''What do you mean by that?''

He shrugged as he closed the door, then started toward the kitchen, where Hallie had gone. ''You're your mother's daughter.''

''I'm not like Sandra!''

''Yeah, right.'' He walked through the dining room and into the kitchen. Hallie was unpacking the groceries in the bag she carried, laying them out on the counter and not looking at him.

He set his bag down next to hers, then rested one hand on the counter, one on his hip. ''Go ahead and say it.''

She didn't pretend she had no advice to offer. Once the bag was empty, she neatly folded it, then looked up at him. ''Be a little patient, would you?''

Had he been impatient? Probably. Had he known comparing her to Sandra wasn't a good idea? Of course. Did he know what an obnoxious response *yeah, right* was under any circumstances? Absolutely.

''I'm going to get changed, then start dinner. If you want something to drink, help yourself, and make yourself comfortable in the living room.''

He went through the door that led down a short hallway to his bedroom, closed the door and changed into jeans and a T-shirt. In the walk-in closet, he dropped his uniform in the laundry basket on the closet floor, then hung his gun belt on a hook inside the door and laid his pistol on the shelf above his head…for all of five seconds. On second thought, he shoved a rodful of clothing aside to reveal a small wall-mounted gun rack. It held two rifles and a shotgun—all it was built for—but the drawer underneath was empty except for a few photographs. He slid his pistol inside, then hesitantly picked up the photos. He didn't look at them, though. He knew their images well—his grandmother, Logan, Sandra, himself.

And Les. Her mother had called her Alessandra, even then, when she was hardly bigger than a wish. He had always preferred sweetheart.

He returned the pictures to the drawer and locked it, then left the bedroom and went down the hall that passed the bathroom and the room he used for storage, then into the living room.

Les had plopped down in the middle of the sofa, her feet were planted on the coffee table, and she was flipping through the television channels.

He stood at the end of the couch and waited for her to acknowledge him. When she didn't, he moved between her and the television. That earned him a hateful look.

"I, uh... Look, I'm sorry. I didn't mean... I'm just sorry, okay?"

She stared at him but didn't speak.

"There's pop in the refrigerator and cookies and chips in the cabinet. Dinner will be ready in an hour or so."

On his way back to the kitchen, Brady opened his mouth wide, then wiggled his jaw side to side. He'd spent less than ninety minutes in Les's presence, and already he'd ground a few layers off his teeth. By the time she went home to Texas, he was going to be in need of serious dental work.

Hallie was still in the kitchen, drinking a diet pop and gazing out the window over the sink. When he stopped beside her to wash his hands, she shifted a few inches away.

"You have a nice view," she remarked.

He didn't look out the window. He saw the pasture out there every day, and had fallen into the habit most evenings of walking out after dark and feeding apples to the horses that grazed there. Instead he glanced down at her. "Yeah, I do."

She was dressed in pastels today—shorts in pale peach and a shirt in peach and mint-green stripes. With her hair in a ponytail that bounced every time she moved, she looked young and innocent, as if her life hadn't gone to hell on her a couple of times already.

He wondered how she managed that. He hadn't felt either young or innocent since he was five years old.

"I assume we're having spaghetti." She gestured toward the food on the counter. "Can I help?"

"Would you rather chop onions or open cans?"

"I'll chop." She washed her hands, then accepted the cutting board, knife and bag of onions. "Do you have a housekeeper?"

"For a place this small?"

"So you cook, clean, do your own laundry and shop for groceries. I'm amazed some smart woman hasn't snatched you up."

"I haven't been available for snatching," he said dryly.

"I've heard plenty of men say the same thing, and they had rings on their fingers and their signatures on the pre-nups before they even knew they were in danger."

"Did you and Max sign a pre-nup?"

"You bet. His lawyer would have had him declared incompetent if he'd tried to marry without one."

"But you still got the house and the Mercedes."

"He offered the house to speed things along. As for the car, it was a birthday present. It was a little extravagant for Max, but I thought it was just proof of how much he loved me. Turned out he just felt guilty about the bimbo."

"And you were never tempted to drive it into his pool or fill it with concrete or anything?"

"Tempted…but, contrary to popular opinion, too pragmatic."

"Popular opinion's not too popular," he commented. "Or accurate."

Her only response was a faint smile.

He emptied a half dozen cans of diced tomatoes and tomato sauce into a Dutch oven, added sugar, then seasoned it with salt, garlic and oregano. Usually he added Italian sausage sautéed with onions and bell peppers, but this time they would have to settle for just the vegetables.

Once the sauce was simmering, they returned to the living room. Hallie sat on the sofa, and Brady chose the easy chair at one end. "So…what did you guys do this afternoon?"

Hallie looked at Les, who was pretending to be engrossed in a rerun of "The Andy Griffith Show." When the kid ignored her, Hallie gave a gentle tug to one of her purple spikes, then said, "I rented a house."

A feeling oddly akin to panic tightened in his gut. "You're only staying a few more weeks. Why would you go to all that trouble?"

She gave him a chiding look. "It wasn't any trouble. For half the money I was paying at Motel Le Dump for one room, I've got five rooms and a huge bath. And it's just far enough outside town to be peaceful and quiet. As far as I can figure, my nearest neighbor is a grumpy undersheriff who likes to keep to himself, so he shouldn't be any trouble, either."

He frowned, considering the houses he could claim as neighbors. There weren't many, and all of them were occupied except… "You rented the Tucker place?"

She poked her elbow in Les's ribs. "It's that sharp mind and those brilliant powers of deduction that made him become a cop."

"Brilliant like Barney Fife," Les replied with a snort.

Brady chose to ignore the insult. "When are you moving in?"

"The furniture we picked out this afternoon will be delivered tomorrow, and I plan on sleeping in my very own bed tomorrow night."

So tomorrow night—and every other night she stayed in Buffalo Plains—she would be sleeping only a five-minute hike away. How easy was it going to be for him to sleep then?

Not at all.

Abruptly Les muted the television. "Did you bring my stuff?"

He was still thinking about Hallie in her bed and him in his own, so close but apart. Blinking, he focused on Les. "Your… Yeah, it's in the truck."

"Can I have it?" she asked with exaggerated patience, as if that had been her question all along.

If the duffel were in his pickup, he would toss her the keys and let her get it. But it was in his sheriff's vehicle, along with handcuffs, Flex-cuffs, his radio, his shotgun and plenty of other stuff he'd prefer she not get into. "I'll get it."

It took him maybe two minutes to get the bag and return. She was waiting impatiently at the end of the sofa, and as soon as he set it down, she hefted it over her shoulder, then looked around. "Where can I put it?"

Feeling helpless, he looked around, too. "I told you, I have only one bedroom. You'll have to sleep in here."

"Oh, that's just great." She flung out her arm to point at the closed door across the hall. "What's in there?"

"Just stuff." It had once been a guest room, but when he found the time, he intended to knock out the wall and enlarge the living room. What did he need with an extra bedroom? Logan was the only relative he could face without the very real threat of violence, and the chances that *he* would come knocking on Brady's door after seventeen years were nil. His only friends were Reese and Neely, who had their own place. He never brought women home with him, and the odds of him ever having a family of his own were slim.

Slimmer this morning than they were tonight.

"I'm fourteen years old," Les complained. "I can't camp out on the sofa like…like a boy. I need my privacy!"

"Maybe…" He glanced at Hallie, who looked as uncomfortable as he felt, then back at Les. "Maybe tomorrow you can pick out a bed, and I-I'll clear a space for it."

"You're damn right you will!" Dropping the duffel to the floor with a thud, she stomped down the hall to the bathroom and slammed the door hard enough to send vibrations through the air.

In the silence that followed, Hallie softly said, "Teenagers. Aren't they lovely?"

Chapter 5

Exhaling loudly, Brady sat down at the opposite end of the sofa. "I'm not surprised Sandra raised a self-centered brat. She intended for her little girl to be a mirror image of herself, and since *she's* a spoiled brat..."

Hallie considered all the things she could say, and settled on the most innocuous. "You married a purple-haired, pierced and tattooed girl?"

"No," he said sullenly, then unexpectedly he grinned. Sort of. "I bet it drives Sandra crazy to look at her."

"And anything that drives Sandra crazy can't be all bad, right?"

The sort-of-a-grin faded. "Why is she so angry?"

Hallie glanced toward the hallway, then stood up. "Let's go see the horses."

On the way through the kitchen, he stirred the spaghetti sauce, then picked up a handful of apples and tossed one to her. She took a bite as she went out the back door and down three steps into the yard.

"Hey, that's for the horses."

"I know. I'm just making sure it's nice and sweet for them."

His yard was broad and long and, she would bet, pretty much self-sufficient. He didn't strike her as the kind to spend his time watering, fertilizing and feeding. Keeping it mowed appeared to be the extent of his green thumb. It was empty of garden-y touches like flower beds, but there was a nice variety of trees—oaks, maples, dogwoods, redbuds and mimosas, as well as a row of crape myrtles on one side and another of forsythia opposite. No doubt it was a pretty place in the spring, as well as the fall. Not that she would be around to see it.

That thought shouldn't dim her pleasure at being there that very moment, but it did. Should that worry her?

They strolled back to the fence, where he gave a low whistle that brought five of the six horses grazing at a trot. Hallie leaned her arms on the top rail of the fence and watched while Brady fed apples to the first two horses.

"You want to feed one?"

"No, thank you." She would much rather photograph him doing it, but her cameras were back at the motel. One of these days she would get back in the habit of taking them with her wherever she went.

"You're not afraid of horses, are you?"

"Nope. I just don't like horse slobber on my hand." She waited until he'd run out of apples, then handed hers over. When it was gone, too, she shifted her gaze to him. "Les is angry with you, and from her perspective, she's got very good reasons. You disappeared from her life when she was a baby. You never called her, never sent her birthday or Christmas cards, never invited her for a visit. You abandoned her, and you bet she's angry about it."

"But I didn't know—"

"We're talking her perspective, remember? She doesn't know what her mother told you. All she knows is she's grown up without a father, and now she's finally met him and he's not at all happy to see her. She came here most likely with some fantasy of telling you who she was and being welcomed with open arms into your home and your life. Instead, you're treating her like some alien being who's more a nuisance than anything else."

He turned so the fence was at his back and leaned there. Accepting that there were no more apples, all the horses but one wandered away. That one, black and beautiful, nudged Brady's shoulder, then stuck his face right up next to Brady's. Absently he reached up to pat the horse.

Lucky animal.

"I don't even know how to talk to her," he said at last.

"Maybe you could start by telling her you're glad she's here, that you welcome this opportunity to get to know her."

"You mean, lie to her."

Hallie wasn't sure which of them her heart ached for more— Les, who would deny it until she was blue in the face, but who desperately needed someone to love her, or Brady, who would also deny it, but who also needed badly to love and be loved. "Would it be such a lie?" she asked softly. "Does she have to prove she's your daughter before you can care about her?"

He didn't answer, but stared off toward the house, his expression troubled and grim.

Hallie touched his arm. "Have all the doubts and questions you want. But for the few days or weeks she's here, can't you pretend to be who she thinks you are? After all, she might really be your daughter, and if you lose her now, you may never get her back."

"And what if she's *not* my daughter?"

She shrugged. "If that proves to be the case, what will it have cost you? A little hope?"

"And what will it cost *her* if I pretend to be her father and I'm not?"

"At least she'll find out you had a reason for abandoning her. That's got to be better than believing she wasn't good enough for her own father to love her." After another moment's silence, she asked, "How old was Les when Sandra told you you weren't her father?"

"Three months."

"Remember how you felt about her before that? She was your family. She depended on you to take care of her, and you were there for her. As far as she knows, that hasn't changed. She's still your family, and she still needs you."

"It's damned hard to reconcile that kid in the house with the baby I used to get up with in the middle of the night for feedings," he said dryly.

"We all grow up. I used to be a prissy little girl who played with dolls and cried if someone looked cross-eyed at me. And look at me now."

He did, his gaze starting at the top of her head and working its way down to her Pearly Pink Pale toes, and in the process warming her almost beyond bearing. "Yeah, and now you're a prissy woman who plays with men and can probably still turn on the waterworks at the drop of a pin."

"I'm not prissy," she said primly, "and at this point in my life, I don't even like men, but yes, I can cry on cue with the best of 'em."

"You like *me*."

Hallie studied him. Even though his mouth wasn't smiling, there was mischief in his blue eyes. Brady Marshall was *teasing*. This must be a day for the record books.

She screwed up her face as if his comment required serious thought. "Well...you *are* awfully cute, and you're a very nice man when you aren't so busy being distant, and you are definitely well worth playing with. Not that I make a habit of doing that."

"So why did you do it with me?"

With a blush warming her cheeks, she pushed away from the fence and started back toward the house. "Refer back to the 'you're awfully cute' part," she said when he caught up with her.

"That's all it was? If you hadn't liked the way I look, you would have chosen someone else?"

"Why did *you* do it with *me?* You could have accepted the beer I offered and told me to get lost."

"Men don't tell women like you to get lost."

"Every man I married did."

"You married fools." He said the words with a dismissive shrug, as if it was so obvious a fact it hardly needed stating. The very matter-of-fact-ness of it salved some little bit of the ache

deep inside her and smoothed over some little bit of the wound
to her pride.

She climbed the first step to the stoop, then turned to face
him. The extra height put her eye-to-eye with him. "So that was
it?" she asked, mimicking his own questions. "If you hadn't
liked the way I look, you would have gone home with someone
else?"

"I liked the way you looked, and the way you talked…" He
took a step up, forcing her to move up one more, too. "And the
way you felt, and the way you smelled…" He took one more
step, and so did she. "And I liked the way you smiled, and the
way it was obvious you didn't make a habit of doing that sort
of thing, and I especially liked the way you—"

She was on the stoop, her back to the wall and the railing
against her hip, and he was mere inches away, leaning closer,
his mustache tickling her ear, when a disgusted snort broke the
mood.

"Jeez, act like adults, would you?" Les said, her voice dripping disdain. "That sauce on the stove smells like it's burning,
and someone named Willl-burrr is on the phone." She did a
creditable imitation of Mr. Ed on the name, then managed to
sound pretty horsy as she stomped away.

More than a little regretful, Hallie smiled at Brady, still close
enough to send her heart rate into double time. "I'll check the
sauce. You talk to Wilbur." Ducking underneath his arm, she
opened the screen door and went into the kitchen. A moment
later he followed, taking the call on the phone mounted near the
hall door.

She stirred the sauce, lowered the heat, then put a pot of water
on to boil, and listened only partly to his conversation. Wilbur,
she was able to pick up, was the night jailer and was apparently
having trouble with one of his prisoners.

It was the sort of homey scene she remembered from her
childhood—her mother fixing dinner, her father talking. It was
the kind of scene she'd envisioned herself a part of when she
grew up and married, but she couldn't recall a single time it had
ever happened. The Madison family joke was that she'd made
a career of marrying well if not wisely. Even in her first mar-

riage, when she was only twenty, her husband had come with a large house, a housekeeper and a cook.

She'd envisioned a lot of things about marriage when she was a kid. That she would have as many babies as they could afford. That she and the children would be the most important things in her husband's life. That they would be together forever. That he would love her dearly, faithfully, endlessly.

What a joke.

Maybe someday her heart would harden enough that she could laugh at it.

When he got off the phone, Brady buttered thick slices of French bread, sprinkled them with garlic and put them in the oven, then set the table in the dining room. Was he as sorry as she that Les had interrupted them outside? Would he have kissed her if she hadn't? Would he try again? If he were any other man, she would say of course. After all, he'd spent two nights with her.

But he'd turned down the invitation for a third one.

And then he'd asked her to lunch, and then to dinner.

With him and his daughter.

Aw, heck, she'd never been any good at figuring out why a man did the things he did or what he might do in the future, and trying only made her head hurt. Better she should stick with something she *could* handle.

Like pasta.

Brady woke up in the middle of the night, groggy, disoriented and unable to kick his brain into gear. For a moment he couldn't figure out what had awakened him, then he heard voices and saw a dim glow at the end of the hallway and remembered.

Les.

Pushing back the sheet, he sat up and pulled on a T-shirt. He'd taken only a few steps, though, before heading back to grab his jeans off a chair and slide into them. There was nothing immodest about boxers—Les had changed into a pair of red-and-blue plaid ones and a T-shirt to sleep in—but it seemed improper for him.

He went down the hall and stopped in the living-room doorway. The light came from the TV. She was curled on her side on the couch, pillows under her head and a sheet tucked around her, and was watching a rerun of an old show he remembered from his childhood. After watching one episode, Logan had turned to him and innocently asked, Are other families really like that?

Had Les ever wondered the same thing? Had she wondered where *her* perfect family was, or what she'd done to deserve the life she had?

After a moment, he walked into the room and sat down on the arm of the easy chair. "Having trouble sleeping?"

Her expression swiftly turned to distrust and wariness. "I didn't have it turned up loud."

"No, you didn't." He gestured toward her. "You're almost too tall to fit on the couch."

"It's okay," she said with a shrug, then added, "For one night."

"I'll try to take off after lunch tomorrow and we'll go shopping for some furniture. I don't know if I'll have time to get that room cleaned out before the weekend, but at least we'll be able to get the bed in there."

"Yeah, sure."

After an awkward silence, he slid down into the chair. It had been almost ten o'clock when Hallie went home, and Les had walked out to the convertible with them. They'd had just enough privacy for Hallie to say one thing—*Remember what we talked about.* Since he had little doubt she would ask him about it the next time he saw her, he took a deep breath and said, "Listen, Les…"

She slowly sat up on the couch, and her entire body grew stiff. She was looking at him as if she expected the worst and hated him for it. Seeing things from her point of view, he couldn't blame her.

"I, uh…" What would he say to her if he knew beyond a doubt that she was his daughter? The answer came easily. Giving voice to it was another matter. "I know you probably can't tell it by the way things have gone, but…I'm glad you're here. I, uh…I've thought about you a lot." That part was true, just not recently. In the first months after he left Texas, both she and her mother had been on his mind constantly. After a while, though, he'd been forced to distance himself from them, just as he'd done with Logan after he'd disappeared.

You're a very nice man when you aren't so busy being distant, Hallie had said. What she didn't understand was that being distant was how he'd survived. His parents might not have taught him much, but they'd taught him how to disconnect, and damned if he hadn't learned the lesson well.

"*She* told you to say that, didn't she?"

Deliberately, he avoided answering. "You know, I've lived my whole life without Hallie telling me what to do. Not that I wouldn't take advice from her if she offered it. She's a lot smarter than she's given credit for." And a lot better with people than he'd ever imagined being.

Les combed her fingers through her hair. It wasn't standing on end now and, except for the color, looked fairly normal. All the earrings were gone, too, as well as the bar through her eyebrow, though the stud in her nose was still in place. He wondered what she would look like as an average kid—what color her hair was, if she was pretty, whether she resembled her mother at all.

Whether she resembled him at all.

There was her height, not that it was a particularly significant factor. Sandra was only five foot five, a full eleven inches shorter than him, so Les didn't get it from her. And Les's eyes were blue. Sandra's were brown. Again, though, that wasn't significant.

"I like Hallie," Les said at last.

"I do, too." And he meant it. Liked her in ways he'd never liked any woman, not even Neely. Liked her. Lusted after her. Looked for excuses to see her.

As long as she understood nothing would ever come of it....

With a feeling that felt uncomfortably like guilt nagging at him, he stood up. "I'm heading back to bed. Six o'clock comes early. Good night."

He was halfway down the hall before she softly spoke. "Good night."

* * *

After turning off the television, Les sat on the couch, arms wrapped around her knees, for a long time and listened. The house was quiet. Once in a while the bed springs creaked down the hall—with a bed that noisy, she'd bet Brady wouldn't be doing any fooling around for a while—but there were no other sounds besides annoying birds outside.

Once she was pretty sure he was asleep, she hauled up her backpack from the floor. The outside pockets held her CD player and a dozen CDs, and inside was everything she'd needed for the trip—money she'd lifted from Sandra's not-so-secret stash, her makeup bag, chewing gum and candy bars, tissues, journal and pen. The journal was leather-bound and had the year embossed on the front in gold. It had been a gift to her stepfather on his last birthday, but since he'd never had an original thought to put on paper, she'd claimed it for her own.

Now she pulled it out and flipped past entries in purple and hot-pink ink, not stopping until the pages fell open naturally. It was a photograph that made them do it. She'd found the original in her baby book, packed in a box in the attic, and scanned it into her computer. After fixing the faded color and red eyes, she'd printed out this copy.

According to the date on the original, she'd been four weeks old when the picture was taken. That meant *he* had been twenty-one. He didn't look much different than he did now. His hair was shorter, he'd put on weight and grown that mustache, and his eyes were bleaker, but she still would have recognized him.

Was part of that bleakness because of the way he'd abandoned her?

She hoped.

Sandra didn't talk about him a lot, but Les knew she hated Brady more than all her other ex-husbands combined. Back when she was a kid, Les had thought it was because he'd broken Sandra's heart. Then she'd figured out Sandra loved money more than people, and so she'd decided Sandra was pissed because she only got part of his money instead of it all.

Les didn't care if her mother did hate her father. She'd just wanted to meet him...and to piss off her mother at the same time.

'Cause Sandra wasn't at a spa in Mexico—she'd come back from there two weeks ago. She was home in Marshall City, and maybe by now she was wondering where her only child was. Maybe she was worried and calling Les's friends—not that she knew who Les's real friends were. She didn't know anything about Les, except that she didn't like putting up with her.

And now she'd met her father, and he didn't want her, either.

But that was okay, she told herself, swallowing over the lump in her throat as she returned the journal to the backpack, then curling up on the sofa. It wasn't like she needed either one of them. She was old enough and smart enough to get by on her own. Parents were a major pain.

And she'd had enough pain already.

On Wednesday, Hallie got moved into her house and Les got her bed. On Thursday, the two of them drove to Tulsa, where they spent the day shopping for linens and the tile for Neely's kitchen. On Friday, feeling guilty for spending all her time living her own life, she took Les with her for the twenty-mile drive to Heartbreak to check on the construction. Then they went into the Heartbreak Café for a late lunch.

The café was empty except for two pregnant women, one on either side of the counter, two little girls and a baby boy. Hallie recognized the twins as the flower girls in the wedding—Elly and Emma Harris. Though their features were identical, they couldn't have been more different unless they'd come from different species. Emma was as prim and prissy as any little girl could be, and Elly was rough-and-tumble and brimming with personality. She looked up from her ice-cream sundae when they entered the café, dismissed Hallie as unimportant, then gave Les a wide-eyed stare.

"Whoa!" the little girl said excitedly. "You got purple hair!"

For the second time, Les reacted self-consciously, mumbling, "Yeah, so what?"

"Do they make that in red? This kind of red?" Elly thrust

out a plastic holster that held a toy gun, its color a strange fire-engine red/bitter orange.

"Yeah, probably."

"Mama!" Elly raced to the pregnant woman on the stool. "Mama, could I get my hair like that, only in this color? Wouldn't 'at be cool? An' then you wouldn't have to be tellin' me to comb my hair all the time, and I would look *neat!* Can I, Mama?"

Her mother smiled patiently. "Honey, I let you wear cowboy boots when it's a hundred and twenty degrees outside. I let you dress yourself, even though your tastes are a bit…ah, adventurous. I even let you wear your cowboy hat with your Easter dress—"

"But not in church," Elly interrupted.

"Right. But, darlin', there's no way I'm letting you color your hair to match your holster. Sorry."

Elly's face fell, and her lower lip poked out. "Guess I'll have to wait 'til I'm growed." Then a sly look crept into her expression. "Unless maybe I can get Daddy to say yes."

The woman behind the counter waved her hand airily. "Have a seat wherever you want. Today's special is— Hey, you're Neely's sister, aren't you? I'm Shay Rafferty, and this is Olivia Harris."

"I'm Hallie Madison, and this—" Realizing Les had slowly drifted behind her, Hallie caught hold of her and pulled her around. "This is Les Marshall."

"Nice to meet you, Les," Shay said. "The special is pot roast with all the trimmings, and the menus are on the tables."

Hallie chose a booth, and Les slid onto the opposite bench. When a young woman came to take their order, Hallie ordered a burger and fries. Les asked for the same. One brow raised, Hallie looked at her long enough to make her scowl.

"Yeah, I ordered a hamburger," Les said irritably. "I'm gonna eat meat. So what?"

"Hey, it makes no difference to me. I'm just surprised."

"Well, don't be."

"Do you mind if I ask when you decided to become a vegetarian?"

For a moment, Les stared hard out the plate-glass window, then the corner of her mouth started twitching. Before she could stop herself, she was wearing a full-blown grin. "When I found out that it drove Sandra freakin' nuts. Brady didn't even say anything. He just started fixing meals that didn't have any meat. But Sandra.... She tries to control everything I do, but she can't make me eat something I don't want."

Hallie leaned forward. "Sweetie, you've got purple spiked hair, a tattoo around your belly button and about twenty extra holes in your body. If that's an example of your mother controlling you..."

"You know what I mean. She wants me to be just like her when she was a kid, only better. She wanted to be in all the clubs, so she tries to make me join them. She wanted to be cheerleader, so she made me try out. Her family was poor and she didn't have nice clothes, so she buys all these clothes that *she* would have wanted and tries to make me wear them, even if they look stupid on me. My bedroom is done the way *she* wanted. I can't even hang a poster on the wall because it doesn't 'go.'"

"So your mother's controlling, and you're rebelling." Hallie smiled. "It's not always easy being the rebel, is it?"

Les shrugged and mumbled something.

"I bet your father couldn't care less if you wanted to cover your bedroom walls in his house with posters." Of course, she would remember to tell him so when he picked up Les this afternoon. "How's it going with him?"

"I think he's afraid to be alone with me. That's why he's always asking you to stay."

It was true that Hallie had had dinner with them every night since Les's arrival. "Darn. Here I thought he might like me for myself, and now you tell me he's really just using me as a buffer."

"Do you like him? Not as a friend, but like, you want to go out with him, have sex with him—you know, boyfriend stuff?"

Hallie wished friendship was all she felt for Brady, but she'd never slept with a friend before. She'd never flirted with a friend before, either, or caught herself thinking about a friend darn near every time her attention wasn't required elsewhere. She'd never lain awake in her bed at night, wondering what a friend was doing or placing bets with herself on whether he'd ever come to her bed again.

But she had no expectations, remember?

And the last time she'd told Brady that, he'd responded in a husky voice, *Maybe you should.*

But he hadn't been volunteering for anything. A mere eight or ten hours later, she'd invited him into her room, and he'd turned her down flat. Oh, he'd softened the rejection by saying he would very much like to go inside with her, but the bottom line remained the same—he'd said good-night twenty feet from her door. And the closest he'd gotten to her since then was when he'd cornered her on his back porch Tuesday evening, when she'd thought he was going to kiss her.

"If it takes that long to think about it, then the answer must be yes," Les said. She looked as if her conclusion pleased her.

"The truth, Les," Hallie began gently, "is I've been divorced three times, and each time's been a whole lot harder than the last. I can't go through that again. So, yes, I like your father a lot and I find him very attractive, but...I'm not looking for another relationship. I just can't do it."

"Sandra says if a divorce hurts, you're not doing it right."

"Well, Sandra's wrong. If a divorce doesn't hurt, you're not doing the marriage right."

The conversation was lighter while they ate. When they finished, Hallie chatted for a few minutes with Neely's friends, then went to the cash register with Shay to pay.

Over by the door, Elly Harris was standing on a bench, leaning over the back of the booth to talk to Les. "What kind of name is Les?"

"It's a nickname."

"What does it mean?"

"Nothing."

"But it's got to mean something."

"It's just less. You know, more, less? Less than nothing? That's what it means."

Shay's gaze was sympathetic as she counted out the change.

For a moment Hallie couldn't move, then Shay folded her hand around Hallie's, closing it over the money, then squeezing it tightly. Hallie smiled faintly, dropped the cash in her purse, then drew a deep breath before looping her arm through Les's. "Come on, sweetie, let's head back to Buffalo Plains. It was nice meeting all of you," she said to Shay and the Harrises. "I'm sure we'll see you around."

The trip home was silent, partly because the top was down and the wind whipped their words away as soon as they were spoken, and partly because Hallie was thinking. As soon as she pulled into her driveway, she put those thoughts into words. "You need a new nickname."

Les's face turned as red as Elly's holster. "It doesn't matter."

"Either you pick out a new nickname or I'm calling you Alessandra."

She folded her arms across her chest. "I won't answer."

"I don't care."

"There's nothing wrong with Les. Alessandra should be beautiful and elegant and speak with a foreign accent, and that's not me."

"Les should be short, fat and bald—to say nothing of male— and that's not you, either." Hallie parked next to the house and shut off the engine, then turned toward the girl. "Is that really why you picked the name Les? Because it's short for your name as well as 'less than nothing'?"

Her jaw clamped tightly shut, Les jumped out of the car and started toward the house, then whirled around and came back. "That's what *she* said, and it's what *he* thinks, so why shouldn't I use it?" Spinning again, she crossed the yard with long strides, took the steps two at a time and flung herself into the porch swing.

Hallie slowly got out of the car, then leaned in to get her purse. Les's words made her stomach hurt—and made her want to punch someone, preferably Sandra. Since that wasn't an option, she took a couple of deep breaths as she climbed the stairs. She unlocked the front door and set her bag inside, then pulled the rocker close to the swing. "I'm sorry your mother said that, but I can promise you your father doesn't think it."

"Yes, he does. That's why he doesn't want to be alone with me, and that's why he abandoned me. He divorced her and just forgot I existed. He never wanted to talk to me, never wanted to see me. He sends a damn check every month. If he thought I was worth the trouble, he'd put a note in there for me once in a while, but he never has, not in fourteen years!"

Reaching out, Hallie unknotted Les's fingers, then took her hands tightly in her own. "Divorce is hard, honey, and there's a lot that the kids involved don't know or can't understand. But Brady's a good man, and his reasons for doing what he did have nothing to do with you. It's not your fault."

"Of course it's not my fault! I was a *baby!* What could I have done to deserve that?"

"You didn't deserve it," Hallie murmured. But Brady didn't deserve the blame, either. How could he have known all those years ago that, after making such a point of convincing him he *wasn't* her daughter's father, Sandra was going to raise the child to believe he was?

"They did what *they* wanted, and to hell with me. They didn't give a damn about me then, and they still don't. And I don't give a damn about them!"

Hallie sighed. She couldn't exactly argue the sentiments with Les, since she had no idea whether they were true. If they were discussing a normal family, she wouldn't hesitate to reassure the child that her parents loved her. But Sandra was far from a normal mother, and Brady wasn't at all convinced he was even a father.

So instead of addressing the sentiment, she focused on the way it had been presented. Leaning back in the rocker, she shook her head and made a tsk-ing sound. "We've got to do something about your language. I'd hate to wash your mouth out with soap every time you swear, but if that's what it takes…"

Les stared at her a moment, unbalanced by the shift in the conversation, then with belligerence that was mostly feigned— or so Hallie thought—she asked, "You and what army?"

"Oh, child, don't tempt me. Ask my sisters—I give only one warning, and then I act. And you got your warning the first time we met." She watched Les work to maintain her scowl. "Let me guess. You started swearing when you realized how much your mother disliked it. And you dyed your hair and got pierced and tattooed because you knew she would hate it. And you started going by Les because you knew she would hate that, too.'' Putting on a bad accent, she said, ''Vell, Miss Marshall, I think ve can safely say you have issues vith your mother.''

''Everyone who knows Sandra has issues with her.''

''But everyone isn't her daughter, whom she's supposed to love and treasure and protect with her life,'' Hallie said gently.

Les stretched out on the swing and tilted her head up to study the ceiling. Hallie watched her and thought about how wonderful a cool ocean breeze would feel. When Neely had shared her honeymoon plans with her sisters, Hallie had thought they were perfect. She was a firm believer that there was no problem a bikini, a handsome man and a tropical beach couldn't make better. Too bad she, Brady and Les were stuck in landlocked Oklahoma.

After a time Les announced, ''I won't answer to Alessandra. That's what *she* calls me.''

The ache in Hallie's stomach eased a bit. ''There are plenty of nicknames for it. How about Ally?''

''Great. Then we'd be Hallie and Ally.''

They were only going to be a part of each other's lives for another week or two, so that wasn't a concern, but Hallie didn't point that out. ''Okay. There's Andie. Or Sandy. Alessandra is the Italian variation of Alexandra, so you could be Alex, Alexa, Lexy or Zandra.''

''Sandy's too close to Sandra, Andie's petite, Zandra is exotic and I'm not.'' Then her expression softened, and her manner became hesitant. ''I-I kinda like Lexy. A Lexy could be five-ten and skinny and flat-chested.''

''Do you want to think about it, or ask your father's opinion?''

''What do *you* think?''

''I like it. Do you think you could get used to it?''

She blushed. ''I, uh…only started going by Les this summer. It won't be a problem.''

After another short silence, Hallie asked, "You want to go inside where it's about thirty degrees cooler?"

"Can't take the heat...or having a hot flash? You know, at your age..."

"At my age?" Hallie gave her a mock outraged look. "I'm going to give you a five-second head start, and then I'm gonna chase you down and tickle you until you cry uncle."

Les—nope, she was Lexy now—looked at her a moment, then without warning, jumped to her feet and dashed inside the house. Hallie was only three seconds behind her. Okay, so she cheated. She was more than twice the kid's age. She needed whatever advantage she could get.

They were on opposite sides of the dining table when the doorbell rang. Lexy grinned. "If you go answer the door, I'm outta here."

Hallie grinned, too. "That's okay. I know where you live. Sometime in the middle of a dark scary night, if something comes scratching at your bedroom window, wailing and moaning—"

"I'll tell Brady, and he'll arrest you—if he doesn't shoot you first."

The doorbell sounded again. Hallie glanced that way, and through the frosted glass, she could see the outline of a tall, broad-shouldered man wearing a cowboy hat. "That's Brady now. Come on. Reintroduce yourself to him." She extended one arm and wiggled her fingers. "Come on. All threats are off for the moment. No tickling."

Lexy hesitated, suspicion in her eyes, then came around the table. Hallie slid her arm around the girl's shoulders and walked into the living room and halfway to the door with her before she disregarded her own assurance and started tickling her.

With shrieks of laughter echoing around them, Lexy collapsed on the couch and Hallie got her best tickling in, until the girl gave in. "Okay, okay," she said, her voice unsteady. "You win. It couldn't have been a hot flash 'cause you're way too young for that, and I swear, I won't ever suggest you might be old again."

Hallie sat back on the coffee table. "Like I believe that."

"This from the woman who gave me a five-second head start that only lasted, like, one second? Who said all threats were off, then carried 'em out anyway?"

Brady cleared his throat, drawing both their gazes to the door, where he leaned one shoulder against the doorjamb and watched.

"Come in," Hallie said, skimming her hand over her hair to make sure her braid was still intact. "We were just having a discussion of things a child should never say to a woman who's fast on her feet and more devious than said child."

"Some discussion. I've broken up quieter domestic disputes."

Hallie shifted her dry gaze from him to Lexy. "Oh, look. The grumpy undersheriff has a sense of humor." Rising from the coffee table, she gave the girl a hand up, then pulled her across the room to him. "Go ahead."

Ducking her head, the girl shuffled her feet, then muttered, "You do it."

"Okay." She slid her arm around the kid's thin shoulders. "Being that it is a woman's prerogative to change her mind, as well as anything else under her control, this young woman has decided to change the name to which she'll answer. Alessandra is verboten, and Les is to be forgotten. From this day forward, she shall be known as Lexy—and if you forget, you'll have to deal with me.

"And dealing with me," she finished with a wink for Lexy and a slow, lazy grin for Brady, "can be hazardous to your health. Can't it, O ticklish one?"

Chapter 6

After his shower Saturday morning, Brady dressed in jeans and a T-shirt, then took his breakfast to the front porch to enjoy the only relatively cool moments of the day. This was his weekend off, though with Reese gone, he would be on call for anything his boss would normally handle. Usually on his Saturday off, he cleaned house, caught up on the laundry, bought groceries and did anything else that needed doing. Today, with Les—Lexy to consider, he didn't know what was on the agenda.

When he'd gone to pick her up yesterday and heard the hysterical laughter inside the house, he'd been surprised. He hadn't known she was capable of laughing like a kid. She was always so wary and on her guard around him. But there she'd been, on her back on the sofa, wiggling and giggling breathlessly, as if she did it all the time.

Hallie hadn't looked the least bit embarrassed when he'd made his presence known—a fact he liked a lot. Les—Lexy hadn't looked embarrassed, either, but wary, distrustful—a fact which he regretted a lot.

Hallie had turned down his usual dinner invitation, so it had been just him and the kid for the entire evening. They'd exchanged maybe twenty words, then wound up watching TV until he'd finally gone to bed. Not a great evening for either of them.

He didn't hear the door open behind him, but the screen door creaked, alerting him to Les's—damn it, he would get this right—to Lexy's presence.

She still wore her boxers and T-shirt, and made her way gingerly across the porch to sit at the opposite end of the step from him. Wrapping her arms around her legs, she rested her chin on her knees and stared out at the street.

"I didn't mean to wake you," he said after a while.

"You didn't. I usually get up early."

"You want some cereal?"

She shook her head. "Can we do something today?"

"Like what?"

"I don't know."

"I'm on call, so I have to stay close to home."

"Then never mind."

"That just means I need to stay in the county where I can respond to any calls. Do you have any idea what you want to do?"

"Is there a pool around here?"

"No, but there's a lake."

"We could go swimming."

"I don't swim, but I can take you. We can take a picnic."

"How can you not know how to swim? You had your own pool growing up."

Her innocent words cranked his nerves so tight he felt sick with it. "Let's just say I don't have a natural affinity for the water."

She fell silent again for a while before asking, "Could I hang a poster on the wall in my room?"

"Sure. There are some thumbtacks in the junk drawer in the kitchen."

After a solemn nod, she apparently found the chipped polish on her fingernails of great interest. She peeled and picked at it until she couldn't do any more damage before swiveling her head around to look him in the eye. "Is it true what Sandra said about your parents?"

The sick feeling came back, only about ten times as strong. and made his hands tremble so much that he had to set his cereal bowl down to stop the spoon from clattering against the dish. "What did she say?"

"That they— That you—" Her gaze flickered tellingly, then her cheeks turned pink and she shrugged and jumped to her feet. "Never mind. Forget I asked. I'm gonna take a shower and get dressed."

He watched her cross to the door in two strides, then forced himself to speak. "It's okay, Les-xy. It's just that...I-I'd rather not talk about some things. They're...hard."

She gazed at him a long time, looking about thirty-four instead of fourteen, then nodded. "I know. I'm gonna get dressed."

After she disappeared inside, he leaned back against the post that helped support the roof and sipped his coffee. A fourteen-year-old girl shouldn't be capable of that old, weary look, and she shouldn't have a clue that it hurt to give voice to some things in life. Damn Sandra and her selfishness...and damn him. He shouldn't have let her run him off so easily. He should have stuck around and demanded proof, one way or the other, of Lexy's paternity. He should have made life impossible for Sandra until she settled the issue to his satisfaction, to the court's and to Lexy's.

But if the proof had pointed to another father, he still would have left Texas, and most likely she still would have had no parent but Sandra. The damage still would have been done.

When he finished his coffee, he went inside and filled the sink with soapy water, put the dishes in, then gazed out the window. Across the pasture was a stand of trees, most of them blackjacks not good for much besides dozing down and, in this case, hiding the Tucker place from neighbors' prying eyes. He wondered what Hallie was doing, if she was an early riser, too, or if she preferred to laze around. He wondered if he sneaked out of the house after Lexy had gone to sleep some night and tapped on her bedroom window, if she would let him spend just a few hours in her bed.

Backing off from the thought, he washed the dishes, then

started a load of laundry, vacuumed and swept. By the time he finished, Lexy had finally come out of the bathroom and shut herself in her room. After about thirty minutes in there, she emerged. He glanced up from polishing the coffee table, then did a double take.

Her hair was still purple, but there were no spikes this morning. Instead, it curled all over her head, giving the appearance of being only about half as long as he'd thought. Her makeup had been toned down, and the outfit she wore was as close to normal as he'd seen so far—denim shorts, a tank top and sandals. Yes, the shorts were short and rode well below her waist, and the tank top was tight, didn't quite reach her waist, either, and lime-green, but they were a vast improvement over her usual style.

"Do you happen to have any shirts that actually fit, or should I add that to the shopping list?"

"Hey, Hallie wears her T-shirts tight, too, but I haven't heard you complaining about hers."

True, and she wouldn't. He hadn't yet seen Hallie in anything he didn't like…though he liked her best in nothing at all. Laughter and a smile—they flattered her most. "You haven't heard me complaining about yours, either. I just asked a question."

She rolled her eyes, returned to the bedroom, then came back a moment later with a white shirt. She put it on, tied the tails just below her waist, then rolled the sleeves to her elbows. "Better?"

"Yes."

"Parents are such prudes." She dropped down on the couch and turned on the TV, then immediately muted the sound. "Can Hallie go with us today?"

"If you want. Have you decided where you want to go?"

"I saw a sign in town the other day that said they were having something downtown with music and food and stuff. You know, like, some sort of street festival."

"The Sidewalk Sale." He'd forgotten about it, mostly because he'd had more important things on his mind this past week. It was Buffalo Plains's annual the-end-of-summer-is-near celebration and back-to-school sale. The first year he'd lived there, he'd walked down the street from end to end one time and felt so out of place among all the families and friends. He'd never been back, except for the one time he'd gotten called in to help Reese break up a fight in the closing hours. "Why don't you call Hallie and see if she wants to go? If she does, we can pick her up on our way."

"Okay."

Hallie was home, and after a few minutes of Lexy's wheedling, she agreed to join them. Lexy grabbed her backpack, then Brady locked up and followed her to his sheriff's department SUV. Leaving the front seat for Hallie, she climbed in the back seat, settled in, then announced, "Now this is more what I'm used to."

He looked at her over his shoulder, and she looked back, as innocent as a pierced, tattooed rebel child could appear. "Jeez, just kidding."

He figured he could trust her on that. Most likely an arrest would have been a quick ticket to the boarding school of Sandra's choice, and who could blame her? No one wanted a juvenile delinquent on their hands.

It took about two minutes to drive to Hallie's house—minutes that seemed endless. He was in damn sorry shape when the prospect of spending a miserably hot day outside in the sun with half the county around sounded like a great idea just because a certain woman was going to be there, too. That fact sent up warning flags all over the place, but it didn't stop his muscles from tightening when she came out of her house, and it didn't stop the need from taking hold in his gut or the hot, achy feeling from growing.

"Hi," she greeted when she climbed into the truck, then settled her camera bag on her lap. "Hey, Lexy, I didn't know your hair was curly. It's so *cute*."

In the rearview mirror, Brady watched Lexy comb her fingers through her hair, a frown on her face. "Sandra hates it. She says it lacks class. She says *she* would shave her head and be bald before she'd ever have curly hair."

How did you tell a teenage girl that her mother was full of crap and not to listen to anything she said? Brady wondered with a scowl. Before he found an answer, though, Hallie responded.

"Oh, she's probably just jealous. You're young and pretty, and you take attention away from her, and women like her don't like that."

"I bet no one takes attention away from you," Lexy said.

Hallie's laughter was light and easy. "Oh, sweetie, I've been invisible at every party I've gone to or given for four years. It's not easy when the guest lists include Julia Roberts, Charlize Theron and Lilah Grant."

"Lilah Grant looks like the queen of the planet Silicone," Lexy said, her voice heavy with disdain.

"Bless you, child," Hallie replied. "Can I adopt you?"

"I wish," Lexy murmured softly.

Though cars lined every street for blocks around the downtown area, Brady had no problem finding a convenient space—his reserved space behind the courthouse. It was one of the few perks of working for the county.

They cut through the courthouse, where he made a quick visit to the sheriff's department to let the dispatcher know he was in town, then stopped on the steps out front to survey the goings-on. All the merchants had tables on the sidewalks in front of their stores, there was an art show on the courthouse lawn, crafts booths were set up in the street and food vendors were located about every fifty feet, and of course, there were people everywhere. In the intersection in front of the bank, a bandstand had been erected, and a kiddie beauty pageant was taking place there now. Later in the day there would be other pageants, as well as live music.

"This is almost as good as the state fair," Hallie said with a beaming smile. "Remember when you were a kid, eating cotton candy and caramel apples and riding the Ferris wheel and the Tilt-a-Whirl?"

Brady shook his head.

"Your parents never took you to the fair?"

The muscle in his jaw twitched. "No."

Hallie was scandalized. Her mother had loved going to the fair even more than the kids had, if that was possible. They'd gotten there when the gates opened on the first Saturday morning and stayed until the gates closed again, and they'd sampled everything from food to crafts to livestock shows to rides. It had been a blast. "Sheesh, that's un-American. It's unnatural."

The corners of his mouth quirked into a thin smile, though that was a generous description. Grimace might be more accurate. "Unnatural. That's my parents," he said in a low rumble before deliberately, transparently, directing the conversation elsewhere. "Lexy, what do you want to do first?"

"Find the funnel cakes. I'm hungry." She set off, and Hallie and Brady followed her into the crowds.

"You're doing better with her," Hallie said.

"She's doing better, thanks to you."

"I haven't done anything special. I just like her."

"I imagine for her, that's pretty special. Her mother, you may have noticed, isn't particularly interested in her."

She smiled at a familiar face, then pulled her camera bag around in front so she could unzip it and remove one of the two cameras inside. When she rezipped it, Brady extended his hand and she passed the bag to him. "I've been wondering about that. How did you happen to marry a woman as utterly self-centered, vain and mercenary as Sandra appears to be?"

He was silent so long that she was about to write the question off when he shrugged. "She knew what she wanted and I was the way to get it. I was...alone. I made it easy for her."

Alone, she knew from her own experiences, often translated to *lonely.* Sandra had been poor, according to Lexy, and she'd wanted money, so she'd set her sights on the lonely rich kid, who'd probably had a miserable relationship with his parents, considering that even now, he couldn't seem to bear any conversation about them without overwhelming tension.

"How old were you?"

"Eighteen."

That muscle in his jaw was twitching again, so she decided to lighten the conversation. "Oh, you must have been easy pickins," she teased. "An eighteen-year-old boy with raging hormones, a beautiful and willing girl.... You didn't stand a chance, did you?"

"I was an idiot and a fool."

"Honey, that's part of being an eighteen-year-old boy. Haven't you learned that yet?"

They joined Lexy at the funnel-cake stand, where Brady paid for the fried batter cake laden with powdered sugar and calories. They walked and ate, window-shopped, traded hellos with people Hallie had met and some she hadn't, and she snapped off a roll of photographs. They stood in the shade and watched part of the talent show, ate fried alligator and sno-cones and talked about things of no consequence.

Hallie couldn't imagine a better way to spend a hot August Saturday.

They were looking at a rack of CDs—at least, Lexy was looking—three blocks from the courthouse when Brady's cell phone rang. He spoke for a moment before disconnecting, then said, "I've got to go to the department for a minute. I'll meet you guys around here when I'm done. You need any money, Lexy?"

"Nah. I've got some."

Hallie turned to watch him go, following his progress through the crowd. She wasn't the only female doing so, she noticed, and felt just a nibble of jealousy. She and Lexy were giving him no choice but to get out of his house once in a while and socialize, and when they were both gone, some other woman was going to benefit from it.

Life wasn't fair.

"Isn't he cute?"

"Hmm," Hallie answered absently.

Lexy poked her in the ribs. "Not my dad. *Him.*"

Hallie turned to look at the CD Lexy was holding. It was the latest offering of one of the ubiquitous boy bands, and the member she was pointing to had dirty blond hair and a scruffy beard—largely because he was too young, Hallie suspected, to grow a decent one.

She looked from the CD to the headphones around Lexy's neck. "You listen to *boy bands?*"

"Good God, no. But isn't he cute?"

Hallie moved closer to hug the girl. "Yes, he's cute. And thank heavens you don't listen to that stuff."

Just then she felt a tug on her camera strap, slung over one shoulder. As it slipped down her arm, she grabbed it in a tight hold, and felt the resistance immediately give. When she whirled around, two young men were trying to move away, but they were making slow progress, thanks to two women pushing baby strollers.

"Sorry," the shorter of the two said. His look was guilty, his manner unfriendly. "My arm got caught when I was trying to get by."

Lexy turned, her backpack swinging against Hallie. "Was that guy trying to steal your camera?"

"I don't think so. I think it was just an accident, like he said." But she had kind of a creepy feeling, and when the shorter man stopped before turning the corner and looked straight back at her, she shivered. "Unless you've found something you want, let's see if we can find Brady."

They ran into him coming out of the courthouse, then spent the next few hours wandering around and enjoying themselves. Finally, when the afternoon sun was at its hottest, they went to Brady's house so Lexy could change into her swimsuit, and then they drove to Buffalo Lake outside Heartbreak.

At the location Brady chose, there were concrete picnic tables, a boat ramp and a small sandy beach. As Lexy headed for the water, Hallie and Brady sat down atop a picnic table under a corrugated tin canopy, a few feet of warm concrete and a small cooler of cold drinks between them.

When Lexy started to strip off her shirt and shorts, Brady apparently found the boat passing by way off to his left quite interesting. With a grin, Hallie said, "You can look now. She's got her clothes off, and she's quite decent."

He gave her a steady look, as if he didn't have a clue what she was talking about.

"Come on, admit it. You were afraid she was wearing an itsy bitsy bikini under there, weren't you?" She knew, because she'd expected something outrageous herself. But it was just your average maillot, designed more for serious swimming than anything else.

"Can you swim?"

"I live in California, remember? Of course I can swim. And surf. And body surf. Never did learn to water-ski, though," she remarked as a boat towing a skier raced past. "Why?"

"Because if she gets into trouble, one of us ought to be able to help her."

"You can't swim?"

"Nope. I do well to manage showers."

"Sounds like you had a traumatic experience." She spoke softly, tentatively. If he wanted to talk, she would be happy to listen, but she didn't want to push him. She'd learned well that bad memories had to come out on their own schedule.

For a long time he sat there, watching Lexy swim parallel to shore with strong, sure strokes. After a time, he turned his head to look at Hallie. "You could say that. When I was about five, my father—"

Abruptly he broke off and straightened, bracing his hands on the table on either side of him, pressing so hard his fingers turned white. "We had a pool, and one day he decided to teach me how to swim. I didn't pick it up easily, so he kept me in the water for hours. I was sick from all the water and chlorine I'd swallowed, and I was so tired I could hardly hold my head above water. He got angry and...he left me there. If the housekeeper hadn't been watching, if she hadn't thrown me a float, then pulled me out...."

He would have drowned.

Hallie was horrified. She couldn't imagine a father doing such a thing to a child. Her own father had been the sweetest, most loving man in the world, and most fathers she'd known were the same. Heavens, Brady himself was proving to be a good father to Lexy, and he didn't even believe she was his child!

Because she didn't have a clue what to say, she impulsively reached for his hand, coaxing and pulling and forcing it free. She wrapped both her hands around it, and after a moment's hesitation, he held on.

"I'd give anything to hear that when your mother found out what he'd done, she killed the bastard, but I know that's not the way the story goes," she said quietly, fiercely.

"No. He's alive and presumably well."

"And that wasn't the only time…" Hallie hesitated, considered changing the subject, then drew a deep breath and started over. "That wasn't the only time he hurt you."

His only response was to tighten both his jaw and his grip on her hand, but only for a moment. Obviously uncomfortable, he pulled loose and stood up, then fixed his gaze somewhere around her feet. "I shouldn't have— Just forget all that, would you?"

"Sure," she lied.

"I'm going to check in with the office. I'll be back."

As he stalked across the grass toward the truck, she didn't point out that both his cell phone and the radio were there on the table beside her. Maybe he intended to use the radio in the SUV…or maybe he just needed a few minutes alone. Telling a story like that for what she would bet was the first time in thirty years had to be tough, especially for someone who kept to himself as much as he did.

And she couldn't find the words to express how touched she was that he'd trusted it to *her*.

He'd been gone five, maybe ten, minutes when Lexy came splashing out of the water. She wrapped a towel around her middle, shoved her feet into her sandals and grabbed her clothes for the quick trek across the grass to the table. "Where's Brady?"

"He had to call in and make sure all's well with the world."

Lexy slicked her hair back from her face. With her makeup washed away, she looked so young and innocent. She was a pretty girl, and she was going to break plenty of hearts someday. Hallie hoped one of them wasn't Brady's.

"You should have brought your suit," she said, dripping water as she took a can of pop from the cooler. "Even warm, the water feels good."

"You know, that's exactly what every thirty-year-old woman wants—to show up in public in a swimsuit with a teenage girl in *her* swimsuit."

"Brady would've appreciated it. He likes looking at you. You guys should go out tonight."

Hallie took out her own pop and swallowed a long cool drink, then dryly asked, "You think?"

"They're having a band at the Sidewalk Sale tonight, and dancing and everything. I heard some people talk about it. You guys should go."

"And what about you?"

"I can stay home."

"Alone?"

Lexy rolled her eyes. "I've done it plenty of times before."

"Not while living with Brady, you haven't. Wouldn't you be afraid?"

"What's to be afraid of? It's Buffalo Plains, Oklahoma, and my father's the acting sheriff. Hell—uh, heck, you'd only be a few blocks away. How long's it take to drive? Two minutes?" Lexy grinned. "So…you wanna do it?"

"It's a funny thing about going out—you need someone to ask you."

"You could ask him."

Of course she could. And he would probably turn her down, and she would feel like an idiot. Or worse, he would accept even though he'd rather not because he wouldn't want to hurt her feelings, and he would spend the whole evening wishing he were someplace else.

Putting on a cheery smile, Hallie said, "My plans for this evening include luxuriating in a bubble bath, then lounging around in my air-conditioned house in my bathrobe and eating ice cream for dinner."

"Dam—uh…"

"Darn," Hallie supplied. "Dang. Drat. They're all good substitutes."

"Darn," Lexy repeated, then stuck out her tongue. "How are you ever gonna get married if you insist on spending Saturday night home alone?"

"Honey, I'm not looking to get married again." And she meant it. She honestly, truly did.

Just maybe not quite so much as she had a week ago.

"Don't you want to have kids and someone to grow old with?"

"I got married three times wanting those things, and all I got was three divorces and a heart that can't break anymore. I plan

to be an adoring aunt to all the kids my sisters will have, and—''
she put on a wicked smile ''—if I feel the need for a man to
grow old with, I got enough cash from this last divorce to buy
one.''

Lexy crumpled her soft drink can and tossed it in a high arc
into the nearby trash pail, then looked past her. ''I was just
telling Hallie that I think you guys should go back to the Sidewalk Sale this evening for the dance. There's this movie on HBO
that I've been wanting to see, but you wouldn't like it, so you
guys can entertain each other at the dance while I watch it.''

Hallie shifted positions so she could see Brady standing on
the opposite side of the table. His hands were on his hips, and
he'd gotten a pair of dark glasses from the truck to hide his
eyes…and his embarrassment that he'd confided in her? Or was
it regret?

''You're too young to stay home alone.''

Lexy mimicked his position. ''I stay alone all the time.''

''Not in my house.''

''Shi—sheesh. Whaddya think—someone's gonna come arrest you for it?''

They stared at each other in stiff silence, and for the first time
Hallie saw a resemblance between them. Lexy's scowl matched
Brady's point for point, and her jaw was just as taut, just as
obstinate. Even the way their mouths flattened in a thin line that
quirked up on one side was the same. Of course, it could be
written off as learned behavior on Lexy's part or mere coincidence, but…it could also be evidence of that indefinable something passed down from parent to child along with the usual hair
color/eye color/body type.

Brady caved first. He drew a deep breath, then exhaled loudly.
''They'll be providing free baby-sitters in one of the empty
stores tonight for the people who are attending the dance. You
can help out there.''

''Or I could stay home and watch my movie.''

''Or we can both stay home and watch your movie.''

Lexy's gaze narrowed, probably calculating her odds of win-
ning, Hallie thought. Then she shrugged. ''Okay. It's a deal. I'll

help take care of the little hoodlums, and you guys can go to the dance.''

"Excuse me," Hallie said and, after a moment, they both looked at her. "Remember me? Home, bubble bath, ice cream, bathrobe?"

"Ask her to go to the dance," Lexy instructed.

"Do you want to go to the dance?" he obediently asked.

Oh, yeah. The last time she could remember wanting to go to a dance as much as she did this one, she was in high school and it was prom time. And that was exactly why she should stick to her plans for a quiet, lazy evening home alone. Wanting something that much wasn't good.

Wanting to be in Brady's arms that much wasn't good at all.

Oh, but the actual being there was fantastic. And could it really hurt? It wasn't as if it was even a real date—heavens, if Lexy hadn't pushed it, he never would have asked her. And considering he'd danced only four times at Neely and Reese's reception, once with the bride and once with each Madison sister, she was likely to spend most of the evening standing on the sidelines or dancing with strangers.

So she'd be an idiot to go on a real date with him, but this kind of fix-up to make the kid happy would be harmless. It would be like going out with a good friend. No risk, no danger, just fun.

Inwardly Hallie grimaced. She was feeding herself such a line of bull. Apparently, idiocy and foolishness weren't the sole province of eighteen-year-old boys.

"Yes," she said against her better judgment. "I'd like to go to the dance with you."

She hoped she didn't live to regret it.

By the time the music started at nine o'clock, the crowd had thinned considerably. All the booths and displays were gone, and the only vendors who remained were selling cold drinks, hot dogs and ice cream. Except around the bandstand, the only activity downtown was in the storefront that had once housed a fix-it shop. Now it was filled with teenagers and grandmothers riding herd on rambunctious kids.

Brady glanced at Hallie beside him. She'd changed into a summery dress that was red and fitted snugly to every one of her curves, and she'd fixed her hair up on her head in some soft, feminine style. She was by far the prettiest woman at the dance.

Definitely the prettiest woman not dancing.

"Well?" He gestured toward the section of pavement that was serving as dance floor.

She smiled at him. "In a minute. Tell me about some of the people here. Which ones are your friends?"

He didn't need to gaze across the crowd. "None of them. I have no friends besides Reese, Neely and Jace."

"And me."

"And you." But he didn't want her for a friend. He wanted…more.

It seemed he'd lived his entire life wanting more. For a time with Sandra, he'd thought he'd hit the jackpot—a beautiful wife, an adorable daughter, enough money to make their every wish come true. And then he'd found out the beautiful wife loved his money but not him, and the adorable daughter belonged to someone else, and what did money matter if he didn't have someone to spend it on?

He wanted…

A grim feeling settled over him. He wanted. That said it all.

"Okay, so tell me about these people you won't let be friends," Hallie said.

His first impulse was to argue the point with her, but he decided against it. Instead, he gestured toward the nearest couple. "That's Easy and Shay Rafferty. She owns the Heartbreak Café. He used to be a champion roper until an accident shattered his hip and cost him three fingers. Now he raises and trains horses. Next to them are Guthrie and Olivia Harris. They've got twin daughters and just had a son last spring, and now Olivia's pregnant again."

"And they couldn't be happier," Hallie murmured.

He didn't ask how she knew. It was so apparent on their faces that even a blind man couldn't miss it. "The blonde over there is Callie Sellers, the nurse-midwife who delivers all the babies around here. And the redhead with the body—" which couldn't be seen for all the men around her ''—is Isabella. She came to visit Callie in May and hasn't gone home yet.'' Isabella was pretty, voluptuous, sexy and played at being nothing more than that, but Brady had spent enough years running away to recognize the signs in someone else.

''And who's that gorgeous charmer with the blond hair?'' Hallie's sly look made it apparent the question was payback for the comment about Isabella's body.

''I've never been the least bit tempted by Isabella,'' he remarked, gazing down at her.

''And I'm sure she's given you plenty of chances.''

''A few.'' The redhead did make a habit of being extra…er, friendly whenever he saw her, but sultry, bold redheads weren't his style. ''Your gorgeous charmer is Ethan James, Guthrie Harris's half brother, and he's dancing with his wife, Grace.''

He watched the Jameses for a moment. They'd met in a bar in Buffalo Plains, spent one night together and gone their separate ways. Sounded familiar. But then Grace had gotten pregnant and Ethan had come back to Heartbreak, and the rest was history. They'd both been scarred by their pasts and scared by their present, but they'd overcome all their hurts and fears and changed each other's lives in the most fundamental ways. More than anyone else, he envied them, because more than anyone else, he could relate to them—at least, as far as the scarred and scared part.

How slim were the chances that Hallie might possibly get pregnant from their two nights together?

So slim as to be nonexistent. Besides, a baby wouldn't change things. She didn't want to get married, and neither did he.

He just wanted.

Suddenly feeling restless and achy, he pushed away from the tree where he'd been leaning and took her hand. ''Dance with me, Hallie.''

She nodded, and he led her across the grass and into the street, where he drew her close. She smelled like cool spring nights and delicate flowers, and she was warm and soft and fitted against him in all the right places. He clasped her right hand in his, and her left hand rested on his shoulder, her fingers flexing, then relaxing.

The time and temperature sign above the bank showed that it was ninety-two degrees, and the air was heavy. Large fans borrowed from the feed store were set up on either side of the street, and from time to time a breeze quickened, ruffling hair and fluttering dresses. Bugs by the hundreds gathered in the halos of the streetlights. All in all, it wasn't an ideal party setting. He'd grown up with second-floor glimpses of ideal parties. Jim and Rita Marshall had been generous, gracious hosts, and they'd taken every opportunity to prove it. If their guests had only known....

But for all the less-than-gracious aspects of the scene tonight, there was only one thing he would change about it—when they left, he wouldn't say good-night to Hallie at the door, then go home to sleep alone.

She had let him in twice before and had invited him another time. What would it take to persuade her to ask again?

And what right did he have to persuade her to do anything? She wasn't the sort of woman a man played with, then walked away from. *I got married three times*, she'd told Lexy, *and all I got was three divorces and a heart that can't break anymore*. She deserved a man who could commit to her, who could trust her, one she could trust to be there for her now and always.

And all he could do was use her, then eventually walk away.

Tilting her head back, she gazed up at him. "You seem a thousand miles away."

Just four hundred or so in Marshall City. And about nine blocks, at the motel. And a half mile, at her house. "Nope," he lied. "I was just thinking you're the prettiest woman here tonight."

"Thank you," she said with a dubious smile. "Though I'm sure every one of these men would argue that point with you."

He scowled at her. "Do I look like the sort of man people argue with?"

She laughed. "You look like a first-class phony. You act so tough and distant and unemotional, but underneath all that you're really a nice guy."

"Have you considered that maybe it's the nice-guy stuff that's phony?"

"No," she said, then rested her head on his shoulder again. Her answer was plain, simple, confident. He liked that.

After a moment's silence, she looked up again. "Can I ask you a question?"

"I don't think even a gag would stop you. You're not just the beautiful sister. You're the tenacious one."

"No, Kylie's the beautiful one. I'm the popular one."

"I've seen Kylie, and while she's pretty, you're the beautiful one. Trust me."

For an instant she looked...stricken? Anxious? Then she gently tugged his earlobe in admonishment. "You're distracting me. I want to ask you... When it's time for Lexy to go back to Texas, are you going to just let her go? Or are you going to stay in touch with her, let her come visit, let her continue to believe that you're her father?"

He'd half expected a question about his family, or the memory he never should have shared with her that afternoon. Now that she'd proven him wrong, he half wished she hadn't. He'd been brushing off questions about his family so long that he was an expert at it. He'd lied to his grandmother, his teachers, the pastor of their church, to Sandra, to Logan and even to himself.

But Lexy wasn't a subject to lie about, other than the necessary lie he was spinning out to the child herself. "Until I find out for sure that I'm not her father, I don't really have a choice, do I? I have to play the part, especially now that I've started."

"Is that going to be so difficult? She told me you've been sending support checks every month since you left, so the financial obligation won't change. Only the emotional one."

"Are you asking if I'm emotionally capable of being her father?" When she shrugged, so did he. "Like I said, I don't have a choice, do I?"

Truthfully, though he still felt awkward when alone with the kid, though he wished she looked and dressed like a normal teenage girl—normal for Buffalo Plains—and though he wished like hell that he didn't feel guilty every time he looked at her for leaving her to grow up with Sandra, he kind of liked the kid.

Well, maybe *liked* was too strong a word. He felt sorry for her. He believed he owed her something.

And he thought if he spent enough time with her, he could learn to love her.

And that could cost him more than he had to give.

"It matters to you whether she's your child, doesn't it?" Hallie asked softly, as if saying the words in a normal voice might have repercussions she wasn't prepared to face.

"Yes, it does." There was nothing wrong with that. In general people loved their own children more than someone else's. It was the way of the world...so why was he ashamed of himself for admitting it?

It was impossible to tell from Hallie's expression whether she was ashamed of him, too. "Wouldn't DNA tests prove it?"

"Yes."

"But...?"

He glanced at all the couples around them. No one seemed to be paying them any attention, although Isabella did raise her head from some cowboy's shoulder and give him a sultry smile and a wink. "Let's take a break."

They made their way to the sidewalk, bought a pop for him and bottled water for her, then started away from the festivities. After four quiet blocks, they came to the Canyon County Public Library. It was an imposing building, sitting in the center of an entire block that was built up behind stone retaining walls to three feet above street level. Steps cut through the retaining wall and led to a walkway then to the main entrance, and stretching across the top of the wall was a sucker-rod fence, a cheaper alternative to wrought iron.

"I need to take some pictures of this," Hallie remarked, drawing her fingers along the fence as they walked. When they reached the steps, she sat down, loosely clasped her hands and said, "Tell me the pros and cons of DNA testing."

He stood in front of her, hands in his hip pockets because he didn't know what else to do with them, and shrugged. "Well, as you're probably aware, accuracy is always an issue. You'll find that defense attorneys are much more convinced of DNA's reliability if it proves their clients' innocence, just as prosecutors are more convinced if it proves their defendants' guilt. However, scientists whose opinions aren't for sale in some courthouse believe it's *very* reliable, even foolproof, and they—''

"Tell me the pros and cons in relation to Brady and Lexy Marshall.''

He crouched in front of her, his knees resting on the edge of the first step. "What's she going to think if I ask for a vial of her blood because I think her mother's lied to her all these years?''

"That you don't want her any more than her mother does. That you're looking for a way out of having anything to do with her.''

"Exactly.''

"But what if the tests prove that it was *you* Sandra lied to, not Lexy? Then you'll know beyond a doubt that she's your daughter.''

"And she'll know beyond a doubt that I *needed* proof. That I couldn't—'' he took a breath, then went on "—that I couldn't want her or love her without it. And how will that make her feel?''

"Still unwanted and unloved.''

He nodded. And he knew all too well how that felt. The insecurities, the lack of self-esteem, the sense of worthlessness, the guilt that there must be something wrong with him if his own parents couldn't love him. It had taken him a long time to accept that he hadn't deserved the things that had happened to him. He didn't know if Logan had ever accepted it.

"So...you're willing to act as Lexy's father, not knowing one way or the other, for...how long?''

The answer stuck in his throat and made his gut tighten. She was talking—*they* were talking about a commitment here, and that was something he'd avoided religiously for the past fourteen years. But it was a different kind of commitment, he assured himself. A kid couldn't destroy him the way a woman could. A kid couldn't break his heart.

Yeah, right.

Hallie was waiting for his answer. After rolling his neck to loosen the tension there, he gave it. "As long as she wants.''

Unexpectedly, she leaned forward, cupped his face in her palms and kissed him. It was as innocent as a kiss could be, her mouth pressed firmly to his for only seconds, and it felt as intimate as a kiss could be. Still holding him, she drew back and murmured, "Right answer."

And then *he* kissed *her*. Hard, hungrily, threading his fingers through her hair, pulling her closer, thrusting his tongue into her mouth. She made a small sound in her throat, a whimper, but when he tried to back off, she clung to him, wrapped her arms around his neck and drew him down onto the steps with her.

In milliseconds he was incredibly turned on, hard and hot, but he had enough presence of mind when she slid her hands down his back to catch hold of them and wrap his fingers tightly around hers even as he maneuvered to get still closer to her. Unfortunately, between the unyielding concrete steps and her snug-fitting dress, he couldn't get anywhere near close enough…which was just as well. It was a public street, after all, and it wouldn't look good to have the acting sheriff arrested for public indecency by one of his own deputies.

With a groan, he ended the kiss and rolled over to sit next to her on the steps. His breathing was ragged, and hers was labored, but not so much that she couldn't speak.

"Tell me something, Brady," she murmured as she finished the task he'd started—taking down her hair—then combed her fingers through it. Clutching hairpins in one hand, she rested her elbows on her knees and her chin on her fists, and asked, "Why won't you let me touch you?"

Chapter 7

Though she would have been the last to expect it, Lexy had had a good time with the kids. Elly Harris and her twin were there, and some girls her own age who lived in Buffalo Plains. They'd been nice enough—mostly interested in her hair and earrings and the stud in her nose—but they'd known each other all their lives. One evening wasn't long enough to bother trying to fit her in. And she was cool with that. She knew what it was like when they got new kids at school back in Texas. They had to stick around a while before they could become part of any group.

The grandmothers had been pretty nice, too, once they got used to her. She didn't really know Sandra's mother—Sandra said she was an embarrassment—and she didn't like Brady's mother. Rita Marshall was cold and sour as a lemon, and she didn't like kids in general or Lexy in particular. That had never bothered Lexy, though, because the old witch didn't like Sandra, either, or Brady. She didn't have a single picture of him in the house. Hell, even Sandra had kept some pictures of him.

But these grannies were different. They laughed a lot and

played with the kids, and she hadn't heard them scream at the kids to shut up even once all evening.

It wasn't even close to midnight, but the party was starting to break up. Ranchers and farmers had to get up early in the morning, Mrs. Tucker had said, so everyone was heading home. Enough of the kids had been picked up that she told Lexy to go ahead and find her father.

"Thank you, Miss Lexy," the old lady said as Lexy slung her backpack over one shoulder. "We appreciate your help."

"You're welcome." She started to walk out, then turned back. "Good night."

"Good night, dear."

There probably weren't twenty people still dancing, and Lexy couldn't find Brady or Hallie in the bunch. She did spot Shay, though, from the café in Heartbreak, and went up to her. "Hi. Um, have you seen my dad and Hallie?"

"No, hon, I haven't." Shay glanced around, then asked loudly, "Has anyone seen Brady Marshall or Hallie Madison?"

A redhead glanced around the man she was plastered to. "Last time I saw Brady, he was heading down that way."

"Thanks." Lexy cut across to the street that ran parallel to Main and looked in the direction the redhead had pointed. It wasn't dark, but it wasn't nearly as well lit as right in front of the courthouse—not that she was scared. It just made it harder to see if they were down there. But, yeah, over on the left she could see someone, and he looked big and tall like Brady and wore dark clothes. Maybe he and Hallie had gone off to make out, she thought with a grin as she headed that way.

She'd gone about a block when she heard footsteps behind her. Quickly she spun around, but she couldn't see anyone. It was silly to get goose bumps over it, 'cause she was close enough to all those people to scream if something happened, and someone would surely come.

In the middle of the next block, she swore she heard voices—low, male, definitely behind her. But again when she turned, there was no one in sight. Maybe sound carried funny at night, or her imagination was running away with her. Or maybe someone really was following her and was hiding in the doorway of some store back there. Part of her really, really wanted to go back to the grannies and the kids and wait there for Brady to come and get her, but that same part was scared to go back past where someone might be hiding. And now she could tell almost for sure that that was Brady up ahead. He was standing on the sidewalk in front of a big building, which meant Hallie was around there somewhere.

So instead of turning back, Lexy just walked faster, and the footsteps got faster, too. For the first time in ages she was glad she was tall like her dad, because it meant she could take really long steps and move really fast. As she reached the corner, she glanced back and saw two men less than half a block away, and with a cry she started running. "Brady! Hallie!"

He turned, and Hallie popped up from the steps where she'd been sitting. He took a half dozen steps toward Lexy, and she launched herself into his arms. "I came looking for you, and these men started following me, and when I stopped, so did they, and when I walked faster, they did, too, and it scared me!"

"It's all right," he said, patting her shoulder kind of funny, like he didn't know how. "What men? Where did you see them?"

"Right back there," she said, pointing, but of course they were gone. "Honest, they were there. There were two of them, and they followed me from the dance. At first I thought I was just imagining it, because every time I turned around, there was no one there, but then I saw them, right there by that sign, but now they're gone."

Brady pushed her away, and she wanted really bad to cry, but then she saw he'd pulled a gun from its holster on his belt. "Hallie, you take Lexy and go to the sheriff's department and wait inside. I'm going to take a look around. Come on."

He hurried them back, stopping at the sign she'd pointed out. There was an alley just a few feet away. Hallie started to tug on Lexy's arm, but she dug in her heels just for a moment. "Be careful," she whispered.

He stopped at the entrance to the alley, looked back and smiled. "I always am."

This time when Hallie pulled, Lexy went with her, too stunned to protest. When she got home, she was going to mark this day in her journal.

For the first time in her whole entire life, her father had smiled at her.

Hallie and Lexy waited at the sheriff's office for nearly twenty minutes before Brady returned. He shook his head in response to their silent questions.

"I really did see somebody," Lexy said, distress sharp in her voice.

"I'm sure you did," he replied. "Maybe they got scared off when they realized you weren't alone, or it could have been some kids, just acting goofy. Whatever it was, don't wander off like that again, okay?"

"I just wanted to find you guys."

"I understand, but next time wait for us to find you."

Hallie stood nearby, silently willing him to say something more—*I worry about you; I don't want anything to happen to you; I need to know you're safe.* But he didn't seem inclined to go any further.

Then he surprised her. Though the action was as awkward as the comforting he'd offered Lexy on the sidewalk, he slid his arm around her shoulders and hugged her. Almost immediately he stepped away, opened the door and gruffly said, "Let's go home."

Hallie followed Lexy out the door with a knot in her throat.

It was a short, silent drive to her house. When Brady shut off the engine and opened his door, she said, "You don't have to get out."

He gave her a level look, one brow raised, then climbed out and shut the door. Not only did he walk her to the door, he insisted on going inside and checking the house. He really did believe Lexy, Hallie realized, and was taking no chances. Though she offered a half-hearted protest, she was glad he didn't listen. She really did believe Lexy, too, and the incident had left her a little shaken.

"You're not going anywhere tonight, are you?" he asked when they'd returned to the front door.

"At midnight? Where would I go?" She smiled unsteadily. "No, I'm in for the night."

"Lock the door behind me."

"I always do. Hey, don't scare me, okay? I live here alone, you know."

"You can come and stay with us."

Now there was an interesting invitation. She'd seen Lexy's daybed-built-for-one, which meant she would be sleeping on the couch. With Brady right down the hall in a room all his own, what were the odds that she would *stay* on the couch? Not good. So she would either seduce him, which wouldn't be a wise thing, considering how important he'd become to her, or she would try to seduce him and he would reject her, which would be painful, embarrassing and possibly more than her ego could take.

"No, thank you," she said politely. "I'll be fine here."

"You have my number at home?"

She nodded.

"Call me if you need anything, okay?" He looked for a moment as if he might kiss her. Sadly, the moment passed. "Go ahead and lock up."

With a regretful nod, she started to close the door, then paused with just enough space to catch a glimpse of him. "In one way, at least, Lexy's adventure turned out good for you."

"What's that?"

"It let you avoid answering my question. But that's okay. I'll just ask again. I'm the tenacious one, remember?"

"We've had that conversation before. In your motel room. Remember?"

Oh, she remembered. It had ended with him on his back and her on top of him and an incredible, wild, frenzied release that had curled her toes and left her too weak to do anything but sleep. "So you only want to be touched when you're naked and in bed and about to get laid."

A look of such sorrow came across his face that her heart ached for causing it. "No. That's not the only time. It's just…" He cleared the hoarseness from his voice, then said in a flat, emotionless tone, "I've got to get Lexy home."

"Sure. Thanks for a wonderful day." Wishing her voice

hadn't quavered on the words, she once again started to close the door, but he blocked it with his hand.

"Hallie—"

She smiled her best smile—the brightest and phoniest one she used when the only alternative was bursting into tears. "Go on. Take your daughter home. I'll see you later." She pushed against him, closed the door and locked it, then leaned against it. Holding her breath, she listened one moment, two, then finally heard his footsteps crossing the porch. One sad cry escaped her before she clamped her hand over her mouth, then dragged in a few deep breaths.

Her days of crying over men who found her lacking were over. So she wasn't the smart one, the capable one, the independent one. She wasn't the spineless, nothing-without-a-man one, either. Whatever problems Brady had with her were his problems.

Her problem was how to get over it.

She showered and put on her nightgown, then curled up on the old oak bed she'd found in a dusty corner of Stella Clark's shop with the binder Neely had given her before the wedding. It contained notes, photographs, sketches, ads torn from magazines and detailed instructions for every room in the new house.

Her sister was so organized it was scary, Hallie thought as she flipped through the pages. Neely could have given the binder to her contractor and been almost as assured of getting exactly what she wanted. Instead, she'd pleaded with Hallie to handle it for her…mostly, Hallie knew, because Neely had been worried about her. In the months following the divorce, Hallie had had a little trouble getting back into life—perfectly reasonable, she thought, for a third-time loser. Though she'd wanted to remain in hibernation in her Beverly Hills mansion, she hadn't been able to turn Neely down.

By the time she left Buffalo Plains—and Lexy and Brady—behind, she might need to return to her isolation. At the rate she was going, she wouldn't be fit for human company.

She reacquainted herself with all of Neely's wants and commands, then closed the notebook. It was nearly one-thirty, and the night was quiet except for an occasional car passing by on the highway. The bobwhites and tree frogs were singing out back, and from the more distant trees came a whippoorwill's cry. It was all so peaceful and could lull her to sleep in a heartbeat if she could just lose the anxious knot in her stomach.

When the phone on the night table rang, it made her jump and sent Neely's binder sliding. She caught the binder with one hand and grabbed for the phone with the other. "Hello."

"You should be asleep," Brady said.

"How do you know I wasn't?"

"I can lie here in bed and see a faint light through the trees over there."

"Why aren't *you* asleep?"

"Too much on my mind."

What? she wanted to ask. Lexy? His ex-wife? His parents? Maybe *her?* But she didn't ask. Wouldn't. "How's Lexy?"

"She's sound asleep. She's convinced herself that it was just a couple kids who happened to be walking behind her and decided to be stupid."

"Do you believe that?"

He was silent for a moment, then he murmured, "No. Buffalo Plains is a relatively safe place, but…things happen."

"Maybe getting scared once in a while is good. Maybe she'll think twice before doing something like that again."

"I hope so. I'd hate to have to put her on a leash."

"I'd pay money to see that," Hallie said dryly. Brady might make a great authority figure, but she had no doubt Lexy could really dig in when something was important enough to her.

"Are you okay?"

She set the binder on the floor, then slid underneath the covers. "I'm fine. Why wouldn't I be?"

"When I left, you seemed…"

She waited, wondering if he had a clue how close to tears she'd come, or why. She'd gotten the why only half right herself. She'd thought she was hurt because, once again, she wasn't enough for the man in her life. But there had been more to it than that. She'd been hurt because *he* was hurt. That look in his eyes just before he'd gone all blank and cold…. It had been enough to break a woman's heart.

"You seemed upset," he finally said. "I didn't mean to upset you."

"No, I'm not upset," she lied. "Did I remember to thank you for a very nice day?"

"Not necessary. Lexy and I appreciated your coming."

"Sheesh, we sound so formal, considering that we're each lying in our beds wearing… What *are* you wearing?"

He made a noise that sounded remarkably like a chuckle. "You ask the most impertinent questions."

She fixed her pillows, then turned off the lamp and snuggled in on her side. "On the contrary, at the moment I think it's quite pertinent." Then she slyly added, "I'll tell if you will."

"I don't need the torment, but thanks for offering." Then… "You turned your light out."

"Hmm. I like the sound of your voice in the dark." She gazed out her window and made out just a glimmer of light in the distance. It gave her a warm, secure feeling to know he was just on the other side of the trees and pasture—only minutes away if she needed him. "If you were a DJ, every woman in the country would tune in."

"You must be tired. You're getting silly."

"I am many things, but I am not and never have been the silly one. In fact, there *is* no silly one in the Madison family."

"I hate those labels you and your sisters hang on each other."

The emphatic tone of his voice made Hallie frown. "It's all in fun. With our names all ending in some variation of Lee—need I mention that our father's name was Lee?—it's just a way to help keep us straight."

"You defend them, but deep inside you don't really like them, either. Most of the ones you get stuck with—or stick yourself with—are putdowns, and they're just so much bull."

She didn't know what to say because she was surprised he noticed. Surprised he cared. Surprised that he was right. Whenever her family started attaching labels, it seemed the ones they gave her were the most insignificant, and she'd often thought it was because they saw her as the most insignificant sister. She was the only one without a college degree, without a career, without a purpose or a plan for her life, and she was the one who screwed up far more often than she got it right. And because *they* saw her that way, it was so much easier for her to view herself that way, too.

"No one really pays much attention to them," she said lamely.

"You do."

Her smile was unsteady and disappeared before it formed. "Not really," she lied again. "Besides, labels can be helpful. All anyone has to say about you is 'loner,' and we automatically know an awful lot about you. All you have to say about Lexy is 'teenage girl.' And all you have to say about me is 'loser.'"

The phone line actually hummed with tension. She shifted uncomfortably, brushed her hair back, then put on the fake cheery voice that went with the fake cheery smile. "Hey, it was a joke."

"And a bad one." He sounded as if he were scowling, an image she could all too easily call to mind.

"Sounds like the undersheriff is grumpy tonight," she teased.

"According to you, the undersheriff is grumpy all the time."

"Not all the time. I can recall at least twice that you were almost perfect."

"Just almost?"

She deliberately kept her tone light. "Well, there was that disappearing act you pulled before sunrise both mornings."

"Pardon me, but I had the distinct impression you didn't want anyone to know I'd spent the night with you."

That was a good excuse for the second time, but not the first. He'd left without a word, expecting to never see her again, and he'd done it, she thought, because *he* didn't want anyone to know he'd spent the night with her.

She wondered if he still felt that way.

And if she would ever get a chance to find out.

The sound of a yawn came over the line, then he murmured an apology. "Sorry. I guess I'd better let you go so we can both get some sleep."

"I'm glad you called." Just talking with him had made the knot in her stomach disappear. She felt relaxed, warm and drowsy.

"I'll see you tomorrow."

"Okay. Good night." She liked his assumption, even though they hadn't made any plans for Sunday. It had been a long time since anyone had assumed she would be a part of his day.

"Good— Aw, hell, go ahead and torment me. What *are* you wearing?"

She shifted under the covers, her satin chemise rubbing sensuously against her skin, then she smiled a naughty little smile. "Nothing at all. Sleep on that, Brady."

With his low groan echoing in her ear, she hung up and settled in to sleep.

It was after nine o'clock on Sunday morning when the phone awakened Hallie. She stared at it, too groggy for a moment to realize that it was the culprit making the awful racket. Finally, her brain kicked into gear and she reached for it. "Yeah."

"Hey, it's me," Brady said. He couldn't have gotten any more sleep than she had, but he sounded alert, brisk and all business, while she could hardly lift her head from the pillow. "I'm sorry to wake you, but I've got an emergency call, and after last night, I don't want to leave Lexy alone. Do you mind…?"

"No, not at all." She sat up and shoved her hair back from her face, then glanced out the window. It was another bright, sunny and hot day. She would give a lot to see a few rain clouds in the sky, and even more to feel raindrops falling on her head, but it didn't look as if it might happen today. "You want to bring her over on your way, or should I come over there?"

"She's not dressed yet. If you could come over…."

"I'll be there in ten minutes."

"Thanks, Hallie. Feel free to crawl into my bed and sleep a few hours more when you get here."

"Great. You invite me to bed when you're not in it. Be careful." She hung up, rubbed her face with both hands, then stumbled into the bathroom. It was a good thing she'd showered the night before. Otherwise, it would take her an hour to get ready. But all she had to do was wet her hair to tame a bad case of bed-head, brush her teeth and put on a minimum of makeup.

With her hair slicked back and a change into shorts and a T-shirt, she was out the door.

She drove the short distance to Brady's street, then turned. Up ahead a car was stopped in the middle of the street, blocking both lanes, and its driver was standing beside it, holding on to someone Hallie couldn't see, presumably trying to get that person into his car. She would have to drive around him on the grassy shoulder, and if she picked up a nail or anything else sharp in her tire because of a spat between some guy and his girlfriend, she would be so—

She hit the brakes, bringing the car to a stop with a sharp squeal, and immediately climbed out. "There you are, Lexy," she said, keeping her voice steady and calm by sheer will. She could see now that the man didn't have hold of Lexy, but had wrapped his fingers around her backpack strap—still a threatening move, in Hallie's opinion. "Who's your friend?"

The girl was scowling darkly, but it couldn't hide the fear in her blue eyes as she jerked her backpack free of his grip, circled far away from him and hurried to the Mercedes. "He's no friend of mine. Let's get out of here, Hallie."

"Get in the car," Hallie directed. She looked at the man's car—small, red, an older model with a mud-covered tag—then at him. He was probably in his early twenties, not as tall as Brady, brown hair, fair skin, everyday white-bread average. He wasn't handsome, wasn't homely, wasn't particularly memorable at all. "You're old enough to know better than to hassle a fourteen-year-old girl on the street."

His grin was too slick, too easy. "Fourteen? No way. You're kidding, right? She can't possibly be— Man, you aren't kidding, are you?" He raised both hands as he backed toward his car. "Hey, look, I'm sorry. I had no idea. I thought she was older. I'm really sorry. Hey, no harm, right? Sorry, kid," he called as he got into his car and drove away, accelerating quickly to about double the speed limit, then turning out of sight.

Hallie slid into her seat and fastened her seat belt before looking at Lexy. "Is your father already gone?"

"Yeah."

"Are you okay?"

"Yeah."

"You sure? Then would you please tell me what in the hell you're doing out here?"

"Heck," Lexy said, twisting her fingers together nervously. "Sam Hill. Blazes. They're all good substitutes."

"This is no time to be cute, Lexy. Why are you out here?"

"I just…I was just coming to meet you, and then that jerk came along and he was blocking my way and wouldn't let me by."

"Did Brady tell you I was coming over?"

"Yeah," she said petulantly. "He said ten minutes, and I waited ten minutes. Then I decided to walk up here and meet you on the way and then maybe we could go do something. Only that—that moron came along first. He kept asking if I needed a ride and saying it was too hot to walk and he'd take me anywhere I wanted to go. I told him I wasn't interested, but he just kept on and when I tried to go around him, he grabbed my backpack and wouldn't let go. Stupid jerk."

Her jaw clenched, Hallie tapped her nails on the steering wheel. She hated to bother Brady when he was busy, but if she waited until he'd finished with his emergency, the odds of finding the guy would dwindle away to nothing. And maybe he really hadn't meant any harm and there wasn't any reason to find him, other than to put the fear of God—and a father with a badge—into him, but after what had happened last night….

She drove the remaining block to the Marshall house and parked behind Brady's pickup. "You do have a key to the house?"

"I found Brady's extra one. He put it in the *junk* drawer, for heaven's sake. You'd think a cop would have better hiding places."

Once they were inside, Lexy tossed her backpack aside and flopped down on the couch to watch TV. Hallie went to the kitchen phone, then called, "Do you know his cell phone number?"

"Nope."

She located the phone book, then dialed the non-emergency number for the Canyon County Sheriff's Department. The woman who answered sounded older than dirt and tougher than nails, and she was none too anxious to help Hallie. "I can't give that number out," she interrupted the first time Hallie mentioned his cell phone.

"I don't expect you to give it to me. But can you get in touch with him—"

"He's on an emergency."

"I know that, and I wouldn't be calling if it weren't important. Can you contact him—"

"Not while he's on a call."

Hallie closed her eyes briefly, then said in her most patient voice, "Okay. Not a problem. I need to see a deputy as quickly as possible at 128 East Cedar about an incident a few minutes ago involving the acting sheriff's daughter."

"One-twenty-eight East— That's Brady's house."

"Yes, it is. Can you send someone?"

"I'll pass it on."

"Thank you," Hallie said sweetly, then she hung up and stuck out her tongue at the phone. She took the long way back into the living room, passing Brady's room and giving a longing glance at his bed. It was neatly made, without a wrinkle anywhere, and she would bet the sheets smelled enticingly of him. Not that she was going to get a chance to find out.

She entered the living room behind the sofa and bent to give Lexy a hug from behind. "You're lucky I don't turn you over my knee and paddle you."

"Huh," Lexy scoffed. "No way. *Nobody* paddles me." But for one sweet moment, she held tightly to Hallie, as if nobody hugged her, either, then she whispered, "I wish my dad was here."

"So do I."

"But since he's not…I'm glad you are."

Hallie closed her eyes to slow the dampness welling, then swallowed over the lump in her throat. "So am I, sweetie." *So am I.*

Chapter 8

There were some things a man should never have to get used to, and the sight of violent death was one of them. Brady kept his gaze on the timber in the distance as Ryan Sandoval, the county's chief criminal deputy, ran down what they'd learned so far—three cousins, partying through the night and into the morning; a dispute over one cousin's girlfriend, who happened to be another cousin's ex-wife; too much booze and an easily accessible loaded handgun. Now one of the cousins was going to the hospital, one was going to jail, and the third was going to the medical examiner's office.

What a waste of three young lives.

"Hell of a way to start a Sunday morning, isn't it?" Ryan commented.

"Hell of a way to start *any* morning...or to end any life. Has the family been notified?"

"Yeah. After calling us, the guy called his father. His parents live just down the road."

Brady started to speak, but a familiar call on the radio cut him off.

"County two, this is county fourteen."

345 SDL DNVJ   245 SDL DNVE

FIRST NAME   LAST NAME

ADDRESS

APT.#   CITY

STATE/PROV.   ZIP/POSTAL CODE

2 free books plus a free gift

2 free books

1 free book

Try Again!

He pulled the handheld from its pouch on his gun belt and pressed the mike button. "County two."

"Hey, Brady, this is Mitch. We got a call to your address—something about your daughter. I don't know anything else, but I'll be there in a minute. Thought you'd want to know."

The muscles in his stomach clenched, and a feeling he hadn't experienced in a long time began building inside him—pure, unadulterated fear. Was Lexy all right? What about Hallie? And why the hell did it happen now, when he was at least ten minutes away?

"Go on," Sandoval said with a sympathetic look. "We've got this covered."

"Thanks." As he returned to his SUV, he told Mitch he was on his way, tossed the radio onto the passenger seat, buckled up as he started the engine, then peeled out in a spray of gravel and dirt.

He made it back to town and to his house in nine minutes, and they were the longest nine minutes of his life. This wasn't good, he warned himself as he crossed the yard to the porch in about three steps. Neither Lexy nor Hallie was in his life for the long haul, and getting this involved with them could only hurt in the end.

Unfortunately, his self wasn't listening.

He took the steps in one stride, jerked open the screen door and burst into the living room. Mitch was sitting in the easy chair, and Hallie and Lexy were on the couch, both apparently none the worse for whatever had happened. As she'd done the night before, Lexy threw herself into his arms.

"I'm sorry!" she cried. "I know it was stupid, but I was sure I'd meet Hallie before I got to the highway, and I would've, too, if that jerk had left me alone! But I'm sorry, and I won't ever do anything like that again, I swear!"

On occasion his job put him in the position of comforting a distraught female, usually when he was making a death notification, and he'd never been at ease with it. Last night, when he'd found himself holding Lexy, he'd been just as awkward. Today... Maybe with practice, as with most things, it got easier, because the urge to push her thin, trembling body away wasn't nearly as strong as the urge to hold her until the shaking stopped.

"Mitch, you want to fill me in?"

The deputy did so quickly.

"Anyone come to mind who matches that description?"

"No one who drives a red car, or would try to pick up a kid on the street, especially your kid."

Brady shifted his attention to Hallie. "And you couldn't make out anything on the tag?"

She shook her head. "I can't even tell you what state it was. It was coated with mud...." Her forehead wrinkled in a frown as she slowly added, "But the car wasn't. It was relatively clean."

So some bastard had deliberately obscured his license tag before he'd tried to force Lexy into his car. Was he one of the men who'd followed her last night? And why? What did two men want with a purple-haired teenager with an attitude?

Mitch got to his feet. "We'll look out for the car, Brady, but..."

But without a make, model or tag number, their only chance of finding it would be pure luck.

Hey, sometimes it happened.

Freeing one arm from Lexy's grip, he shook hands with the deputy. "Thanks, Mitch. I appreciate it."

Once the door closed behind the deputy, Lexy drew back. "I know you're pissed."

"I'm not—" He considered it and decided that now the fear was almost gone, pissed was exactly what he was. "I told you you couldn't stay alone. I called Hallie to stay with you. I did that for a reason."

"Yeah." She ventured an unsteady grin. "But I thought it was because you wanted her to be here when you got back."

That wasn't his reason, merely an added benefit. But he kept any hint of that out of his expression and continued as if she hadn't spoken. "So as soon as I was gone, you went out by yourself and damn near got kidnapped."

His voice got louder with each word and made her flinch at

the end. Hanging her head, she said, "Hallie cussed, too, and she never cusses."

Well, almost never. He'd heard a few words from her...but he liked that she didn't swear. It was sweet, refined...and exactly the opposite of Sandra and his mother.

He seated her on the couch, then took the chair where the deputy had sat. "Have you had any problems like this at home?"

Lexy shook her head.

"No one ever hassles you?"

"Just Sandra and Adam."

"Adam...her husband?" After her nod, he asked, "What does he do for a living?"

"I don't know. But he makes a lot of money and has a lot of creepy guys working for him."

That didn't sound encouraging. Brady made a mental note to find out what he could about Adam Napier the next morning. "When this guy grabbed you, what did you do?"

Lexy shrugged. "I told him to let go. He didn't, and I tried to pull loose, and he tried to talk me into getting in his car, and then Hallie came."

"If it ever happens again, if you think some stranger's even thinking about touching you, scream. Kick. Bite. Kick him in the testicles. Gouge out his eye. I guarantee, when you're standing there holding it, he's gonna leave you alone."

"Ewww, that's gross."

"Maybe so, but it's not as gross as getting raped or beaten or murdered. Damn it, Lexy—! Do you know how lucky you are? Do you have any idea what he could have done to you?"

An uncertain look came over her face. "I—I don't think he meant to hurt me."

Brady swore under his breath. "Men don't force girls into their cars if they don't mean to hurt them."

"I—I—" She shuddered, rubbing her wrist, then jumped to her feet. "I'm gonna go clean up." Her boots made clomping noises as she crossed the living room to her bedroom, then headed toward the bathroom.

"Daughters are the reason fathers get gray hair," Hallie said softly.

Brady sighed, then dragged his fingers through his hair. "I'm glad you were there."

"If I'd been a couple minutes earlier, I could have caught her before she left the house and it never would have happened."

"Don't blame yourself because there's some bastard around here who likes little girls."

"Do you think that's all it is?"

He moved to the sofa, propped his feet on the coffee table and tilted his head back to gaze at the ceiling. "Hell, I don't know. Why Lexy? Her appearance is sure to draw attention. People may not notice a teenage girl with brown hair in shorts and a T-shirt, but they damn well won't forget seeing *her*. I just can't figure…"

After a moment's silence, Hallie said, "Well, you've had an eventful morning for your day off. Did everything turn out okay with your emergency?"

"There isn't any 'okay' for that situation. A man got drunk and in an argument, and killed one cousin and wounded another. They grew up together, have been best friends all their lives, and now…"

"I'm sorry. Do you need to go back there?"

He shook his head. "Nope. Barring any other emergencies, the rest of the day is mine. I think I'll get my leg irons out of the truck and chain Lexy to the couch. She can watch TV, listen to her music, sleep if she wants. What do you think?"

"I think she might take your self-defense advice to heart, and your eyes are too pretty to risk."

He directed a hard look her way. "My eyes aren't pretty. That's a girly word."

"Well, I'm a girly person, so I can use girly words." She mimicked his position, which required moving a foot or so closer. Now less than half a cushion separated them. "That night in the bar, I thought your eyes must surely be as dark as the rest of you, but then I saw they were this incredible blue…and shadowed. Wounded. Haunted."

Brady could tell she was looking at him, but he didn't turn

his head to meet her gaze. He was too comfortable the way he was, to say nothing of the fact he didn't want her to see whatever was in his eyes at the moment. She was too good at noticing things no one else ever did.

"So now you're playing the strong, silent type," she teased as she fixed her gaze elsewhere.

"I *am* the strong, silent type."

"It's easy to be silent when you've intimidated everyone into not asking questions for you to answer. I, however, am not easily intimidated—at least, by you—because I am the—"

He turned only his head to look at her and warned, "No labels."

She turned her head, too, and smiled a little. Her hair was combed straight back from her face and secured in a ponytail— a severe style that not many women he knew could pull off. Instead of looking severe on her, though, it emphasized the delicate, elegant lines of her face.

Damn, she was beautiful.

Her smile slowly faded, and her hazel eyes took on a dazed look as her lips parted on a soft breath. It took no more than that to make him hard, to make him want her more than he could recall ever wanting anything. He remembered all the reasons why he shouldn't, all the risks in getting involved—caring too much, losing too much, getting hurt again—and at that moment he didn't care. He wanted to make love to her, to be as intimate with her, both in bed and out, as a man and woman could be. He wanted to face all the risks and dangers.

He just didn't know how to do that and survive.

But one more kiss....

As he started to move toward her, her expression turned heavy with regret. She scooted away, turning on the sofa so she faced him, so her legs in front of her kept him from getting close.

"You don't want me to kiss you?"

"Oh, I want that and a lot more…but it wouldn't be wise."

He knew she was right but asked anyway. "Why do you say that?"

"You don't want to get involved."

"Neither do you." Then he added, "And you don't want to get hurt."

"Neither do you."

"But casual affairs aren't in your nature."

She smiled ruefully. "You were my first—and look how casual it's turned out. I told you, I'm the Madison family screwup. I can't even do a one-night stand right."

"You can blame that on me."

"I don't want to blame it on anyone. If I'd gotten it right, I never would have gotten to know you and Lexy, and that would be my loss. In my stronger moments, I know I've already risked more than I can afford. One of these days, Lexy is going to go home. One of these days *I'm* going home. And I'll miss both of you very much when that happens."

"And in your weaker moments?"

"In my weaker moments, I want to adopt your daughter, and beg, plead, seduce—whatever it takes to get just one more night with you."

One more night. Was it really so much to ask? They wouldn't be doing anything they hadn't already done. Three nights together wasn't likely to cause any more problems for them than two nights, was it? They were adults. They knew what the future held. If they accepted it, if they both went into this with their eyes open and expecting nothing more, wouldn't it be all right?

No. Their first night together, they hadn't even known each other's names. They'd been total strangers, and the sex had been purely physical. The second time they'd known a lot more about each other. He'd danced with her, held her in his arms in front of her entire family. He'd known about her three divorces, her pain, her insecurities. There had been some emotional connection.

Now they knew each other entirely too well. They were past the stage of having sex. If he made love to her, it would have to mean something and there would have to be at least the potential for a future.

But he couldn't offer that potential. As much as he liked her, as much as he liked the changes she and Lexy had brought to his life, he knew they weren't permanent. More, he knew he was neither ready nor willing to try to make them permanent. There were still things she didn't know, things he wasn't prepared to deal with.

And if he spent another night with her knowing that, she would be hurt, and he would suffer for it.

He pushed himself to his feet and started toward the kitchen. "If weakness is a problem, you need to eat to keep your strength up. You want an early lunch or a late breakfast?"

"Hmm…late breakfast."

"Yes, ma'am." He saluted her just before he left the room. Detouring to his room, he locked up his gun, hung up his gun belt and put the handheld radio in its charger, then went to the kitchen and opened the refrigerator. A breakfast to keep Hallie strong…. He set out eggs, cheese, bacon and sausage. That should make a good start.

But damned if he didn't wish they could both choose to be weak.

Just one more time.

"This is *not* my idea of fun."

Giving Lexy a chiding look, Hallie offered the sales clerk her credit card, then waited while the woman ran it through. "What's wrong, sweetie? Did you miss your nap today?"

"You're not funny."

"I wasn't trying to be. Tell me—did you get your lovely disposition from your father or your mother?"

"I didn't get *anything* from Sandra but a hard time."

"Uh-huh."

"If you'll sign here," the clerk said, then gestured toward two men at the end of the counter. "Tell them which vehicle is yours and they'll start loading it for you."

"It's the blue pickup right in front." She'd borrowed Brady's truck for this trip into Tulsa to pick up the tile for Neely's bathrooms and entry, and to choose and order the wood flooring for the rest of the house. Though she'd tried her best to avoid it, she'd caught herself more than once wishing it was her own house she was shopping for, with the prospect of sharing it with her own family.

The house part she could do. She still had zero desire to return to Beverly Hills to live. She hadn't given it much thought—the idea of leaving Oklahoma was one she preferred to avoid, since it also meant leaving Brady and Lexy—but one of these days soon she would. Maybe she would just hang a map of the country on a wall, close her eyes and throw a dart at it, then live where it landed.

Or maybe she'd find someplace not too terribly far from Heartbreak and Neely.

And Buffalo Plains and Brady.

And what? Exchange awkward greetings with him when she went to visit Neely and Reese? Maybe even have another one-night fling in a year or two? Or maybe find out on one visit that he was seeing someone else, and learn on another that he was married?

Perhaps, instead, she would make her home on whatever little bit of American soil was as far away from Buffalo Plains as possible without leaving the country.

"Hallie." Reaching across, Lexy waved her hand, with nails painted black, in front of Hallie's face. "Hey, snap out of it. She's been finished, like, forever. Let's go."

Giving a start, Hallie tucked the credit card and receipt in her wallet, then followed Lexy outside. As soon as they were settled in the truck, the girl said, "Let's go to a movie."

"Sorry. Not this time."

"Oh, come on. I just spent *three* hours with you in the floor place. Now let's do something fun."

"We were only there two hours—" Hallie glanced at the clock on the dashboard "—well, two and a half. Now I've got to deliver this tile to the guy who's going to lay it."

"Shouldn't he be picking up his own tile?"

"I don't know. I've never built a house before. But he's doing some special patterns that require a lot of cutting, and he asked me to pick it up for him, so I did."

"You just do everything anyone asks, don't you? Your sister says, Come watch over my house, and you drop everything and come. Brady says, Watch over my kid like she's three years old, and it doesn't even occur to you to tell him no. Except me. I ask to go to one lousy movie, but no, we can't do that.''

"Sweetie, I have thousands of dollars' worth of tile that took five weeks to get in from the manufacturer in the back of this truck, where anyone can reach it. I can't park outside a movie theater for two or three hours and just leave it there.'' She pulled onto the expressway that would take them back to Buffalo Plains and Heartbreak, merged into the traffic, then glanced at Lexy, slouched in the passenger seat. "And why shouldn't I help out my sister and your father? Why shouldn't I spend time with you? I *like* you.''

"Oh, yeah, sure. *Brady's* the one you like. You're just trying to get on his good side.''

She'd already been on his good side, Hallie thought with a faint smile—and, heavens, was it *good.* Of course, she would never say anything like that to Lexy. "Is it PMS, normal crankiness or just being a teenager that's got you in such a mood?''

Lexy's only response was a frown, then she pulled the ever-present headphones over her ears and reached inside her backpack to turn on the music.

Hallie didn't mind. She turned on the stereo and switched the setting from Brady's preferred country music to rock, then hummed along with the familiar tunes.

When they reached the outskirts of Buffalo Plains, Lexy removed her headphones. "Can we stop by the house? I gotta pee.''

"Such a refined and gracious request,'' Hallie teased as she turned onto the side street that was the quickest route to the Marshall house.

When she pulled into the driveway behind her Mercedes, Lexy unbuckled her seat belt and opened the door. "You can wait here if you want. I'm just gonna—'' sarcasm glinted in her eyes when she glanced at Hallie "—make use of the facilities, then change clothes.''

Good, Hallie thought silently as she nodded. After her relatively…er, ordinary clothes the past weekend, today Lexy had chosen black leggings that ended midcalf, a black tank top and, over it all, a sheer black dress printed with purple flowers. In keeping with the theme, every single earring she wore was a skull or dagger, and her lipstick was a purple so deep it appeared black in a certain light. It had been all Hallie could do to contain her shudder when she'd first seen her.

Black was hell—uh, hard on a person when the temperature was over a hundred, Lexy thought as she closed the pickup's door and started across the yard. When she'd gotten up this morning, it had seemed appropriate, considering that she had officially been gone a week and still there'd been no calls from Sandra.

How dense could her mother be? How could she possibly not know that the first place Lexy would go was to her father? Probably she did know, and just didn't care. And that was okay, 'cause Lexy didn't care, either. She could never see Sandra again, and it wouldn't matter to her at all. She was a lousy mother. Hell—heck—Lexy could take care of herself better than Sandra. She'd been doing it practically all her life. And she liked it here with Brady and Hallie. She kinda liked Buffalo Plains and Mrs. Tucker and the kids she'd met Saturday night, and that deputy Mitch who'd come to the house yesterday had been awfully cute. She'd liked him a whole lot.

But she'd still thought Sandra would have called by now.

Scowling because it hurt even though she didn't care, Lexy climbed the steps, then propped the screen door open with one foot. Brady had let her keep the key she'd snitched after she pointed out that not having it meant she and Hallie had to stay at his house all day or they couldn't come back once they'd left. Now she opened the door, took a step inside and froze.

Holy— Heck, darn, drat— Hell!

The living room was a mess. The pillows and cushions from the couch and chair were thrown all over the place, and the armchair lay on its side. The end tables were turned over, the lamps they'd held broken, their drawers emptied. All the books and videos from the shelves against the wall were on the floor, the fireplace mantel had been swept clean, and the few green plants had been dumped from their pots, stomped and broken.

And it didn't end there. She could see her own clothing scattered in the hallway, and in the dining room broken dishes and stuff from the cabinet drawers were everywhere.

Aw, hell, Brady was going to blame her for this, even though he would say he didn't. How could he not? His life had been perfectly normal until *she'd* come along. And now this....

And what if the people who did it were still around?

She backed out of the house and let the screen door bang, then backed to the edge of the porch. Instead of bothering with the steps, she jumped to the ground and reached Hallie's window in seconds. "Someone broke into the house, Hallie! It's all torn up! You gotta call Brady!"

Sandra would have questioned her and doubted her and gone to see for herself to make sure she wasn't lying, but not Hallie. She dug in her purse for her cell phone and started dialing without question. Lexy liked that.

Hugging her arms to her chest, Lexy leaned against the bed of the pickup and waited. If weird stuff didn't quit happening, Brady was going to send her away for sure, and he'd probably never let her come back. He was expecting her to leave soon anyway, though he hadn't asked her about it lately. But she didn't want him to decide before then that she was more trouble than she was worth.

Within seconds of Hallie getting off the phone, they heard a siren coming their way from the east side of town. It seemed like just seconds after that, though it must have been at least a couple minutes, when Brady turned onto the street from the highway to the west. Deputy Mitch arrived right after Brady, and they went in the house together, leaving Lexy and Hallie in the driveway.

"He's awfully good-looking, isn't he?" Hallie asked.

"Who?"

"Mitch."

Lexy copied one of her father's favorite looks—that long, steady, measuring gaze. "A little young for you, isn't he?"

Hallie's grin was wicked. "I like 'em young."

When Lexy didn't respond, Hallie poked her with her elbow. "Come on, lighten up. Everything's okay."

"Easy for you to say. Some idiot out there isn't stalking you."

"You're safe, Lexy. Your dad and I would never let anything happen to you." She slid her arm around Lexy's shoulders and hugged her close. Even though it was miserably hot and they were both sticky, it felt really good and—and motherly, Lexy thought. Not that she had much experience with motherly stuff. That wasn't one of the things Sandra was good at.

After a while, Brady came back out, looking real serious. "They kicked in the back door. It looks like they broke everything they could get their hands on, but as far as I can tell, nothing's missing."

"I have to deliver this stuff to Neely's tile guy," Hallie said, "but when I'm done, we'll come back and start cleaning up."

"No. I don't want you guys here alone. I'll do it this evening." He looked from her to Lexy. "Why did you come back here?"

"I have to use the bathroom. Can I go now?" Lexy asked.

"Yeah, sure. Be careful of the broken glass."

Hallie watched until Lexy was inside the house, then turned her attention to Brady. She'd seen plenty of men in uniform, but there was something quite amazing about him in *his* uniform. It fitted as if tailor-made, and the colors—green and khaki, with a tan cowboy hat to match—flattered him. Of course, she hadn't yet seen him in anything that didn't fit perfectly, and she doubted the color existed that wouldn't flatter his dark skin and hair.

Ah, the advantages of being to-die-for gorgeous.

"You look tired," she remarked.

"Not tired. Just puzzled. Why in hell would someone break in and not take anything? I mean, obviously they were searching for something, but *what?* All Lexy brought with her was a duffel bag of clothes, and God knows, nobody wants to steal them. What else could a fourteen-year-old girl have?"

"You're assuming this is connected to what happened Saturday night and yesterday morning," Hallie said quietly.

"I've lived here more than six years, and I've never had any trouble. Then Lexy comes to town and—" He gestured toward the house, then shook his head.

"But she's a kid. She's not even from around here."

"I know. And maybe it's time to send her back where she belongs."

Hallie stared at him, but he refused to meet her gaze. He looked so serious, so grim and cold. "You can't do that."

"Hey, we all knew from the day she got here that she had to go back sometime," he snapped. "Now seems like a good time."

"And what if this continues and you're not there to protect her?"

The muscle in his jaw started twitching. "Her mother will be there."

"*Sandra?* You're kidding, right?"

Wearing a chagrined look, as if he couldn't believe he'd suggested Sandra as a protector, he shrugged. "Her stepfather will be around."

"The man with all the creepy guys working for him? Oh, yeah, that makes me feel so much better. By all means, put her on the next bus that rolls through town and send her home to the parents who obviously love and protect her as if she were their most precious possession—the parents who thought it perfectly reasonable to put her on the damned bus in the first place!"

Finally he did look at her, his expression belligerent. But his eyes…his eyes were filled with shadows and worry. "So what do you suggest? I let her stay here, and hope we can catch these guys before they get her or you?"

"They're not interested in me."

"You're with her virtually all the time. If you get in their way…."

Hallie focused on breathing deeply, easing the tension and anger—and, yes, fear—knotted inside her. It was another hot day, and the sky was clear from horizon to horizon, a soft pale lazy blue that invited stretching out underneath it and relaxing. It was too bright a day to let darkness take control.

Calmer, she laid her hand on Brady's arm, bringing his attention to her. "Have you considered the possibility that this is just a run-of-the-mill, garden-variety break-in? Even a perfect little town like Buffalo Plains must have them from time to time."

"We get our share. But *nothing* was stolen."

"Maybe they didn't have time. Maybe they were looking for cash, jewelry—something small and easy to hide. Maybe—" She broke off as he solemnly shook his head. "She'll think you're looking for an excuse to get rid of her."

"She'll have to understand—"

"She's a kid, Brady, who's spending time with her father for the first time in her life. She's not going to understand."

"Then she'll just have to live with it."

When he started to turn away, Hallie tightened her grip on his arm. He turned back to look at her, and she quietly asked, "*Are* you looking for an excuse to get rid of her?"

He hadn't been cold a few minutes earlier, she realized. *Now* he was cold—hard, icy, unemotional except for the contempt that darkened his eyes. His movements tautly controlled, he loosened her fingers, then removed her hand from his arm and backed a few steps away. "Make your delivery, bring my truck back, then go to hell."

"Brady—"

As he crossed the yard to the steps, he gave no indication of hearing her. When he ran into Lexy at the door, he slid his arm around her shoulders, turned her and took her inside with him.

Then he closed the door.

Hallie stood there, stunned by his reaction. Under the circumstances, it had been a fair question. After all, it was one thing to pretend to be Lexy's father for a few weeks when life was normal. It was another when the girl apparently had enemies who made the situation dangerous. Almost every parent would risk his life to protect his own child. But how many would do the same for someone else's child?

Brady would.

Hallie wanted to go inside and apologize, to tell him she was worried—not just about Lexy, but about him and Lexy. But when she moved, she didn't start toward the house. Instead, she climbed into the driver's seat, started the engine and backed out of the driveway. Neely's tile guy lived a mile or two west of town and had a workshop out back. As she drove, she located the directions in her purse, then concentrated on following them.

When she'd agreed to help out Neely by spending these few weeks in Oklahoma, she'd thought it would be exactly what she needed—quiet, a slower pace, no familiar faces, a little bit of a job to make her feel useful and plenty of time for planning her future. She'd imagined that September first would roll around, and she would be healed, renewed and ready to face the world. She would know what she wanted to do and where she wanted to be, and life would be worth living again.

Ha!

Wait a minute. Silent wasn't emphatic enough. *"Ha!"* she said aloud, and was satisfied with the scorn and disdain she packed into the one word.

She'd been living in Fantasyland.

But where else would the flighty sister live?

Chapter 9

His house was a mess, and his life wasn't much better.

Brady stood in the middle of the living room, hands on his hips, and looked around. He'd cleaned up all the broken glass, put right the furniture and returned the books and videotapes to their shelves. Two trash bags held everything the punks had broken, and that was just from this room. Lexy had straightened her room and was working in the dining room now, and she was more than a little sullen about it.

He knew she hadn't overheard his conversation with Hallie that afternoon, because he'd found out later she'd been in the kitchen, talking to Mitch while he dusted around the door for fingerprints. Still, she'd been full of questions when she'd realized that Hallie had left without her, and when Hallie brought back the truck and picked up her car, then left again without a word to them, she'd gotten downright petulant.

"Lex? Let's take a break."

She came in from the dining room and stood at the end of the couch. With the table lamps broken and no overhead lights in the room, his only option for lighting had been to pull out the two oil lamps he kept for occasional power outages during the heavy spring and summer thunderstorms. They cast flickering shadows and gave the room a cozy, if dim, atmosphere.

Too bad he didn't have anyone to get cozy with.

"Why don't you find something good on TV, and I'll stick a frozen pizza in the oven," he suggested.

With a shrug, she dropped down on the couch and turned on the television. He went into the kitchen, stepping over pots and pans, canned goods and empty canisters, the contents of which had been dumped in the sink. He supposed he should be grateful for that, since they could have just as easily dumped the flour, sugar and coffee all over the floor.

But at the moment, about the only thing he could find it in him to be grateful for was the fact that Lexy and Hallie hadn't returned while the intruders were still there.

He put a large pizza in the oven and set the timer, then began picking up everything on the floor that didn't belong there. He'd just gathered an armload of pans when Lexy spoke from the doorway.

"Hallie volunteered to help with all this, so where is she?"

His gaze shifted automatically to the window, where no lights showed on the other side of the pasture. That was a good question. The only two rooms in her house whose lights he couldn't see from his own house were the bathroom and the dining room. It was doubtful she was sitting over there in the dark and unlikely she'd gone to bed this early. Though she'd met a lot of people, he couldn't think of any she knew well enough to go out with, and there was no place open for shopping at this time of night.

Of course, there was always the bar where he'd met her.

He immediately dismissed that idea. She didn't make a habit of picking up men in bars.

Even though she'd picked him up in one.

But that had been significantly out of character for her.

And where was it written that she was restricted to only one out-of-character act?

She wasn't the type.

But that hadn't stopped her with him.

"I imagine she's home or…doing something."

"But she's not *here*. Why? What did you say to her to make her not come over?"

Not much, he thought bitterly. Just *Go to hell.*

Of course he hadn't meant it. He'd been angry— No. The least he could do was be honest with himself, if no one else. He'd been hurt that she, of all people, could ask that question of him. *Are you looking for an excuse to get rid of her?*

She knew him better than anyone, and yet she doubted him. She believed he would pretend concern for Lexy's safety when his real agenda was to remove her from his life.

Which meant she didn't know him at all.

"What makes you think I said something?" he asked, avoiding looking at her as he ran water into the sink.

"Because she never would have left like that if you hadn't. Because she would have said goodbye, and she would have come back, like she said she would, unless *you* did something to keep her away."

It must be nice to know that someone had such faith in you, Brady thought as he began washing the pots and pans. But it wasn't fair that Lexy had that faith in Hallie and not him. He was her *father,* for God's sake, while Hallie was only…

His words echoed in his head. He was no closer today to knowing whether he was her father than he'd been the day she showed up in town. How had he forgotten that? Was he getting too comfortable with the role he was playing?

He couldn't afford that.

He just wasn't sure he could stop it.

"Well?"

He looked at her over his shoulder. Before they'd started cleaning, she'd changed into a pair of faded cutoffs and a Marshall High School T-shirt that was about three sizes too big for her. It was such a normal outfit that he hardly even noticed the purple hair or all the piercings. He hadn't suspected that she even owned such clothes.

Turning back to the sink, he asked, "Why don't you go watch TV?"

"Why don't you answer my question?"

"I don't know where Hallie is."

"That wasn't the question. It was what did you say to make her leave the way she did and not come back?"

"What we talked about is between her and me."

"When it means *I* don't get to see her, it involves me, too."

Impatience surged through him and made his voice sharper than he'd intended. "Just let it drop, Lexy. It's none of your business."

She gave him a go-to-hell look, then spun around and stomped into the living room. A moment later she switched the TV to her favorite music channel—if that discordant, arrhythmic din could be called music—and raised the volume to ear-splitting. His nearest neighbors were an elderly couple who were both hard of hearing, but he wouldn't be surprised if even they could hear it. But instead of yelling at Lexy to turn it down—no doubt the response she was hoping for—he gritted his teeth and worked at ignoring it.

He'd washed about half the dishes when the timer went off. After drying his hands, he took out the pizza, cut it and dished up three slices each on two plates, then carried them along with two soft drinks into the living room. "Turn that down while we eat."

She pretended not to hear him, so he set down the food, then used the remote to crank down the volume to a respectable level.

He'd eaten one piece of pizza and started on another one before he finally broke the silence. "When does the new school year start?"

She mumbled three indistinct sounds that gave the definite flavor of *I don't know.*

"Does it start in August?"

"Hm."

"Toward the end of the month?"

She shrugged, then gave him a sweetly sarcastic smile that reminded him so much of her mother he couldn't stand it. "Counting the days until you're free of me?"

"No." Drawing a breath, he forced himself to go on. "Believe it or not, Lexy, I've liked having you here." After living totally alone for so many years, it was a big change, having someone to come home to, to share meals with, to entertain and be entertained by. He didn't want to even think about how empty his life was going to be once she and Hallie were gone. He would have to learn living alone all over again, and instinct warned him it was going to be a hell of a lot harder this time than the first time.

"But…?"

He shook his head. "No 'but.'"

"There always is. But you've had enough now. You want your life back. You're tired of the hassle."

He shook his head again. "There's no 'but.' Sorry to disappoint you." After a moment, he added, "I was thinking…maybe you could come back at Thanksgiving."

Her jaw literally dropped open as she stared at him in astonishment. She hadn't expected an invitation to return. She believed he was her father, but she'd thought that once this visit was over, he wouldn't want to see her again.

Hallie was right. If he tried to send Lexy home now, before her visit was scheduled to end, she would never buy the story that he was concerned about her safety. She would believe he was using the break-in and the attempted kidnapping merely as excuses to get rid of her. She'll just have to live with that, he'd told Hallie—an adequate response if they were talking about a normal kid with a normal upbringing and a mother who loved her. But Lexy's life had never been normal, and she'd never known with any certainty that *anyone* had ever loved her.

He knew how that could damage a person. He knew all too well how it could affect a person's entire life.

And whether she was his daughter or someone else's, he didn't want her to grow up like him.

"Thanksgiving," she echoed. "S-sure, th-that would be grea—okay." Then she grinned sheepishly. "Nah, that would be *great.*"

"Then we'll get your airline reservations before you go home, okay?"

Still grinning, she bobbed her head.

They polished off the rest of the pizza, then returned to the cleanup. By eleven o'clock, everything was back in its place and, except for all the missing breakables and the two-by-four nailed across the back door to secure it, the house looked none the worse. Brady glanced around the kitchen, then yawned. "I'm going to bed."

"I think I'll watch a little TV first." Lexy started out of the room, then came back, raised onto her toes and brushed the slightest of kisses to his jaw. "Good night," she muttered, her face turning red as she hurried away.

He stared after her a long time before turning down the hall and into his bedroom. He didn't bother with a light, but undressed in the dark and slid underneath the top sheet. He could see out the window that the Tucker farmhouse was dark, which very well might mean Hallie was in bed asleep. Or in bed not asleep. Or in bed and not alone. Or maybe she wasn't there at all. Maybe....

He rolled onto his side, away from the window, and closed his eyes. He'd been satisfied with living alone the past six years, until first Hallie, then Lexy, had come into his life. Of course he'd been needy those years, though he didn't like to admit it.

But when had he become so greedy?

The sound of the screen door opening was soft, familiar, but so out of place in the middle of the night that it woke Brady from a restless sleep. The night's silence was heavy as he listened to a bird's call, a gurgling from the refrigerator in the next room, the tick of the kitchen clock. Then came more sounds that didn't belong—the scrape of metal on metal, the creak of the front door, a couple of little bumps as the screen door closed.

He sat up on the side of the bed and eased into the jeans he'd taken off a few hours earlier. From the closet he grabbed a T-shirt, then unlocked the gun cabinet and removed his pistol. Sliding the safety off, he held it close to his side as he moved cautiously into the hallway.

Light flickered from the living room. Lexy must have fallen asleep watching TV, he thought, but the hairs standing on end at the back of his neck said it wasn't her sneaking around. He passed the dark bathroom and was approaching the living room when a shadowy figure stepped into the hallway, stopping in front of Lexy's bedroom door. It was a man, dressed all in dark clothes, and just as he reached for the doorknob, Brady brought his pistol up and took aim.

"Hold it right there," he said quietly. "Get your hands up where I can see them."

The man froze, then slowly raised his hands. He was gripping a flashlight in one.

"Drop the light and move into the living room."

"Hey, look, I'm not up to anything," the man said as he obeyed and Brady followed. "I just came to see Les. She said you'd be asleep by now. She left the front door unlocked for me because, hell, I'm too old to be climbin' in windows."

Not believing him for an instant, Brady stopped just inside the door. "Put your hands on the back of the sofa and spread your feet apart."

The guy turned to face him. "Hey, come on. You got a problem with her and me, you need to talk to her about it. I just came to see her, like she told me. I'm not doing anything wrong."

Brady recalled Hallie's description of the man who'd hassled Lexy on the street—early twenties, brown hair, fair skin and not particularly memorable except for a slick grin. It was a damned accurate description, right down to the grin. "Put your hands on the back of the sofa," he repeated coldly, "and spread your feet."

The man's gaze flickered from Brady's face to his weapon, and he swallowed hard before turning to obey.

Brady had just taken a step toward him, intending to pat him down, then get the truth out of him—one way or another—when the floorboards behind him creaked. Instinctively he stepped to the side as he turned, but he wasn't quick enough to avoid the flashlight that smashed down on his right wrist. The force of the blow sent him staggering into the window behind him, where the shattering glass threw him off balance. He sank bonelessly to the floor, pain washing over him with such intensity that his stomach churned. He was barely able to see for the stars bursting in his brain, but he could see enough to tell that he'd dropped his gun and it had skittered across the floor, out of his reach.

"Did you get it?" the second man asked.

"No."

The second man swore. "Jeez, do I have to do everything myself?"

"Hey, you screwed up, too, the first time."

The second intruder turned toward Lexy's room, and Brady forced himself to his feet. His right hand was useless, but that didn't stop him from grabbing the smaller man by the collar and half lifting, half throwing him toward his partner. The man stumbled into the end table, and the light flickered wildly as the oil lamp swayed with the impact. His smile nothing less than evil, when the man regained his balance, he picked up the lamp, hefted it above his head, then smashed it to the floor between them and Brady.

The glass shattered and oil spread across the wood floor in a fiery puddle before flames shot up, their heat forcing Brady back a few steps. Across the room the bastard threw the second lamp toward the kitchen, where it, too, exploded into flames. Laughing, both men ran from the house.

Brady banged on Lexy's door, rattling it open. "Lex! Get up!" He reached her bed in two steps and gave her a shake. "The house is on fire! Come on, we've got to get out!"

She blinked, looked at him, then her eyes opened wide. A roar came from the living room as the flames consumed everything in their path. He dragged her from the bed, and she scrambled into sandals, grabbed her backpack, then raced down the hall ahead of him. When she would have turned into the kitchen, he grabbed her shirttail and pushed her into his bedroom. "The back door's nailed shut, remember? Use that chair to break out the window and screen."

While she grabbed the ladder-back chair in the corner, he went to the phone in the kitchen and called 911. A moment later, coughing from the smoke, he returned to the bedroom and closed the door.

"Come on, Brady, we gotta go!" Lexy shrieked from the window.

"Go on, and wait right outside. I have to get something..." In the closet, he grabbed the two rifles and the shotgun from the rack and dropped them on the bed, then dragged a canvas bag filled with ammunition from the corner.

"Forget the guns!" She was bouncing on the balls of her feet at the window. "The smoke's coming in under the door! Please, Brady…!"

As long as he was saving things, he added his gun belt, tossed his two Stetsons to Lexy, then returned to the closet for the only truly important items—the stack of photographs he kept locked in the gun cabinet. He slid them into his pocket, then reached the window as flames licked through the gap under the door. He lifted Lexy to the ground, wrapped the sheet around everything on the bed and handed it out, then slid out himself.

A fire engine and the chief's truck were pulling up as they came around the front of the house. "Anyone inside?" the chief yelled.

"No, it's just us."

"If you have your keys, we'll move your trucks out of the way."

Brady started to reach into his pocket for his keys, but the pain sent nausea washing over him. "Lex, can you get my keys?"

"What's wrong— Oh, God, what happened to your arm?"

He gazed down at her as she tossed the keys to the fire chief, then dryly said, "You're a sound sleeper, aren't you?" Sliding his good arm around her shoulders, he walked her out toward the street. There he looked her over, head to toe. "You okay?"

She nodded, then burst into tears.

As he pulled her against him, he realized he'd been wrong earlier. If he'd lost the photographs, he wouldn't have lost anything truly important. Photographs could be replaced.

But Lexy couldn't.

When Hallie was upset, she didn't sleep well. After catching Max and Lilah together, she'd lost so much sleep that she'd begun looking haggard in spite of the best cosmetics money could buy—and haggard was *not* a good look for her. Tonight she'd done everything to ensure a good's night rest—taken a long, relaxing hot bath, lighted tension-relieving aromatherapy candles, drunk two cups of chamomile and valerian tea, listened to the most soothing jazz CD she owned.

And none of it had worked. She was still wide awake.

Rolling onto her side, she gazed out the window toward Brady's house. She'd managed not to look over there even once in the past two hours. The last time the house had been dark and still, and she'd wondered if he and Lexy had missed her tonight even one-fourth as much as she'd missed them. Probably not, she'd decided. People didn't tend to get as emotionally attached to her as she did to them. She had always hoped that was a flaw in the people she got attached to, but she was beginning to think it was a flaw in her. She just wasn't the sort of woman people really committed to. Even her own mother and sisters could go months without thinking of her, while they were on her mind practically every day.

Someone was up at the Marshall house, she saw, with lights blazing from every window. She wondered if Brady had gotten another emergency call, or if Lexy was sick, or—

Stiffening, she leaned closer to the window. There was a whole lot more light than there were windows over there, and it was flickering, rising, falling, like a—a—

Oh, God, like a fire.

She jumped from her bed, pulled a jumper on over her chemise, then shoved her feet into shoes. She was halfway to the front door, clutching her keys in one hand, when the phone rang. She hesitated, then kept going. If it was important, the caller would leave a message or try again.

It took only two minutes to reach Brady's house, though she had to park half a block away. There was a fire engine in the driveway, as well as sheriff's vehicles up and down the street. Everyone was standing idle, though. Just a glance showed that nothing could be done to save the house. All the firefighters could do was douse the flames if they started to spread.

She found Brady and Lexy standing arm-in-arm at the edge of the yard and hesitated. What could she offer that they might possibly need? A place to stay? Brady would probably prefer Motel Le Dump over her guest room. Concern? They had enough concern for each other. Support? No doubt that was why all the deputies were there.

They didn't need her at all…but she needed to see for herself that they were all right.

Taking a deep breath for courage, she crossed the last ten feet and circled around in front of them. "Brady, Lexy, are you guys okay?" she asked, and they both automatically reached for her, enveloping her in a three-way hug that filled the emptiness inside her with an incredible sense of warmth and satisfaction.

"Oh, Hallie, they came back and burned our house down!" Lexy exclaimed. "They tried to kill us, and they hurt Brady!"

Her nerves clenching, Hallie pushed back and looked at him. "Where?"

"It's nothing."

"They broke his arm," Lexy said, "but he's too stubborn to go to the doctor."

In the insufficient light from the street lamp, his arm certainly looked broken to Hallie. His wrist was swollen to twice its size, it was badly discolored, and his fingers were cool to the touch.

She gave Lexy a reassuring smile and a wink, then said, "The key to dealing with a stubborn man is to be so stubborn yourself that he'll give in and do what you want just so you'll stop pestering him. So, Brady, do you want to show that you're also an intelligent man and save us both the trouble?"

His blue eyes were shadowed with pain as he gazed down at her. "Don't let this go to your head," he warned, "because it doesn't mean you've won. I just don't have the energy to argue with you tonight."

"Sounds like a victory to me."

He insisted on talking to several of the deputies first, then allowed Hallie and Lexy to help him into the passenger seat of his sheriff's department SUV. "Reese fired the last deputy who let his girlfriend drive his patrol unit," he remarked as she slowly drove past the other vehicles.

"But Reese isn't here. And you're not a deputy. And I'm not your girlfriend." Though she wouldn't mind playing the role for a time. A few weeks or…oh, a few decades sounded about right. "Where are we going?"

He gave her directions to the nearest hospital, some thirty miles away, then related the events of the night to her. "I should have expected someone else," he said, chagrin in his voice. "I shouldn't have let him sneak up behind me."

"You're right," Hallie agreed. "After all, you *are* a super-hero...or so you seem to think."

He scowled at her, but it took more energy than he had to spare, apparently. "It was stupid to think it was just one guy. I mean, there were lights inside, and my pickup and this truck parked outside. Just one guy isn't knowingly going to break into a house occupied by a cop."

And generally, it seemed to her, no one would break into an occupied residence—a cop's or not—unarmed. Brady and Lexy had been very fortunate that the second intruder hadn't had anything deadlier than a flashlight in his hand.

"Did you lose everything?" she asked softly.

"Lexy got her backpack," he replied.

Lexy spoke up from the back seat. "And Brady got his guns and bullets. We're about to be burned to a crisp, and he's getting bullets. Can you believe it?"

He tilted his head back. "Ammunition will explode in a fire, and I had a hell of a lot of it. I didn't want to put the firemen in any more danger than usual."

"Oh. Okay. I apologize for thinking you were crazy." Lexy reached up to pat his shoulder, then sat back. "Damn—I mean, darn, I don't have any clothes. Just my pajamas."

Good, Hallie thought. "I'll take you shopping tomorrow—" Remembering how angry Brady had been that afternoon, she broke off, then lamely finished, "If that's all right with your father."

There was a moment of awkward silence, then Brady murmured, "Better you than me."

It wasn't much, but at least she could accept it as an indication that he didn't intend to keep her out of their lives. Maybe it was pathetic, but she was grateful for it.

They must have made quite a picture walking into the emergency room thirty minutes later, Hallie thought. She wore no makeup and hadn't combed her hair; Lexy wore blue-and-red plaid boxers, a green T-shirt and flip-flops; and Brady was un-shaven, barefooted and smelled of smoke. No one paid them any mind, though, as they whisked Brady away for treatment.

Nearly an hour had passed before he returned with his right arm encased in a cast from elbow to fingertips. He looked so handsome…and so fatigued. Hallie was starting to feel that way herself.

As soon as they got to the truck, Lexy lay down in the back seat and was softly snoring before they got out of town. Hallie glanced at Brady. "Why don't you recline the seat and try to get some sleep?"

"I'm okay."

"Yeah, you really look it."

"Hey, let's not see who can be ornerier at three-thirty in the morning, okay?"

"Okay." She let a few minutes pass in silence before slyly glancing his way. "But I'd win."

"Darlin', it wouldn't surprise me in the least."

She kept the truck's speed five miles an hour above the posted limit. Even so, it seemed to take forever to get to Buffalo Plains. When she turned into her driveway, she gave a soft, weary sigh of relief. It was after 4:00 a.m., and she was fairly certain she would be able to sleep now.

"You don't have to put us up," Brady said, rousing as she shut off the engine. "We can stay at the motel."

She paused in the act of removing the keys from the ignition. "I'll take you there if that's what you want, but…you'll be more comfortable here, and I…I would be more comfortable with you here."

After a moment, he reached across to open his door. Hallie leaned between the two seats to give Lexy a shake. "Come on, sweetie. We're home. Let's go in and get to bed."

As soon as they got inside, Lexy collapsed on the couch and started snoring again immediately. Hallie removed her flip-flops, lowered her backpack to the floor, slid a pillow under her head, then covered her with a sheet from the hall linen closet.

"The guest room is here," she said, leading Brady down the

narrow hall to the left of the fireplace, "and my room is right here."

"Are you giving me a choice?"

She kicked off her shoes and left them just inside the door, then met his gaze. "Why would I do that? You haven't been exactly eager to repeat our encounters of those two nights."

"Don't kid yourself, Hallie. You know I want you."

"But...?" Hugging her arms to her chest, she smiled tautly. "There's always a 'but.' But it would be wrong, but I might expect something from you, but you don't want to complicate things."

When he continued to look at her but said nothing, she shrugged and reached past him to turn on the guest-room light. "Come on. I'll help you get settled."

The only furniture she'd bought for the guest room was a small table and a bed—not because she'd expected actually to have a guest in her few weeks in town, but because she'd found a great iron bed in one of the shops. Someday she would have her own house again, and surely at least once in her lifetime she could count on someone coming to visit.

She turned on the lamp on the night table, then folded back the covers and plumped the pillow. When she glanced back at Brady, she saw that he hadn't moved from the hallway. "Well?"

Slowly he entered the room, going to stand on the other side of the bed. "I'm a big boy. I can undress myself."

"You've got a broken wrist. Besides, I've seen you naked before."

He shook his head. "No, you haven't."

"Okay. I've touched you naked. I've been naked with you. Whatever, there's no reason for false modesty."

He ignored her remark and changed the subject. "I'm sorry about what happened."

Her breath catching in her chest and her palms growing damp, Hallie chose to misunderstand. "I bet. Lexy said if they were going to burn the place down, it was a shame they didn't do it before you guys spent all those hours cleaning up. I don't blame her—"

"I'm talking about what I said to you."

"Oh, that." She reached out to smooth a wrinkle in the sheet as if the conversation was no more significant than that. "Don't think you're the first man who's told me to go to hell. I'm used to it."

"Stop it, Hallie." His tone was rough, harsh. "I never should have said it. I just thought…I thought you knew me better than that. I was…disappointed."

She could certainly sympathize with that. She'd had her share of disappointments, plus several other people's. "I shouldn't have said anything. After all, Lexy's *your* daughter. I'm just…nobody." Smiling brightly in spite of the tears that blurred her vision, she headed for the door. "I'd better let you get to bed. I know you must be exhausted." She turned off the overhead light and ducked through the door into her own room.

She'd made it halfway to her bed when Brady caught hold of her arm and swung her around and hard against his body. "Damn it, Hallie, no more putdowns. You're the most important person in our lives."

Don't believe him, her little voice warned. *You damn well better not believe him.* She had no doubt he meant it at that very moment, but moments didn't last. Heartache did. Pain. Sorrow.

Forcing herself to lift her head, she met his gaze. "If you're not planning to sleep with me in that bed for what's left of the night, would you please leave my room?"

Slowly he released her and took a step back, then another. "I can't stay." His voice was low, heavy with regret, and created a dull heaviness inside her.

"Why not?"

"It's almost dawn." He gestured toward the window, then offered the weakest of smiles. "I'm like a vampire. I only do it at night. In the dark."

"Why?"

As he stared at her, she identified a number of emotions flitting through his eyes—anger, frustration, pain, fear. He was a big, strong, brave man who carried a gun and could intimidate most people with no more than a look. What could he possibly be afraid of?

After a moment, he turned away. He leaned against the edge

of the dresser, and his left hand clutched the curved edge as if the contact might somehow give him courage. He opened his mouth several times without getting any words out, grimaced, then, striving to sound casual, blurted out, "Did I ever tell you that my parents' favorite pastime was beating the hell out of my brother and me?"

Through sheer will, Hallie kept a low moan inside. She wanted to be shocked and disbelieving. She wanted to think that he'd had a relatively ordinary upbringing...even though she'd already known that wasn't true. A father who left him to drown and a mother who didn't kill the bastard for it—there was nothing ordinary about parents like that. And that was only one incident. She didn't want to know that his entire life had been filled with such incidents. She didn't want to imagine the horror he must have lived with all those years.

She just wanted to kill his parents.

Though she felt queasy with anger and the fierce need to protect him, she made an effort to keep it from her face as she sat primly on her bed. Her hands were folded in her lap, her bare feet propped on the side rail. "No, you didn't," she said evenly. Judging by the panicky undertone to his voice and the desperation he was trying so hard to hide, she would bet he'd never told anyone but Sandra.

"Yeah, well...it was, and I've got the scars to prove it."

So that was why he shied away from being touched. Why he only made love in the dark. Why he hated his parents and never wanted to set foot in Texas again. Why he didn't let people get close. With such a betrayal in the most fundamental relationship a child ever had, it was a wonder he'd been able to fall in love with Sandra—and then she'd betrayed him, too. If Hallie ever had the opportunity, she swore she would make the woman wish she'd never been born. "And you think if I see or feel these scars, I'll find them repulsive."

"Repulsive. Sickening. Grotesque." He shrugged as if it didn't matter. "You wouldn't be the first."

Just as he wasn't the first to underestimate her.

"I snore," she said, her tone conversational, "and if my nose is the least bit stuffy at night, I drool, too. I have a scar here—"

she pointed to a spot on her leg ''—where I fell off my bike when I was eight. I only eat the cream centers of Oreos and throw out the chocolate cookies, and I pick all the nuts out of caramel corn. My little toes are crooked, I never can remember to put the little twistie thing back on the loaf of bread, and I hide my chocolate kisses if anyone else is around. Though I haven't told Lexy yet because I don't want to encourage her, I've got a tattoo right here—'' turning, she tugged the shoulder of her jumper down to reveal the moon, star and fairy on her left shoulder ''—and I also wear a small, tasteful sapphire in my navel.

''I always read the ends of books first. I can't carry a tune. I have a birthmark shaped like California on my right hip. Yogurt makes me sick, and the mere thought of exercising makes me feel faint. My left breast is smaller than the right one, I have a tendency to carry ten extra pounds on my hips, and I haven't been fashionably thin since I was ten. The last time I voted was for senior class president and Marcy, the head-cheerleader twit, won in spite of my campaigning for her opponent. I'm not—''

''What are you doing?'' he interrupted, sounding seriously bewildered.

''I'm listing my flaws for you. You told me yours. It's only fair you should know mine.'' She watched him, holding her breath. His reaction would determine how this conversation—and this relationship—would go. If he responded with the seriousness the subject deserved, they had problems he might never get over. But if he could treat it more lightly…there was hope for him—for them—yet.

As much hope as a short-term relationship could afford.

He scowled at her. ''Those aren't flaws. They're personality quirks and superficial imperfections, and they hardly compare to scars.''

''Superficial only if you're not the one sleeping beside me when I'm snoring, or the one who always has to eat sandwiches on stale bread, or the one who likes the nuts in caramel corn, too. And if ten pounds sounds superficial to you, that's because you've never had to escort me to the Oscars in front of the whole world when I looked like… What was the word Max used? Oh, yes. A *cow*."

He stared at her a long time, his brow knitted, his narrowed eyes making him look lethal…and wickedly sexy. Finally, his mouth barely moving under his mustache, he asked, "Want me to punch him?"

Relief whispered through her. "You might break your other hand."

"It would be worth it."

"I appreciate the offer, but Max is so insignificant in my life now that he's not even worth punching." As she said it, she realized it was true. She still had plenty of heartache, insecurities and regret, but none of it was over Max. That was over and done with. Finished. On the cutting-room floor.

"So…" She rose from the bed, closed the blinds and shut off the overhead light, then tugged the jumper over her head, careful not to catch her chemise, too. "Back to my original request. If you're not going to sleep in my bed—and it can be nothing more than sleep; I know you've been through a lot—will you please leave my room?"

His gaze moved over her, from her uncombed hair to her toes curling on the rug next to the bed. Though she knew she didn't look her best, the warm, appreciative look in his blue eyes suggested that he didn't particularly care.

Then he swallowed hard and pushed himself away from the dresser. "Remember that saying—be careful what you ask for?"

"Because you just might get it," she finished for him. Which part might she get? Him in her bed? Or another lonely night alone?

He bent and turned off the lamp on the table behind her, then his sleeve brushed her bare arm as he started toward the door. Holding her breath, she followed his movements by the whisper of bare feet on wood, then disappointment sank like a rock to settle in the pit of her stomach as he closed the door quietly.

Well, that answered that. Just another night alone.

In a life filled with them.

Chapter 10

Brady stood at the door, palm pressed flat against the wood, forehead resting there, too. After his experience with Sandra, he had sworn he would never tell anyone about his parents beating him as long as he lived. Though he'd felt sick when he was trying to get the words out, it hadn't been as hard as he'd expected. That was to Hallie's credit. Maybe it was because she'd been through some tough times herself, or because she didn't make a big deal over things.

Or maybe it was because he trusted her more than any woman he'd ever known.

Wanted her more.

Cared for her more.

But telling was a big step from showing, and showing was where it would make a difference...or not. He really wanted to hope it would be *not,* but he couldn't shake the fear that it would matter. She was accustomed to beautiful people with perfect bodies, and his was damned *im*perfect.

At times he could acknowledge that it was a stupid insecurity. He was thirty-five years old. He knew not everyone judged people on the way they looked. He knew he amounted to a hell of a lot more than a mass of scars. But at other times…. Sandra had done such a number on his ego. She'd thought the scars were ugly and repulsive, and she'd made him feel that way, too.

But Hallie wasn't Sandra.

Slowly he turned from the door. Just enough illumination from the lightening sky filtered around the blinds to allow him to see the big oak bed and Hallie standing beside it, her back to him. Part of him wanted desperately to run, but he'd spent his whole life running from one hurt or another, and what had it gotten him? Nothing but a desperate longing to be part of something, part of some*one*.

From across the room came a whisper of sound. "Damn, damn, god—"

"You know, I wasn't kidding at the wedding reception about Oklahoma having a law against swearing. It's called outraging the public decency."

She whirled around in a rustle of satin. For a moment there was such emotion in her expression—sadness, disappointment, surprise—then it disappeared behind a cool smile. "But I'm not in public, and you don't look outraged."

He shrugged. "Hey, any excuse to put a beautiful woman in handcuffs."

After a minute or two ticked by in silence, she gestured. "I thought you'd gone."

"If you want me to, I will. But if you don't mind, I'd rather stay here. There's just one catch." While she waited, he tried a smile that was a miserable failure. "You'll have to help me with my clothes."

She tossed her head. "I thought you were a big boy who could undress himself."

"You *know* I'm a big boy…but I need your help." *And you.*

She took a few steps toward him, then stopped and waited for him to close the distance. When he did, she took hold of his shirt hem and peeled it up, over his head and free of his left arm, then carefully slid it over his cast. She tossed the shirt aside, and he shifted uncomfortably. He'd never felt so exposed, so much at risk. Facing armed killers and almost certain death at

Reese's house a few months earlier had been easier than standing without the protection of his shirt in front of this woman.

She smiled provocatively. "If I were a cruel woman, I could take great pleasure in dragging this out."

He moistened his lips, cleared his throat. "Yes, you could. But you understand that one day soon my wrist will stop hurting, and then turnabout is fair play."

Hooking her index finger in the waistband of his jeans, she slid it from side to side. "How bad does it hurt?"

"Not much at all." Truth was, the throbbing was almost completely blocked out by the panicked urge to grab his shirt, her quilt, anything to wrap around himself. "I'm a superhero, remember? Broken bones don't faze me." After a pause, he swallowed hard, then continued. "However, show me a belt...."

Through no more contact than her fingertip rubbing against his belly, he felt the tension streak through her. "Was that their weapon of choice?"

"My father liked his fists. My mother preferred a belt. More pain, no broken bones requiring trips to the emergency room. A kid can only fall and break so many bones before the doctors start to suspect either abuse or some rare medical disorder."

"My friends from the great Lone Star State tell me Texas has a he-needed-killin' defense for murder. Sounds as if that would apply here."

"I've wished them dead many times, but I never had what it would take to kill them." He smiled faintly, or at least he meant to. It felt more like a grimace. "I used to think that was some kind of failing in me."

"No. It just meant they could beat the hell out of you, but they couldn't take away your honor, your decency or your humanity."

She undid the button on his jeans, then unzipped them before sliding her hands inside to guide them down. She did it efficiently, modestly, which didn't stop him from responding as if she'd boldly caressed him. After discarding the jeans, she raised one brow. "Boxers on or off?"

"I'm not making love to you with them on."

"You don't have to do that."

He slid his fingers into her hair and tilted her face to his. "Yes, I do. I need you, Hallie. I need to feel you under me—well, on top of me. I need to hear those little noises you make when it feels so good you can't stand it anymore. I need to kiss you and taste you and smell you and feel you..." He brushed a kiss to her lips, took a breath that smelled sweetly of her, then kissed her again, sliding his tongue into her mouth. She opened to him immediately, slid her arms around his neck and clung to him as if she couldn't bear to let go.

The bed was only a foot behind her, but it took them forever to reach it. He lay down first, easing back into the center of the mattress. With her blond hair tumbling around her face, she knelt beside him and slowly inched his boxers down, then gave him a tantalizing smile as she removed her gown. For a moment, all he could do was stare—not at her body, though that was well worth ogling, but at *her*. Her lovely, delicate face. Her lazy, sexy smile.

How could any man willingly give her up? Choose to live life without her?

How could *he* give her up?

And why in hell should he have to?

"Brady?" A shy look came over her as she knelt there, naked, before him. "Are you okay?"

He drew a deep, shuddering breath. He hadn't been okay, not for more years than he could recall. But at that moment, damned if he didn't feel about as *okay* as a man with a broken wrist who'd just lost everything in a fire could feel. "Once you quit tormenting me and come over here, I'll be perfect."

For a moment she studied him, as if torn between continuing the torment or obeying. Then, as pure sensual sultriness replaced the shyness in her manner, she shifted to kneel astride him, reaching between their bodies with her long, delicate fingers to guide him inside her. Then she did exactly what he'd requested of her. She came over...and over...and it was perfect.

Shoving her hair back from her face, Hallie rolled onto her side and groped on the night table for the clock. Once she found it, she had to rub her eyes to bring the numbers into focus.

Sleepily she set it down again. It must need new batteries. It said it was nearly eleven-thirty, and she hadn't slept until eleven-thirty in…well, forever. Only when she'd had a really big night the night before and needed the extra hours to recuperate, and the last time she'd had such a night was when she ran off and married her first husband.

Setting the clock down again, she collapsed on the bed and rolled over…and remembered everything—the fire, the hospital, Brady's admission, their lovemaking. No wonder she was still in bed at practically noon and still tired. She hadn't gotten there until sometime around 5:00 a.m. and hadn't gone to sleep until several hours later.

And she'd sure had fun.

Brady lay on his stomach, the sheet pulled to his shoulders, his right arm propped on a pillow that was balanced half on the nightstand. His face was turned toward her, and his breathing was steady, slow, deep. It sounded peaceful and could lure her back to sleep in a heartbeat if she let it.

If she wasn't curious.

She hadn't yet seen his back and the scars that caused him such torment, but there was something so sneaky about lifting the sheet and taking a peek while he slept. Not that she would be doing anything wrong. After all, he'd let her undress him, and he'd slept naked beside her. He'd known there was a chance she would awaken before him, that she might catch a glimpse.

Not that it even mattered. She hadn't fallen for the smooth perfection of his skin, so how could she care that it was neither smooth nor perfect? Besides, popular opinion to the contrary, she wasn't shallow enough to care. Her mother had taught her that beauty truly was in the eye of the beholder, and life had confirmed it for her.

And she thought he was beautiful.

Pillowing her head on her arms, she studied him for a time. He could be so fierce and distant when he was awake, but asleep he just looked tired. Vulnerable. She could imagine how much he must hate feeling vulnerable, and how vulnerable he must have felt that morning when she'd undressed him.

For a wooden nickel she would go to Marshall City, Texas,

smack Sandra and destroy Brady's parents, then pay the city fathers whatever it would take to eradicate their name from the town and its history. Their only legacy would be the plot of dirt where they were buried.

Which would make her feel better, but wouldn't do much for Brady. It wouldn't heal the scars or make him forget.

A sigh escaped her an instant before she realized he was awake. He hadn't moved other than to open his eyes, and he looked…wary.

"Good morning," she murmured with a lazy smile. "How do you feel?"

"Like I've been run over by a truck."

"I hope you're referring to the tussle at your house, the broken wrist and the fire, and not to making love with me."

His smile started slowly and curved only one corner of his mouth before stopping. "Absolutely. You were the only good part of last night. You made up for all the rest." He shifted, moving his right arm carefully, to lean on his elbows, and the sheet slipped down his back.

Though she tried, Hallie couldn't have not looked to save her life. Her gaze darted automatically to all the warm brown skin now exposed—skin that was crisscrossed from side to side, from his shoulders to his waist, with long pale scars. Some were thin, hardly more than a line stretching across his back, while others were heavy, ridged and puckered. The differences, she assumed, had to do with the age of the scars and the severity of the injuries that caused them. And there were so many. There wasn't a single place on his back where she could lay her palm entirely on undamaged skin.

She couldn't begin to imagine the terrible pain he must have suffered. She wanted to weep, to hold and protect him, to find some way to heal him, and she wanted to hurt his mother—hurt her *bad.*

"It's not a pretty sight, is it?"

Her gaze jerked back to his face. His tone was wry, his smile even more so, as if it really didn't matter. But in his eyes was anxiety, uncertainty and that damned vulnerability. As touched as she was that he could show that side of himself to her—both literally and figuratively—she hated that *anything* had the power to make him feel defenseless.

She wasn't certain how to respond. She could deny that the scars were ugly—and proof that evil did exist. She could shrug them off, insist she'd seen worse. Or she could tell the truth.

"No," she said quietly. "It's not pretty. And it's made up my mind for me. I'm going to Texas, and I'm going to make your parents disappear from the face of this earth. I have the money to do that, and I think Max has the connections."

For a long still moment, he just looked at her, his expression wavering between wariness and amusement. The latter won out. "You think Max has that kind of connections?"

"You know that Mafia movie that came out last year—the Golden Globe winner? He both directed and produced it. You should have seen some of the shady characters he was having meetings with. I suspect most of them had years of experience at making offers people couldn't refuse."

He rolled onto his side and used his good arm to pull her body snug against his. "So you've gone from consorting with mobsters to consorting with a cop."

She brushed her lips over his beard-stubbled jaw. "I *never* did this with a mobster."

After pressing a kiss to her forehead, he rubbed up and down her spine in slow easy strokes. She let her eyes drift shut and thought about sleeping another hour or two, but there were still things she wanted to know, questions she wanted to ask. With a great effort, she opened her eyes and focused on him. "What happened to your brother?"

For just an instant his hand stilled on her back, then resumed the relaxing massage. "Logan ran off just before his sixteenth birthday. He'd committed some infraction—there were so many of them, I don't even remember what—and I took the blame for it. That's what an older brother does, you know? I was bigger, tougher. I could handle it better than him. So our mother punished me, and…I guess he just couldn't take it anymore. He packed whatever he could carry and took off in the middle of the night. I haven't seen or heard from him since."

So he'd been betrayed not only by his parents and his wife,

but also by his brother—the brother he'd literally suffered for. How awful Logan's leaving must have been for Brady…but how impossible it must have been for Logan, seeing his brother beaten in *his* place. If he were anything at all like Brady, he would have preferred enduring the pain himself over the helpless heartache of being responsible for his brother's pain.

"Have you tried to find him?"

"A time or two. Not seriously. He left me a note the night he took off—one line. *Damn you.* He ran away from me as much as from our parents. The least I can do is respect that."

Hallie stared at him in dismay. "Brady, he didn't mean that! He was a *child!*"

"We were never children."

His tone was so even and casual, but the words and the truth behind them sent a shiver through her. She responded by snuggling even closer, as if he could protect her. But all she needed protection from was his memories. Everything he'd gone through made her sick at heart.

And yet he'd survived—not without scars, both inside and out, but he was a kind, honorable, respected and admired man. He didn't have many friends, but Neely and Reese loved him. Lexy loved him. And Hallie….

Deliberately she redirected her thoughts from too-dangerous-on-a-lazy-morning territory. "Tell me you have at least one good memory from your childhood."

He took a moment to think about it. "My grandmother—my mother's mother—lived down the road from us in a little white farmhouse with dark green shutters, a porch across the front and a swing on the porch, and she smelled of fresh-baked bread and roses. Every time I went over there, we'd sit on the porch swing and she would hold me in her lap and tell me stories, feed me cookies and make me feel safe…. She died when I was five."

And thirty years later he'd bought his own little white farmhouse with dark green shutters, a front porch and a swing.

And last night those bastards had destroyed it.

She was trying to think of something else to ask when a knock sounded at the door. "Are you guys ever gonna get up so we can eat?" Lexy called.

Predictably, Brady turned crimson. "Aw, hell, I meant to be back in the guest room before she woke up."

Hallie slid out of his arms and located her chemise on the night table. Funny. She didn't remember putting it there. She certainly didn't remember folding it. "She's fourteen," she said as she tugged the garment over her head, "and she probably knows more about sex than you and I did when we were twenty—and we were both married. She wouldn't have been fooled."

She turned to get his clothes, but there was no sign of them. No T-shirt carelessly tossed aside, no jeans left in a pile on the rug, no boxers tossed heaven knows where.

"I've got Brady's clothes," Lexy called. "What do you want me to do with them?"

Opening the door, Hallie gave the girl a bright smile. "Your dad cooks and cleans and you do laundry? You guys are a prize."

"I only do laundry when all my clothes go up in smoke." Lexy handed over a messily folded stack of clothes. "It's lunch-time, and we missed breakfast."

"We'll be right out."

Hallie closed the door, then set the clothes on the dresser. Brady was lying on his back, the cover pulled up to somewhere around his nose, but it couldn't hide the color in his cheeks. "She came in here while we were asleep," he said with a scowl.

"Yes, she did, and she washed all the smoky smells out of the only clothes you own, so show some gratitude, grumpy."

"Why don't you come over here and make me?"

She sashayed to the bed and climbed right up into his lap. "I know some tricks that will turn Mr. Grumpy into Mr. Happy like that—" she snapped her fingers "—but not until I get a shower and some food." He'd just slid his hand under her gown to cup her bottom when she wriggled away and off the bed. "Give me ten minutes, then we'll fix your cast so you can shower, too."

Brady watched her leave the room before he slowly sat up. He wrapped the quilt around him, then reached for his jeans to get one of the pain pills the ER doc had given him. The pockets were empty, of course, so he put the jeans on, left the bedroom and followed the tinny sound of music escaping headphones through the kitchen and into the dining room. Lexy sat at the table, headphones covering her ears, a journal closed in front of her and an assortment of items on the table.

He pulled out the chair across from her. There was the paper packet of pills, his keys, his badge and wallet, along with seventy-eight cents. The only other things he'd stuck in his pockets were the photographs, and they were in Lexy's hands.

"Hey." When he got no response, he reached across the table and waved his fingers in front of her.

She looked up, offered a tight smile, then pushed the headphones down around her neck. "Hey. How's your hand?"

"Better. You want to turn that down?"

Sliding her hand into the backpack that hung on the next chair, she shut off the music, then unhooked the headphones. "I, uh…I found these in your pocket." She thrust one photo toward him. "Who is that? It looks like you, but not."

He glanced at the familiar face, taken Logan's sophomore year in school. Funny. His brother was thirty-three now—if he was even alive—but Brady still thought of him as a fifteen-year-old kid. He couldn't imagine how Logan the man would look.

Maybe like him, but not.

"That's my brother, Logan."

Lexy's eyes widened, and he realized the bar that usually extended through her brow was gone. Lost in the fire, he hoped. "You have a brother? I have an uncle? That's so cool! Where is he? Can I meet him? Does he know about me?"

"I haven't seen him since right after that picture was taken. He ran away from home and never came back."

"Oh. Well, that's still cool I have an uncle. Uncle Logan." She grinned, then tossed out another picture. "Who's that?"

"My grandmother. Your great-grandmother."

"Huh. I didn't think either of your parents came from mothers. Bet she's dead, 'cause she's pretty old in this picture, and it's an old picture."

"Yeah, she's been dead a long time."

"Was she Jim's mother or Rita's?"

"Rita's. But she wasn't like Rita at all. You would have liked her, and she would have loved you."

"Really." Lexy looked intrigued by the idea for a moment or two as she shuffled through the remaining photos. Finally she laid one on the table between them and waited.

Brady smiled faintly. If he closed his eyes and let himself remember, he would still be able to smell the scents he'd quickly come to associate with Lexy—baby powder, baby shampoo, burped-up apple juice and that sweet, innocent, indefinable *something* that had filled him with such…love.

Until Sandra had taken it away.

"That's you and me."

"I know," she murmured.

"You were ten weeks old."

"You looked like a baby yourself without the mustache."

"That's why I grew it."

She moved to sit in the chair at the head of the table, so she could see the photo, too. "You looked—" She drew a breath, then rushed the words. "You looked like you liked me."

"Nah, I didn't like you," he said, putting on a careless tone. Then he looked at her. "You were my daughter, my baby. And I…" They weren't difficult words—just sounds that could mean everything or nothing at all. People said them all the time, and no one needed to hear them more than Lexy…except possibly him.

"I—I loved you." His face grew hot again, but she didn't seem to notice.

"Then why did you leave me? Why did you forget all about me?"

"I didn't forget you. You were a baby, Lexy. I couldn't take you with me." As far as he'd known, he'd had no right to take her. No right ever to see her again.

"Then why didn't you stay in town? Why didn't you stick close by so I could see you?"

"I couldn't. Between your mother and my—my parents, I couldn't stay."

She sat back in her chair. "So it was Sandra's fault. Of course."

"No, it wasn't—" How many lies did he want to tell her? He was already playing father to her, when odds were even that he wasn't. If he was, Sandra had cheated him of fourteen years with her. Either way, she'd denied Lexy a father. All the problems and hurts were Sandra's doing. Did he really want to lie to defend her?

Before he'd reached a decision, Hallie's voice drifted through the air. "Brady, I'm out of the bathroom. If you want to take a shower, I'll help you cover your cast."

"Okay." He gathered the photos together, then left them on the table as he stood up. Pausing beside Lexy, he laid his hand on her shoulder. "I didn't want to leave you, Lex, and I never forgot you. You got caught in the fallout when things went **bad** between your mother and me, and I regret that more than I can say."

She nodded, then forced a smile. "Hey, I'm here now. That's what counts, right?"

"Now, and whenever you want in the future." He awkwardly hugged her, then headed off for his shower, to be followed, he hoped, by lunch. He needed all the energy he could get. They had a lot to do that afternoon—shopping, Hallie had reminded him with unholy glee—then tonight, bed. Just the two of them. Again.

He met Hallie in the bathroom, where she gestured for him to sit on a wooden stool. The air was steamy and smelled of flowers and citrus, and the same fragrances clung to Hallie, who wore nothing more than a bath towel knotted between her breasts with a smaller towel holding her wet hair on top of her head.

"I've had plenty of broken bones," he remarked as she secured a plastic bag over his cast, "but I don't remember them being such a nuisance before."

"How many is 'plenty'?"

He shrugged. "I told you my father liked to use his fists to discipline us—to the tune of five broken ribs, three arms, one collarbone, a dozen or so fingers and one skull fracture."

Her jaw tightened, and for a time it seemed she'd stopped breathing. He slid his good arm around her waist and pulled her to stand between his knees. "It's all right."

She wrapped her arms around his neck and held him tightly. "You're a hell of a man, Brady."

No…but he was a survivor. And that was something.

After a moment, she stepped back. "You're ready for your shower. If you need anything, just yell. And—" her eyes took on a wicked gleam "—I'd be happy to shave you if you decide you don't like the desperado look. Frankly, though, I find it one heck of a turn-on." With that, she turned and strolled from the room.

Brady was grinning as he turned on the water, adjusted the temperature, then stepped under its spray. He didn't reach for the razor hanging there, though.

After a remark like that, he might never shave again.

The next few days passed uneventfully—though the nights…my, oh my. Hallie couldn't remember the last time her nights had been so amazing that she'd wanted to hurry through the day to get to them. She and Brady made love, which was incredible, but even more special, they talked late into the night, with shadows surrounding them and only the thin light from the moon seeping into the room. She told him things about her marriages that she'd never been able to share with her sisters for fear they would think she was an even bigger idiot than they'd known. He found a few more good memories from his childhood, mostly having to do with Logan, and they talked about Lexy and her future.

But not *their* future.

Probably because they didn't have one—at least, not together.

He went back to work on Thursday, claiming he was ready and that the rain falling since dawn, though desperately needed, would give the department extra calls. Lexy had teased that it was to escape all the shopping. In one and a half days, they'd replaced her wardrobe as well as much of his, and he'd bought new uniforms and picked up a new pistol. Too bad he hadn't had that pistol one of the times his mother had picked up a belt, Hallie thought. The idea of someone putting the fear of God into the woman gave her a great deal of satisfaction.

"You know, this isn't bad," Lexy announced.

Hallie didn't look up from the cookbook she was flipping through while making a grocery list. "What isn't, sweetie?"

"*This.* You, me, Brady, living here. Like a real family."

Then Hallie did look. "You and Brady *are* a real family."

"And you. We want you to be part of it, too."

Maybe she did, but Hallie wasn't so sure about Brady. Oh, she knew he cared for her...but that was a long way from what she wanted. And he'd made it clear from the beginning that he had less than no interest in anything permanent. Of course, people could change their minds, and sometimes when he looked at her in a certain way, or when he revealed some intimately painful memory to her, she was sure he had. But other times... He was so careful not to talk about permanence, commitment or love.

Truth was, she didn't know if he'd changed at all or if thinking so was merely wishful on her part. Maybe he was simply taking advantage of what she offered so freely—nursemaid, baby-sitter, landlady and lover, all in one. Maybe she should have held out for something concrete in return.

But she *had* something—a family. Maybe not real, maybe only temporary, but the stuff her dreams were made of.

"Are you in love with my dad?"

"Do you think I would tell you if I were?" She hadn't even admitted it to herself yet. As long as she didn't put a name to what she was feeling, it would be easier to recover from if it ended in failure. An affair ending badly could be painful, but it had nothing on a loved-him-and-lost-him broken heart.

Or so she told herself.

Lexy gave her a sly look. "No matter what Sandra says, I bet he'd be a good husband. And then you could be my stepmother, and when I come back for Thanksgiving, you'd be here, too."

"Well, you'll see me anyway," Hallie said, striving to sound cheerful. "Neely's invited all of us to come for Thanksgiving."

"But I don't want you here with your sisters. I want you here with Brady. He needs us. He's too alone, and he's lots happier with me and you than he is by himself."

"You think?" Hallie asked dryly. She closed the cookbook, then tore her shopping list from the notepad. "Get some clothes on and let's go to the grocery store. You and I are going to learn how to make the best chalupas you've ever had.''

"I've never had chalupas."

"Good. Then they'll be the best no matter how they turn out."

Lexy headed off to the guest room, which she'd claimed for her own. Hallie was about to leave the dining table when she noticed the girl's headphones hanging on the back of a chair. The kid wore them more often than not, and frankly, Hallie was tired of seeing them attached like some sort of semi-permanent headgear.

She hesitated a moment, then grabbed the headphones and followed the cord to the CD player in the front pocket of the backpack. Clutching them in one hand and the CDs in the other, she went to the pantry, dumped them all on the lowest shelf and arranged a stack of boxed goods in front of them. Of course, Lexy would miss them, but maybe they could negotiate a fair-use agreement before Hallie gave them back.

They were on their way into town when Lexy gave Hallie another of those sly looks. "Oh, gee, it's just about lunchtime. Maybe we should drop by the courthouse and see if Brady has plans for lunch."

"Maybe he's had enough of our company in the last few days."

"If he has, he can always say he's got work to do. Come on, Hallie. Look at me. Look how *ordinary* I look. Doesn't that deserve some kind of reward?"

Her outfit was definitely ordinary—a pair of denim shorts that reached halfway to her knees with a tank top, sneakers and socks, all in white. Her hair was still purple, though the color was fading nicely, and she'd left it in its naturally curly state. Her tattoo and belly ring were covered, and the only other foreign objects stuck in her body were in her ears—simple silver balls and hoops.

"Okay," Hallie said with an exaggerated sigh of defeat. "We'll stop. But if he cringes, hides under his desk or races out the back way when he sees us, we leave again. Agreed?"

"Agreed."

She found a parking space on the side street in front of Stella Clark's antique shop, then gave another great sigh as the skies opened up and the gentle rain turned into a downpour. She had no objection to getting a little damp, but with this deluge, she would look like a drowned rat by the time she reached the courthouse.

Fumbling around the seat, she finally came up with an umbrella. She opened her door and popped it up, then splashed around the car to share its protection with Lexy. Huddled together, they crossed the street and were halfway to the courthouse when, without warning, something slammed into them from behind. The umbrella went flying and Hallie stumbled forward, trying without luck to catch herself. She rolled to the side and landed facedown in the waterlogged grass, but not before cracking her head on the base of the lamppost there.

Pain streaked through her, turning everything dark, muffling the voices around her. There were two men, she thought dazedly, and Lexy, screaming and swearing as fluently as any teenage boy. "What are you doing?" someone else shouted, and another voice chimed in. "Leave them alone!"

Hallie tried to roll over, to get up and help Lexy, but lifting her head sent pain and nausea through her in great, heaving waves. Tears burning her eyes, she sank back down and willed the throbbing to settle into mere agony.

She was dimly aware of a screech of pain from somewhere nearby, followed by running footsteps and squealing tires. Their attackers were gone. Good. Now she could rest....

"Hallie! Hallie, can you hear me?"

She frowned, wanting the noise to go away. She had what her mother used to call a sick headache, and she needed a dark room, a soft pillow and sleep.

Then came a softer, pleading voice. "Oh, please, you have to be all right! This is all my fault!"

"Brady? Lexy?" She managed to open one eye, then the other. Lexy was kneeling on one side, looking as if she'd just stepped out of the shower, tears dripping down her face, and Brady was on the other side. He was wet, too, his hair glistening, his uniform shirt plastered to his body. Around them were a dozen or more faces she didn't recognize.

She reached up to wipe a drop from Brady's jaw. "Hey, it's raining."

"Yeah, it's raining," he said grimly. "How do you feel?"

"I have a headache." She raised her hand to her forehead, but he caught it and clasped it tightly in his.

"You hit your head when you fell. You've got one hell of a knot there."

"I…fell?" She was trying to work that far back in her shaky memory when a terrible sound split the air—and her head. Wincing, she held tighter to him. "What's that awful racket?"

"It's a siren. The ambulance will be here in a minute."

"Ambu— Oh, my God, Lexy!" She tried to sit up, but Brady pushed her back down, and Lexy took hold of her other hand.

"I'm okay," the girl said with a sniffle. "But they got away with my backpack. I tried to hold on, but the strap broke and they got it." She smiled weakly. "You would've been proud of me, Hallie, I did just like my dad said. I screamed and bit and kicked one of them in the ba—testicles."

Hallie matched her smile. "So that explains that squeal of pain."

"Yeah. If I'd had my combat boots on, I could have done some real damage. With just my tennis shoes, he managed to get away."

"Yeah, but he was limping real good," someone remarked.

The siren abruptly shut off, and Hallie closed her eyes gratefully. A moment later the paramedics shooed everyone away, poked and prodded and asked her a few questions. Once they'd strapped her onto a gurney, Brady crouched next to her.

"They're taking you to Dr. Walker's office a few blocks over," he said, gently stroking raindrops from her cheek. "From there we'll see if you have to go to the hospital. Lexy and I will follow you over, okay?"

"Okay," she whispered. "But please tell them no siren. It hurts my head."

"No siren," he agreed. Then he did the most extraordinary thing. In front of his daughter, his deputies and more than a few townspeople, he bent over and kissed her on the mouth. Not just a peck, but a possessive, claiming sort of kiss.

Hallie knew she was smiling stupidly as the paramedics wheeled her away, but she didn't care. A kiss like that in public just might be worth a conk on the head.

Or two or three.

Chapter 11

Seth Walker had been a doctor for forty-eight years, and he'd spent all but two of them practicing right here in Buffalo Plains. He'd delivered most of the people in town and had patched up car wrecks, tractor injuries, drunken brawls and domestic disputes. He was a good doctor, according to his patients, but he was seventy-some years old and feeling it. He'd tried to get another doctor to come in and take over his practice, but when that had failed, he'd made a deal with Dr. Hansen over in Heartbreak to bring in Callie Sellers, a nurse practitioner, to work for them both.

Callie had started out mostly delivering babies, but as the two doctors got older, her practice expanded. She was as good as most doctors and better than some, and in emergencies, she proved it—such as when she'd removed a bullet from Reese's shoulder a few months ago. It might have exceeded the scope of her duties, but an MD couldn't have done it any better.

Brady stood in the corridor with her outside the treatment room where the paramedics had taken Hallie. Callie's friend, Isabella—the sexy, sultry redhead who brought out the protective instincts in most women—was curled on a sofa nearby, a milkshake on the table beside her and *People* in her hands, paying them little attention.

"Mugged?" Callie exclaimed. "Right outside the sheriff's department in the middle of the day? Are these guys idiots?"

Brady shrugged. "Lucky idiots. They got away. Ran out into the street, and when Mrs. Marketic stopped to keep from hitting them, they forced her out of the car and took off. The sheriff's office and the highway patrol are looking for them, but they've probably already ditched that car for another."

"Is your daughter okay?"

Brady's jaw tightened. "She's got some scrapes where they shoved her down. Mostly, she's worried about Hallie." And he was worried about both of them. *They're not interested in me,* Hallie had said after the break-in at his house, and he'd pointed out that she was with Lexy all the time. *If you get in their way...*

And today she had.

The exam-room door opened and Lexy stepped into the hallway. "She's ready," she said, her voice subdued. The first thing Callie had suggested was getting Hallie out of her soaked clothes, and Lexy had volunteered. Though Brady would have preferred doing it himself—he knew he could do it without aggravating her pain, but wasn't so sure about anyone else—it had seemed important to Lexy. In his truck all the way over, she'd kept saying it was her fault Hallie had been hurt. Even now she looked as if she might burst into tears any moment.

The nurse went into the room. As the door slowly swung shut, her cheerful voice filtered out. "Hi, Hallie, I'm Callie. If you'd come in a half hour earlier, our receptionist, Sally, would have been working. That would have been fun, huh?"

As the door closed with a thump, Isabella looked up from her magazine. "I understand you have a bit of a crime wave going on, and most of it's directed against the two of you. Is small-town sheriffin' so boring that you have to drum up business by going out and making new enemies?"

"Boring is the best way for it to be," Brady said as he slid his arm around Lexy's shoulders.

"Or maybe it's not you at all. It seems like those Madison girls come to town and everything just goes all to hell."

"It's not Hallie's fault," Lexy said defensively.

"If you say so." Isabella stood up gracefully and walked past them to the next treatment room. She was barefooted and wore jeans and a sleeveless sweater, and she couldn't have looked more elegant in an evening gown and diamond-studded heels. She returned with two large towels and a blanket. "You look cold. So, Brady…this is your daughter. Proof of the old adage—you might not get what you want, but you'll get what you deserve."

The smile accompanying the words was brittle, and there was a curious bitterness in her voice that made Brady think that old bit of wisdom was directed to her, not him and Lexy. He'd suspected from the first time he'd met her that she was running away from something. What had she wanted, and what had she deserved?

The question disappeared from his head in an instant when Callie came out of the exam room. "I've taken some X rays, and I'm going to develop them. You can go in with her now."

Lexy, wrapped in the blanket, shot into the room. Brady finished toweling his hair, then followed more slowly.

Hallie was lying on a padded gurney, wearing a hospital gown, tucked under a thermal blanket, and looked about as pale and washed-out as the blanket. She managed a smile for them, but it was obvious she felt like hell.

So did he. He'd been at his desk when he'd heard Lexy's screams, but he'd written it off as kids playing in the rain. After a long, hot, dry spell like they'd had, kids tended to do that. Then Wilda, the dispatcher, had shouted that someone was being mugged right outside and he, along with a state trooper and the deputies who were in the office, had gone running.

He hadn't had a clue *who* was being mugged until he'd seen Lexy, soaked and disheveled, scrambling across the sidewalk to Hallie, and his heart had stopped beating. It hadn't started again until she'd opened those pretty hazel eyes and said his name, and he'd known in that instant he was a goner. He might not have found the courage to face it before, but kneeling there beside her in the rain, it had been impossible to avoid.

He loved her.

Was in love with her.

He'd sworn never to trust anyone again, never to love anyone again, and he'd spent the past fourteen years making sure no one ever got close enough to put him at risk. And somehow Hallie had just slipped in. She'd bypassed every one of his defenses and made a place for herself in his life before he'd had the sense to worry.

She'd made a place for herself in his heart.

And now she was lying there, injured, because he'd failed to protect her.

When he reached her, he went to the head of the bed where no rails blocked his access and bent to kiss her cheek. Keeping his face close to hers, he softly said, "I think I have a solution to this problem I have with worrying every time you and Lex are out of my sight."

"Oh, yeah? What's that?"

"I have a cell in the Canyon County Jail with your names on it. I'm just going to lock you up and keep you safe."

"You can't do that," Lexy scoffed.

He glanced up at her. "Honey, I'm the acting sheriff. I can do damn near anything. We'll call it protective custody."

"I thought the idea was to lock up the bad guys," Hallie murmured.

"Soon as we can find them. But as long as they're running free, I really like the idea of you two behind bars."

"You couldn't come spend the night with us," she pointed out.

"Refer back to the 'acting sheriff' part of my earlier statement." He straightened as Callie came back in.

"How's that headache, Hallie?" the nurse asked, sliding a couple of X rays onto the light-box.

"On a scale of one to ten, it's about a fourteen."

"We'll get you fixed up soon. Hey, Isabella, come in here, please."

The redhead appeared in the doorway. "Yes, ma'am?"

"Come look at these."

She didn't budge from the door. "Oh, gee. X rays."

"Come over here, please."

"Nope. Not gonna do it."

Callie gave her an exasperated look. "I don't want to send her to Tulsa if she doesn't need to go. She's been through enough already. But I want a second opinion."

Brady looked from Callie to Isabella. "You're a nurse, too?" She'd been present when Callie removed the bullet from Reese's shoulder, but the extent of her participation had been lavishing attention on the patient. She hadn't so much as touched a bandage.

"No, I'm not a nurse," she said flatly, then turned to leave.

"*Isabella.*"

Brady watched her. So did Hallie, Lexy and Callie. After a long, tense moment, the redhead sighed and stalked across the room to the light-box. She studied the films for a moment, then said in a no-nonsense voice, "Everything looks fine. There's no evidence of any linear or depressed fracture or other deformities, no subdural or extradural hemorrhage, no subgaleal hematoma. Just a little soft-tissue contusion here." She gestured toward a spot on one X ray. "Give her a head-trauma sheet and send her home. Satisfied?" Spinning around, she disappeared down the hall.

"She's a doctor?" Brady asked, surprise evident in his voice.

Callie nodded.

"But why—?"

"Don't ask, okay? But if she says you're all right, Hallie, trust me—you're all right." Callie pulled a mimeographed sheet from a file on the counter and offered it to Brady. "For the next twelve hours or so, be on the alert for any changes in her vision, the onset of a headache other than what she's already got, drowsiness, irritability, agitation, nausea, vomiting, seizures. If she has any of that, give me a call ASAP—my numbers are on that sheet. Other than that, give her a couple of aspirin tablets when you get her home, and an ice pack on that knot should help reduce the swelling."

"Thanks a lot, Callie," Brady said.

"Anytime." The nurse gestured toward a white plastic trash bag. "Lexy, her clothes are in that bag. Wear the gown home, Hallie, get some rest and take it easy."

With help from Lexy, Brady got Hallie settled in the truck. "So," he began hopefully, "now we go to jail?"

"No," Hallie and Lexy answered in unison.

"Come on, it's not so bad. You can have a television, and we'll provide you with three hots and a cot."

Hallie gingerly turned her head to look at him. "If I thought for a minute you were serious, I'd sma—" Breaking off, she paled, then turned a delicate pink and looked away.

"It's okay to say 'smack,'" he said softly.

"I've never struck anyone in anger—well, except the occasional sister when we were kids."

"I know."

When they got home, Lexy got Hallie into bed while Brady put together a lunch of sandwiches and chips. They'd just finished eating when the doorbell rang. "I'll get it," Lexy said, popping up from the bed before Brady could speak.

He took advantage of her leaving to move closer to Hallie. Lifting the ice pack she'd put on her bump after she'd polished off her lunch, he gave a low whistle. "You've got one hell of a goose egg there, darlin'."

"Tell me about it. It's a good thing I'm not vain enough to care."

He wrapped his fingers around hers, then studied her a long time before asking, "Are you really okay?"

"I'm fine. You know, the stupid thing is, I deliberately fell in that direction because I didn't want to scrape the sidewalk with my face. Apparently, I underestimated the distance to that lamppost." A chagrined look came across her face. "Maybe I am vain after all, in addition to being clumsy. I couldn't regain my balance, I couldn't get my hands out to catch myself…and I couldn't help Lexy at all." After a moment, she raised her tearful gaze to his. "What if they'd gotten away with her instead of just her bag? I couldn't have stopped them. I couldn't have protected her."

He gathered her into his arms and gently stroked her hair. "That's not your fault. One of those guys is most likely the same one who broke my wrist, and, sweetheart, I'm a hell of a lot bigger than you and was armed at the time. Don't blame yourself. Lex is okay, except for worrying about you.''

"Hey." Lexy appeared in the doorway. "There are some deputies here to see you, Brady." Then she grinned. "Including Deputy Mitch."

"Ooh, the cute one," Hallie murmured.

Brady stood up and gave her a stern look. "He's too young for you," he said, then transferred the look to Lexy. "And he's too old for you. Why don't you stay here and keep Hallie company?"

"Sure."

He went down the hall to the living room, where Ryan Sandoval and Mitch Connors were on the couch and Canyon County's lone female deputy, Lucy Manning, sat in one of the two armchairs. He took the other one.

"How's Ms. Madison?" Ryan asked.

"She's okay except for a headache and a knot on her head."

"A trooper found Mrs. Marketic's car at a gas station out on Highway 28," Ryan announced. "But there's no clue where the bad guys went from there. The best description anyone was able to give was that they were both Caucasian, male, early-to-mid-twenties, and one was taller than the other. Both were wearing jeans and windbreakers, with the hoods pulled up over their heads. Nobody saw where they came from—but everyone saw where they went."

"I think Mrs. Marketic was more shaken up than anyone," Mitch put in. "When they yanked her out of her car, she was convinced she was going home to meet the Lord."

Brady smiled faintly. The woman was in her seventies, a hypochondriac if ever there was one, and frequently thought she was on her way to heaven.

"You know of any reason these guys would try to grab your daughter? Could it be some enemy she made at home?"

"She says she doesn't have any enemies," Brady said with a shake of his head. "She's never seen these guys before, she doesn't know their car, she doesn't know anything."

"What was in the backpack?" Lucy asked.

"Makeup, candy, tissues. A couple of ink pens. About two

hundred bucks in cash. The key to my house they burned down." He grimaced. "Not a bad consolation prize, I guess, since they couldn't get her."

"You're sure—" Ryan broke off and exchanged looks with the other two deputies before awkwardly continuing. "You're sure she told you everything?"

Brady settled back in his chair and rested one ankle on the other knee. He knew from personal experience that suggesting a child had lied to a parent wasn't easy. Most parents believed they could tell when their kids were lying, and most, in his experience, didn't have a clue. He had no doubt Lexy could lie to him and make him believe it was God's honest truth, but his instincts said that wasn't the case. "I can't be sure without having inventoried the backpack. But am I willing to take her at her word? Absolutely."

Ryan looked embarrassed. "I had to ask."

"I know."

"So...Mrs. Marketic's car is being dusted for prints, and we're looking for any abandoned cars in the downtown area. The guys had to get there somehow. Other than that..." Ryan shrugged as he got to his feet.

Other than that, there was nothing else to do, except hope that if the bastards came back again, the cops caught them before they did any more damage. So far, they hadn't had any luck at that.

Brady walked to the front door with them, stepping out onto the porch. There, Mitch said, "Someone will be coming by on patrol pretty often."

"Yeah. And if all else fails, there are a couple empty cells down at the jail," Lucy said with a grin.

"We'd have to put them in handcuffs and leg irons to get them there," Brady said dryly. "Thanks a lot, guys. If you need anything, or if you find out anything, call me. I'll be here."

He watched until they were out of sight, Ryan and Lucy heading back into town, Mitch turning toward Heartbreak. Then he breathed deeply of the steamy, clean scent of the rain. He'd always liked rainy days. Except for the increase in fender-benders, he found the gray skies and steady splash of water soothing—perfect for being lazy, watching old movies and dozing at odd times.

He could use some soothing now.

Actually, he could use Reese and his cousin, Jace, and someplace as secure as a fortress to stash Hallie and Lexy.

And he could use some answers. He had too many questions, and that made him edgy.

A floorboard behind him creaked, and he turned to see Hallie standing in the doorway. She wore her nightgown—another short, slim satiny thing, this one a rich lavender shot through with silver threads—with a robe in lavender, silver, pink and pale green. Her blond hair hung loose around her shoulders, and her face, washed free of whatever makeup had survived the rain, had a little color back in it. She looked so slender, so delicate.

Just the sight made his chest hurt.

"You're supposed to be in bed resting," he said, his voice huskier than he'd intended, thanks to the lump in his throat.

"Somebody's sleeping in our bed." She came to stand beside him, and he automatically slid his arm around her. "Lexy was worn out by all that's happened, so she's taking a nap."

"She's worried about you."

"I know. She's sweet."

They both watched the rain and the occasional car on the highway for a time before he casually asked, "How secure is that mansion of yours out in Beverly Hills?"

"Plenty, I suppose. It's a gated community, we've got a twelve-foot wall around the grounds, a top-notch alarm system, security patr—" Abruptly she looked at him, her eyes narrowed in suspicion. "Why?"

"I was just thinking you and Lex might be better off someplace else."

Pulling away, she sat down on the porch swing. When he joined her, she leaned back against him and drew her feet onto the weathered wood. "I think Lex and I are safest right here with you."

"There's no way those guys could track you to California. Even if they did, you'd be tough to get to."

"You don't *really* want us to leave."

"Of course not. But when I saw you both on the ground today…and right outside the damned sheriff's department…." He sighed, then pressed a kiss to the top of her head. "I don't want either of you hurt again. I thought I could keep Lexy safe, but obviously I can't."

"So we'll be very careful. We'll watch for these guys. Lexy and I will walk everywhere back-to-back, so there won't be another sneak attack."

She tilted her head back so he could see her sly amusement with the image of one of them always traveling in reverse. Cupping his hand to her jaw, he bent and kissed her. Under the circumstances, he intended nothing more than a brief taste, but she sighed deep in her throat and drew his tongue into her mouth, and he couldn't resist.

Awkwardly, they maneuvered into a more comfortable position, with her bottom on his lap, and his arm around her back. As he stroked and probed and she sucked hard at his tongue, he slid his good hand inside her robe and cupped her breast, applying just enough pressure to make her nipple swell against his palm. And it wasn't the only thing swelling. His arousal pressed against her bottom, making her wriggle, which in turn made him swallow a groan.

When his lungs were about to burst from lack of air, he ended the kiss—not easy when she protested wordlessly and clung to him. "We can't do this," he murmured.

She gave him a smile so womanly and wicked that it alone could have made him stone-hard. "Why not?"

"For starters, we could get arrested. Remember that outraging-the-public-decency law?"

"Privacy's only a few steps away."

"My daughter's asleep in our bed."

"So we can use hers. Or the couch. Or that wonderfully sturdy oak table in the dining room. Or we can take a bath together in that big ol' clawfoot tub. Just you and me, some sweet-smelling soap, our bodies slick and wet and steamy…."

His breath caught in his chest and the temperature of the blood pumping through his veins redlined. His muscles knotting, he lifted her away and deposited her carefully on the bench beside him. "You went through a traumatic event just hours ago. You need rest."

She leaned against the swing's arm and stretched out one leg across his lap, with her foot landing in a very sensitive spot—and naturally, she couldn't keep it still. "All right," she said primly. "I'll rest. And you'd better do it, too, because, honey, sooner or later Lexy's going to get out of our bed, and then you're going to need all the energy you can get."

"Promises, promises," he murmured.

This was one he had little doubt she would keep.

The search of the muggers' getaway car turned up nothing—no fingerprints, no backpack and contents carelessly discarded, no wallets conveniently fallen from hip pockets. One of the deputies had located the car the man who'd tried to grab Lexy off the street had been driving that day, but it had turned out to be stolen from Oklahoma City, with a Colorado tag that had also been reported stolen. They found nothing of value in it, either.

Hallie sat at the dining table Saturday morning, the remains of her breakfast in front of her, and listened to Brady's end of the conversation as he spoke with one of his deputies. For a man whose job was protecting people and solving crimes, it frustrated him no end that he couldn't solve *these* crimes, especially when the crooks weren't particularly smart. But who needed smarts when they had luck?

And these were two lucky bastards.

After hanging up the phone, he took a drink of coffee, then asked, "What do you want to do today?"

She and Lexy weren't exactly under house arrest. They'd gone to the grocery store the day before, and to dinner at the SteakOut last night. Of course, Brady had gone to dinner with them, and the cute young deputy named Lucy had driven them to and from the store. Isn't this an abuse of authority? Hallie had asked as they'd wandered down the aisles, and Lucy had adamantly said no. Brady had helped protect Neely, the deputy had pointed out, and he would do the same if it was *her* family who was in danger. They were a small department, and they all looked out for each other.

Consider it preventive law enforcement, she had suggested. If the presence of a uniformed officer dissuaded the two punks from coming around again, then it also saved all the man-hours required to investigate a second assault.

Truthfully, Lucy had won Hallie over when she'd implied that Hallie was part of Brady's family. Wouldn't she love to be!

"I have to go over to Neely's house," she said now to Brady. "I haven't been keeping an eye on things the way I should have." She'd called Dane Watson Friday morning to make her excuses, but he'd already heard all the gossip. He'd told her not to worry, that he would call if they really needed her input, but she felt she owed it to Neely. She wasn't living up to the favor she'd promised her sister, and if something turned out wrong with Neely's dream house because of her, she would kick herself.

"Okay. Anything else? Go to the lake? Have a picnic? Catch a movie?"

"How about lunch at the café over in Heartbreak?" She wanted to go someplace where, at least for a time, life would seem perfectly normal, and Shay's place, according to Neely, was the most normal, routine, life-is-good place around.

"Okay." He rose from the table and precariously balanced their dishes in his good hand. "Bet I can be ready before you."

"That's a loser bet." He wore jeans and a T-shirt, and needed only shoes, socks and his pistol before he walked out the door. She, on the other hand, was still in her robe.

She detoured into the living room, where Lexy was sprawled in an easy chair, one long leg hanging over the side and swinging, while a movie played—loudly—on the TV. "Hey, Lexy, we're going over to Neely's house."

The girl didn't take her gaze from the screen. "Okay. I'll see you when you get back."

"No, kiddo, *we* are going. All of us. Throw on some clothes."

"I don't want to go. It's just a house. It's boring."

Hallie picked up the remote from the arm of the chair, then perched there herself. The scene on the TV screen was filled with bright flashes and incredible noise, and the dialogue was quick, peppered with obscenities and difficult to comprehend at nine o'clock on a Saturday morning. But she didn't need to understand. "That's one of Max's movies. I'll tell you how it ends on the way. Come on." She pointed the remote at the television and pressed the power button, and Lexy sprang to her feet.

"I was watching that!"

"You can catch it next time it's on."

"You mean if your plans don't interfere. I don't want to go to that stupid house. I'm not a baby. I don't have to have someone with me every minute of every damn day!"

Feeling at a disadvantage sitting while Lexy towered over her, Hallie stood, too. "Yes, sweetie, right now you do. I know it's a pain, but it's something you have to accept. Go on and get dressed, okay?" As she spoke, she laid her hand on Lexy's arm, and the girl angrily spun away.

"You can't tell me what to do all the time! You're not my mother!" Lexy stomped off down the hall, her bare feet making an impressive amount of noise on the wood floor. A moment later, the slam of her bedroom door echoed through the house.

Hallie didn't move. She certainly wasn't Lexy's mother, was her first thought. Though the girl would have been a whole lot better off if she were, rather than Sandra. At least then she never would have felt rejected and unloved.

Her second response was hurt. She knew it was silly—what did it matter if some teenage kid blew up at her?—but it hurt all the same. Lexy wasn't just some teenage kid; she was someone Hallie cared about deeply. The way, her little voice whispered, a mother cared about her daughter.

And she had no right to feel that way. She was a part of Lexy's life only by virtue of being the temporary woman in her father's life, rather like all those stepfathers her mother kept introducing to, then removing from, their family.

"What was that about?"

She looked up to find Brady standing in the dining-room door, a dishtowel in his hand. She put on a smile for him. "It was your daughter being a teenager. No big deal." After a shrug, she added, "She doesn't want to go to Heartbreak. Maybe you two should stay here, and I'll go alone."

He shook his head.

"No one's interested in me," she pointed out. "If I hadn't spent so much time with Lexy, they never would have noticed me."

Stubbornly he continued to shake his head. "I'll talk to her."

"It's really not necessary, Brady. We can just stay here. Let her watch the rest of her movie."

He came into the room and pressed a kiss to her forehead as he passed. "I'll talk to her. Go on and get dressed."

Feeling more like the kid than the kid apparently did, Hallie obeyed, taking the longer route through the dining room and kitchen to her bedroom. As she went, she sent a silent wish for good luck Brady's way.

He would probably need it.

Lexy was lying on her bed, her feet propped on the headboard, her gaze fixed on a water stain on the ceiling. She knew it was just a matter of time before one of them came looking for her— Sandra never let a disrespectful remark pass without punishment—but she wished they would just leave her alone. Just because she was a kid, no one *ever* left her alone when she wanted.

When there was a knock at the door, she could tell by no more than the sharp rap that it was Brady. "Go away," she said loudly, so of course he opened the door and came inside.

At least he'd bothered to knock first. Since Sandra's bedroom was the only one with a lock, she always just walked right into Lexy's room, so once Lexy had used part of her allowance to buy a lock for the door. It was just a chain, like on motel doors, but took her hours to put it up. The first time Sandra had tried to come in and couldn't, she'd gone ballistic. She'd made Lexy take it off, and then made her pay to have some guy come in and fix the holes in the door and the jamb.

But it had been worth it, she thought with a secretive smile as she remembered the way Sandra's face had turned all splotchy red and she'd sputtered like some cartoon character because she couldn't put into words how pissed she was.

Brady went to the window and sat down on the sill facing her. "What's up?"

"Nothing."

"So that's your everything's-fine-with-the-world face?"

She scowled at him. "I was watching that movie, and she just turned it off."

"She asked you to get ready to go. You should have done it."

"No, she didn't. She *told* me. 'Throw on some clothes, we're going,'" she said in a squeaky, whiny voice that sounded a lot more like Sandra than Hallie. "I don't *wanna* go."

He rubbed his jaw for a moment, like he was trying to think of a way to take Hallie's side without making it look like he was taking her side. "I know all these restrictions aren't a lot of fun, but it's not Hallie's fault. She's really gone out of her way to help us out—doing things with you, spending time with us, taking me to the hospital in the middle of the night, letting us move in here. She didn't plan on any of this when she came here, but she hasn't complained at all."

"She's only doing it 'cause she likes sleeping with you."

If she were in a better mood, Lexy would think it was funny that he was embarrassed. Like she wasn't supposed to know what they were doing in the next room at night? Heck— She scowled harder. Hell, she'd known about sex and everything since she was, like, ten years old.

"That's not true, Lex. She's done it because she likes you— us—a lot."

"Then why is she still planning to go back to California?"

"Is that what this is about?"

She rolled onto her side, stuck her arm under her head so her earrings wouldn't pinch and stared at the poster on the wall. Hallie had seen her looking at it when they'd gone shopping after the fire, and had bought it for her. It was a bigger-than-life picture of Devin Daley, the guy who starred in one of her favorite TV shows. He was in high school on the show, but Hallie, who'd met him, told her he was really twenty-three.

Lexy didn't know why anyone would want to pretend to be a kid after they weren't anymore. She just wanted to make it to twenty, 'cause being a teenager wasn't turning out to be a hell of a lot of fun.

"Lex?" Brady sat down on the bed beside her. "Are you worried that Hallie's going to leave before you do?"

Hallie had started talking about going home more often. *When I get back to L.A., I'll get you an autographed picture of Devin,* she'd said when she'd paid for the poster. *I need to get a hair appointment when I get back home. I'll get Max to give me the director's cut of that movie for you after I go home.*

Lexy didn't want her to leave at all—and *she* didn't want to leave, either. Living here, just the three of them, was so totally different from living with Sandra and Adam. Brady and Hallie were so much cooler, and they liked each other a lot, and they even seemed to like her.

But not enough to even think about asking her to stay. She knew Sandra wouldn't let her—then she'd lose all that child support money Brady paid—and besides, she never agreed to anything Lexy wanted.

But it would be awfully nice if they at least wanted her to stay.

"You'll see her again," Brady said.

"Yeah."

"Hey, neither of you are gone yet. Let's not dread the future so much that we can't enjoy the present, okay?"

"So I should just ignore the fact that we'll both be leaving here soon? Is that what you're doing? Pretending that it's not gonna happen? That you won't miss us? That you won't especially miss her?"

For a minute he looked so anxious that she wished she hadn't said anything. To make up for it, she sat up and hugged him tightly. "I'm sorry. Give me five minutes—" which really meant fifteen "—and I'll be ready to go."

"Okay."

And just before he stood up…he hugged her back.

The way a father should.

Chapter 12

Thanks to Lexy's piddling around, by the time they reached Heartbreak, it was lunchtime, which required a stop at Shay Rafferty's café. Before they even placed their order, Shay had offered Lexy a part-time job. *Very* part-time—three, four hours max. Brady felt funny about leaving her there, but the lawman in him pointed out there wasn't much safer than being in a crowd where a stranger would stand out like a neon sign.

So now Lexy was learning the ins and outs of waitressing, and he and Hallie were on their way to the Barnett place. The property was just outside Heartbreak's town limits, and it was a pretty piece—all pasture and timber, with a thicket of scrub oaks between the road and the house offering privacy. He'd expected someone from the crew to be there working, but the only living souls around were Reese's horses in the pasture out back.

After parking in the driveway, he and Hallie climbed out. She headed immediately for the new house, digging in her bag for keys as she went, but he remained by the truck, looking at the place where the other house had stood. It wouldn't be fair to call it old, since Reese had been living there only a few months when it got shot all to hell.

Brady had known from his patrols where the place was, but he'd never actually been there until the day in June when Reese called and asked for his help in protecting Neely. He'd moved in for a couple of days, and when the trouble was over, they'd all moved out. Neither Neely nor Reese had wanted to sleep in a house where so many people had died violently, and he didn't blame them.

He became aware of Hallie's approach a moment before he heard her shoes crunching on gravel. She stopped beside him, keys in hand, and quietly asked, "Is this the first time you've been here since…?"

"Yeah." He kept looking, though there was nothing to see. Every bit of glass, wood, concrete and stone was gone, and with the recent rain, grass was already sprouting in the dirt.

But he could still see every detail. In the short time he'd stayed there, he'd been able to make his way around the entire house in the dark, and he'd known the lay of the land as well as Reese. He'd wanted to come out of the confrontation with Neely's enemies alive, and he'd succeeded…barely.

"Neely was locked in the safe room that night," he said softly, referring to the specially constructed room that could stand up to the severest of tornadoes—and gunfire, too, they'd proven. "Reese and I had killed five or six men when they disarmed us both. Reese had been shot just a couple days before, and when they figured out where she was, they tried to force him to give them the key to the room by putting pressure on his wound. He was in agony, but there wasn't a key to give them."

It was another hundred-degree-plus day without a cloud in the sky overhead. Off to the northwest, though, the horizon was lined with dark gray. Rain would be good—they were still inches behind on the usual rain—but a thunderstorm would be even better, especially if folks had the sense to stay out of it.

Sweat trickled down his forehead, and he felt it, tickling and annoying, inside his cast. He really didn't need to be standing out here in this heat talking about something that was over and done with and should be forgotten until the trial for the two surviving men rolled around. But he didn't move, and neither did Hallie.

"They took us, both handcuffed, into the bedroom," he finally went on. "They tried to shoot their way in and couldn't, so Forbes, the bastard who was behind it all, ordered Reese to tell Neely to open the door. He wasn't going to—he figured he could keep his mouth shut until he passed out from the pain. But instead of trying that again, they put me on my knees, put a .45 to the back of my head and said they would kill me on the count of five." He smiled wryly. "They made it to four before Reese gave in."

He let the rectangular plot of dirt go blurry and put himself back in time in that memory. "I was so pissed with him. Of course, I didn't know Neely had a gun, and I didn't know she was capable of smiling at a man standing this close—" he indicated the distance between him and Hallie "—and blowing him away."

With a shudder, she slid her arms around his waist. "They would have killed you."

"I know. But I wasn't afraid. Maybe all those times I thought my parents were going to kill me paid off."

"You're a brave man."

He shook his head. "I just did what I had to do."

Keeping one arm around him, she turned him in the direction of the new house. "You believe what you want, and I'll believe the truth."

He liked that she believed in him in spite of himself. He didn't think anyone else ever had, other than Neely and Reese.

"What about your house?" she asked. "Are you going to rebuild, or go back to living in an apartment?"

"I have forty acres. Right now it's leased to a neighbor, but I'll probably see if I can buy out the lease, and build a place. Not anything like you're used to," he said with a sidelong look, "but with a bedroom and bath for Lexy. She can spend more time in the bathroom... She came in one day while I was in the shower. I asked her if privacy was a foreign concept to her, and in a real snooty Sandra-type voice, she said no, but living with only one bathroom was."

Hallie laughed. "Regardless of where I live, I'm not a snob, but I agree with her on that. I grew up in a house with five females and only one bathroom. On my list of vital necessities for a house, a second bathroom comes before a kitchen, living or dining room.'' She climbed the steps to the porch and unlocked the front door before glancing back at him. ''So you're going to stay a part of her life.''

''If she wants me to.''

''You know she does.''

''I know she does right now. I don't know about next month or next year. As she gets older, she may lose interest, or her mother may change her mind.''

''I won't embarrass you by getting all mushy, but I think what you're doing is admirable and Lexy's very lucky to have you for a father, whether you are or not.''

No, he was the lucky one, in more ways than he could count.

The door opened into a small foyer. The temperature was a few degrees cooler inside, and the smell of fresh-cut wood sweetened the air. On the right a doorway led into a hall, there was a closet straight ahead, and on the left, wide double doors led into the room that filled the center half of the house. Large bay windows looked out on the lawn and the woods out front, and in back plenty of arched windows bordered the kitchen cabinets and framed a view of the barn and pasture. On the east end was the master bedroom and bath, the laundry room and the entrance to the garage, and on the west end, two bedrooms and two more baths. Apparently, Neely shared her sister's idea of vital necessities.

The floor plan was similar to the other house, though the new place would be half again as big. And in the old house, the living room and kitchen had been separate rooms, while here it was one massive space. One nice space. It would be great when Hallie and Neely finished with it.

He wondered if he could persuade Hallie to stick around through the building of *his* house.

''So are they doing everything they're supposed to be doing?'' he asked after following her through the house and ending up in the master bath.

''Yeah, everything looks fine. Isn't this tile beautiful?''

The floor was a mosaic of pale earthy colors—rose, dusky

blue, mossy green, tan and lavender and russet—in an intricate star pattern, with smaller versions of it on the tub surround. "It's nice," he murmured.

"It'll be repeated in the kitchen tile and in the wood floor in the foyer—an idea I may have to rip off when I get my own house."

He leaned against the doorjamb while she checked out the fixtures. "Where are you going to find this house?" He'd been aiming for a casual-conversation tone, and he thought he'd achieved it, not that it mattered.

"I don't know," she said without glancing at him. "Someplace far from Los Angeles."

How about Oklahoma? he wanted to suggest. It was halfway across the country from L.A., close to two of her sisters, reasonably close to the third one and their mother. And to him.

But he didn't know how close she wanted to be to him.

"Come on," he said. "Tell me what your ideal town is like."

She leaned against the peach-colored counter, resting her hands on the curved edge. In her short, snug, pale green dress, she fitted right in with all the soft colors around her. "My ideal town.... It would be small, but big enough to offer most of the things I need. The people would be friendly, and it would be safe. Kids would ride their bikes and play, and everyone would know their neighbors. The schools would be good, and most people would like their jobs, and there would be this real sense of community."

"I know the place you're talking about. It only exists on a Hollywood backlot."

"Oh, I don't know. What about you? What's your ideal town?"

"I'm satisfied with Buffalo Plains." And that was true. Not happy, but satisfied. He would need Hallie and Lexy in his life on a permanent basis to be happy there or anywhere. After a moment, he moved a few steps closer. "What about your ideal house?"

"Something very homey. Do you know I got lost in the Beverly Hills house for the first month we lived there?" She tilted her head to one side while she thought, and the bruise on her forehead became visible. Between her makeup and her hair, it was hardly noticeable, but he couldn't forget it. He hated that it was there.

"No frills," she went on. "No impressive architectural details, no showplace. White or pale yellow outside, a big, wide porch with wicker chairs. Large rooms, lots of windows, lots of wood and stone. At least three bathrooms and three or four bedrooms, for all the nieces and nephews I plan to have visit me once Neely and Reese start producing them."

"Why not fill them with your own kids?"

Her laughter couldn't hide the sadness in her hazel eyes. "I'm thirty years old and a three-time lose—" At his scowl, she substituted, "And three times divorced. I swore to myself there would never be a fourth divorce, and the only way to guarantee that is never to have a fourth marriage."

"Or to make sure you marry the right man." He wondered if there was any chance in hell he could be that man.

"I thought I did that—*three* times. Obviously, my judgment isn't the best. So, as the old saying goes, three strikes and you're out."

"How about fourth time's the charm?"

"It's *third* time—and believe me, Max wasn't that much more charming than numbers one and two." She pushed away from the counter and slipped past him. "Are you about ready to get back into some air-conditioning?"

No, he wanted to say. He wanted to talk. Wanted to find some argument that would change her mind. Wanted…just wanted.

But as he became aware of an itch down inside his cast and the fact that his shirt was sticking to his skin, he started after her.

The northwesterly clouds had advanced while they were inside, but in the local area, it was still blazing hot and dry. They had a wind now, though he was hard put to say whether it made things better or worse. At least it dried the sweat, but it also seemed to suck the air right out of his lungs.

"You know, the Southern California desert winds have nothing on this breeze," Hallie remarked as she locked the door, then paused at the top of the steps. "I didn't realize Oklahoma was part desert."

"Nah, it's not that bad."

She raised one brow. "All you need is a tumbleweed rolling across here to complete the illusion."

"Would you settle for a dust devil?" He pointed to where a mini-tornado was whirling across the pasture just inches above the ground.

She watched until it disappeared in a shower of dust drifting down. A faint smile curved her lips, and a certain look had come over her face. Contentment, Brady thought. He'd seen her wearing that look more often lately. But how could she be so contented and yet not even consider staying?

Finally she looked back from the field and smiled at him. "We've got probably another couple hours before Lexy's ready. What do you want to do?"

"Let's go for a drive. I'll show you my land."

After making certain she'd locked the door—she had a tendency to get distracted easily these days, she thought with a smile—she followed him down the steps and to the truck. As soon as he started the engine, she turned the air conditioner to high, then redirected the passenger vents directly toward her. As the frigid air washed over her heated skin, she closed her eyes and gave a sigh of relief. "Oh, that feels good."

"God gave us summer so we wouldn't complain too much about winter," he remarked as he backed around.

"Where I live, winter means you put on a jacket or sweater."

"Well, darlin', then you've been living in the wrong place."

"I know. And I intend to do something about it."

At the end of the driveway, instead of turning left toward Heartbreak, he turned right. After less than half a mile, the paved road ended, giving way to dirt and gravel. Even after Thursday's rain, the SUV's wide tires sent up great plumes of dust behind them.

"I guess when you live out here, you give up on the notion of having a clean car, don't you?" she asked.

"Nah. You just have to revise your notion of cleanliness down a few degrees. Our hottest, dustiest times are during our annual drought, of course, so washing your car every day isn't always an option. In fact, water gets rationed every couple years around here.''

"California's had their problems with water, too. And power. And smog. Crime. Traffic."

"Kinda makes you wonder why anyone would want to live there."

She made a childish face at him, then turned her attention out the window. The gently rolling hills were covered with pastures dotted with cattle and horses, and separated here and there by thick stands of trees, mostly those scrubby oaks that seemed to serve little purpose other than taking up space. They weren't pretty, and most of them were too small to bother with for firewood. There were more houses than she'd expected for the first five miles or so, but the farther they got from town, the more sparse they became.

"How does Marshall City compare to Buffalo Plains and Heartbreak?" she asked after seeing enough scenery.

"Marshall City sucks."

She gave him an irate look, and he relented. "It's probably twice, maybe three times, the size of Buffalo Plains. It sits on top of what was once one of the biggest oil fields in Texas. That's where the Marshall family made their fortunes."

"Fortunes?"

With a grin, he shrugged. "You win some, you lose some. It's kind of a hobby with Texas oilmen. My father realized that the way to stop losing it was to diversify. Thanks to him, the trust funds our grandparents left Logan and me have provided enough money for each of us to live comfortably for the rest of our lives."

Or to support a daughter who might not be his, Hallie thought. How many fathers out there refused to pay child support for kids that *were* theirs, kids they'd lived with and raised, then left when they left their mothers? Lexy really was incredibly lucky.

"What about the house you grew up in?"

His mouth thinned. "It was straight out of *Gone With the Wind.* Three stories, white, columns, verandahs. My parents liked being the first family of Marshall City."

Because it was too nice a day to dwell on bad memories, Hallie deliberately shifted the subject in a different direction. "There's a house just outside Heartbreak," she began.

"Big place? On top of a hill? That's the Taylor place."

"And the Taylors are…?"

"Well, they *think* they're the first family of Heartbreak. They're definitely the most well-off. The men raise cattle, and the women raise trouble. Inez, her sister-in-law and her daughter have set the standard for all that's good and proper in town, or so they think—and, no surprise, no one measures up but them."

"The kind of people who are fun to play with," Hallie said with an evil smile.

"Only if you have a warped idea of what constitutes 'play.'"

Slowing, he turned into a rutted lane that ended at a barbed-wire gate. Though he reached for his seat belt, Hallie unfastened hers first. She slid to the ground, then lifted the wire loop that secured the gate and swung it open. Once he'd driven through, she closed it, then climbed in again.

"Did you notice there's no road here?" she asked conversationally.

"Did you notice we've got four-wheel drive? We make our own roads when necessary."

He pointed the truck toward a distant hill to the northwest and set off across the pasture. There was a faint hint of a trail, she realized before they'd gone far. It wasn't used often, but it *was* used.

The cattle paid them no attention beyond a disinterested gaze as they drove past. That was okay. Hallie was interested enough by herself. She would love to come out here with her cameras. There were so many great shots—the cows placidly munching their feed. The skeleton of a dead tree all alone on a ridge. The texture and stark shapes of the shallow arroyos cut into the ground by runoff. The outcroppings of sandstone. The abandoned barn, its boards turned silver after decades of harsh sun, its entire structure tilted ten or twelve degrees off center but still standing. The sun rising over the wooded hills to the east or setting over the undulating pastures to the west.

At the top of the highest hill in the immediate vicinity, Brady stopped the truck and they got out. There were trees on either side of the clearing, and an incredible view all the way around. She could see several church steeples in Buffalo Plains, and could make out a small section of highway that she thought…yes, was just north of her house and west of Brady's.

"When the leaves are off the trees, you can see the courthouse from here," he said quietly, "and back there in the trees is a spring that feeds a creek running down the west slope."

"It's beautiful. It's a great place for a house." Why did that stir up a funny, achy feeling in the pit of her stomach? Why did she find it so easy to envision the ideal house she'd described sitting right on this very spot? With a winding drive twisting its way down the hill to the highway below, and with horses of their own grazing in the fields. But this was *Brady's* property, meant for *his* house. This was where *he* belonged.

She still had to find the place where she belonged.

He moved to stand behind her, sliding his arms around her middle and resting his chin on her head. "You think Lexy will like it?"

"Lexy's happy living in a little two-bedroom farmhouse. She doesn't care where you live. She just wants to be there with you." *But ask me if I would like it,* she silently urged. *Ask me what I think, because the answer's the same. I don't care where you live. I just want to be there with you.*

She was in so much trouble. Neely and Reese were due back in a week, and after spending a few days with them, Hallie was supposed to leave. But how could she go when her family—in her heart if not in fact—was here?

Maybe she could take a cue from pretty Isabella, she thought with a thin smile, who'd come for a visit and stayed. But staying didn't mean staying with Brady. He'd entered into this affair with the understanding that it would have a definite end. Three weeks and a day or two, and she was supposed to be outta there. It wouldn't be fair to him to say, Sorry, I've changed my mind about leaving. It certainly wouldn't be fair to expect him to continue the relationship beyond that three-week point.

And it would be impossible to stay and *not* have that relationship.

The next time any of her sisters asked for a favor, she was going to turn her down so fast her head would spin. She would offer money, household staff, hired help, but she would never put herself in a risky situation again.

Slowly the sweet, ticklish sensation of Brady's mustache brushing her ear pulled her out of her gloomy thoughts and made her smile as she tilted her head to the side.

"You ever make love outside?" he asked in a whisper that sent a shiver through her.

"No."

"Me, either. Want to give it a try?"

She shifted and felt his arousal, long and stiff, against her hip. The funny, achy feeling returned deep in her stomach, but this time it had nothing to do with not belonging with Brady. No, on the contrary, this time it was because she most assuredly did belong, at least for the moment. At least for this.

As his hand slid up to cup her breast, she reached back to tug his head close enough for an awkward kiss. "I don't suppose you have a blanket in that truck?"

"Of course I do. The Canyon County Sheriff's Department is prepared for any emergency."

"This isn't an emergency," she pointed out.

He rubbed his erection hard against her. "It is for me, darlin', and it's getting more desperate with every passing minute."

"Oh, well, then, by all means, get the blanket," she said in her sultriest voice. "I'd hate for you to suffer unnecessarily."

He went to the back of the SUV to get the blanket. While he was there, Hallie undid the back zipper on her dress, then stepped out of it, folded it neatly, and hung it over the dusty mirror. Her bra followed, then her panties. She was glad she'd chosen dressier sandals this morning, with thin straps and a heel. Standing on top of a hill under the bright August sun, naked but for her sandals, felt silly enough. If she'd been wearing her usual clunky, thick-soled sandals, the feeling would quickly switch from silly to idiotic.

As he came back, Brady stopped short and uttered a profanity that vibrated the air with its intensity, and instead of silly, she felt beautiful. Desirable. Womanly. She offered him a provocative smile, then in response to his profanity, she softly taunted, "Promises, promises."

His blanket was a quilt that was worn, soft and had been well-used. She wondered who had made it—Reese's mother or grandmother, perhaps, or a relative of the sheriff who had preceded him. If life was different and she could imagine any future she wanted for herself, she would imagine herself making such a quilt some day, sewing it on the dining-room table of the pale yellow house that would stand right here, quilting it on the broad porch in a wicker chair. It would be in bright colors and would cover her oldest child's bed until it got old. Then it would be relegated to frequent use as a picnic or making-love-under-the-sun quilt.

She would be the housewife she had never been, the mother she'd always longed to be. She would cook and clean and volunteer at the kids' schools, and she would have dinner on the table when Brady came home from work. She would do laundry and help with homework and have Neely and Reese and their kids over for dinner every Sunday after church.

Such fanciful imaginings for a woman who would be leaving Oklahoma alone in a week and a few days.

Alone.

Pushing the thought into the darkest corner of her mind, she watched as Brady spread the quilt in the sun. Then, while he watched, she strolled lazily across the uneven ground to him. He looked as if he wanted to say something but couldn't, so he put the words into a kiss instead—fierce, claiming, possessive, greedy. He stabbed his tongue into her mouth and pulled her against him, his hand roaming over her bare skin, caressing, tickling, arousing.

When they broke for breath, she gave a husky laugh. "What's wrong with this picture?"

His amazing, incredible blue gaze slid from the top of her head to the tips of her toes, and a wicked grin curved his mouth. "Not a damned thing."

"Thank you...but I disagree. I'm naked."

"Yes, darlin', you surely are."

"And you're not."

"I will be." He lowered her to the quilt, then lay beside her. For a moment, he remained on his side, head resting on his left fist, and simply looked at her. His gaze was so intense, she could feel it, she swore, as if it possessed a physical component. After a moment, she closed her eyes, smiled awkwardly, then rolled onto her side and drew her knees up.

"You could give a woman a complex," she chided him.

"I can give you a whole lot more than a complex." Gently but firmly, he pushed her knees down, then rolled her onto her back again, and he leaned over her, pressing a kiss to her nipple. Instantly it swelled and hardened, and a corresponding need tugged deep inside her. "You like that?" he asked.

She managed a careless shrug. "It was okay, but I think you can do better."

"You think?" He repeated the action, only this time it lasted longer, and he caught her nipple between his teeth, nipping at it. "Is that better?"

"Hmm."

His mustache tickled as he offered a third kiss, flicking his tongue across her nipple before drawing it into his mouth and suckling it with enough pressure to curl her toes. Gasping, she slid her fingers into his hair, then tugged him closer even as she arched against his mouth. She couldn't speak to save her life, but he seemed to understand what her whimpers meant, because he repeated the kiss on her other breast.

Every nerve and muscle in her body was stretched taut before he finally let her help him undress. Her hands shook as she fumbled with his zipper, but once she got her fingers inside his jeans to caress his arousal, the shakiness was suddenly all in *him*. Swearing, he tried to remove her hand as well as his jeans, but she was intent on having her chance to play.

"Hallie...damn, babe, you've gotta..." His face paled and his eyes squeezed shut as a low groan escaped him.

She smiled sweetly, removed her hand and sat back on her heels. "I've got to do what?"

"That. Again." He drew her hand back where he wanted it and curved her fingers around him, then groaned again.

Finally they discarded the last of his clothing, and he stretched out on the quilt and filled her in one long, hard thrust. She gave a low, satisfied smile. In her make-believe future, they would do this every chance they got, and it would be just as incredible every time.

But forget make-believe. He was here now, the sun was beating down on them, the breeze blowing across their skin, and he was starting to move in a tormenting, tantalizing way. Long strokes, deep and forceful, but lazy, as if they had all the time in the world. As if they could make love forever.

He kissed and stroked her, and she returned the favor, gliding her hands over smooth warm skin and rough scars heated by the sun. She loved the feel of him beneath her fingertips—the silky skin, the coarse hair, the hard muscle, the thud of his heart, even the scars. She loved everything about him.

She loved him.

And in a week and a day or two, she was supposed to say goodbye to him.

The shift in his rhythm was subtle at first, then more pronounced as he began thrusting harder, faster. Clinging to him, she met every stroke, took every inch of him, and when the tension became too great to bear, she closed her eyes, relaxed and let it all wash over her—the hunger, the need, the heat, the pleasure, the pain, the promise of sweet satisfaction.

He pushed into her one last time, and with a groan, he stiffened and strained. His climax hit only seconds before her own, rocking and trembling and leaving them both fatigued, their hearts pounding, their breathing ragged.

After a time he rolled to his back beside her, then began fumbling with his jeans. She wanted to protest that it was too soon to get dressed, that she wanted more, but she couldn't find the words. Then she realized dimly that he wasn't getting dressed but rather searching for his cell phone.

Funny. She'd thought that ringing was in her head, caused by decreased blood flow to her brain and pleasure worth dying for.

He spoke to the caller—Lexy, she guessed from his end of the conversation—for a few minutes, then hung up and grinned at her. "You know which sister you are?" When she shook her head—all she had the energy to do—he went on. "The sexy one. The amazing one. The my-God-how-do-you-do-that-to-me one."

She summoned a smile from somewhere and lazily replied, "I aim to please."

Suddenly his expression turned serious, and he bent to kiss her. It was another of those fierce, possessive kisses, but something was different. It was as if this time…as if he was making a promise. A commitment.

And *that* was wishful thinking.

He got to his feet, shook out his boxers and jeans and wriggled into them. "Lex is ready. Guess we'd better head back that way."

"I don't suppose you'd get my clothes for me," she said in a sweet voice, batting her lashes at him.

"And miss the opportunity to watch you walk over there to get them?" He gave a shake of his head. "Oh, honey, obviously you've never watched yourself walk naked in heels."

"I tend to not look at myself naked very often. You know, you've seen it once; what's the point of seeing it again?"

"That's because you don't appreciate your body the way I do." He put his shoes on, then headed for the truck, pulling his T-shirt on as he went. A moment later he returned with her clothing.

She quickly dressed, helped him shake out and fold the quilt, then followed him to the truck. She could use a tall glass of iced water about now, plus a snooze with Brady in her comfy, cool bedroom. Then whoever awoke first could take his or her sweet time awakening the other, and they could do the deed—and experience the pleasure—all over again.

But that wasn't going to happen today. They didn't make love during the day with Lexy around. She wasn't sure if that was a little parental hangup on Brady's part, or if hormones and circumstances just hadn't jibed yet.

"So you think a house here would be nice?" he asked as he turned the truck in a wide circle, then started back the way they came.

"I think it would be great."

His responding smile was more pleased than it should have

been. After all, it wasn't as if she would be living there with him. Oh, maybe she'd get to spend a night or two there on future visits, but she wouldn't even count on that. She didn't think she could be a part-time part of his life.

"Did Lexy say how she liked her first day's work?"

"She said it was 'cool.' She earned as much in tips as she did in pay, but her feet hurt."

Rather than follow back roads all the way to Heartbreak, he took a shortcut to the highway. From there, they made good time, traveling a steady ten miles an hour over the speed limit. And why not? Who was going to give the acting sheriff a ticket?

When they reached the Heartbreak Café, most of the cars that had lined Main Street were gone, and fewer than a dozen customers were visible through the plate-glass windows. Hallie saw Shay, leaning on the counter and talking to a slender brunette, but there was no sign of Lexy.

"Want me to go in and get her?" she offered.

"Sure."

When she went inside, the bell over the door rang. "Hi, Shay. Is Lexy around?"

Slowly Shay straightened, and her smile disappeared. "She's gone, Hallie."

In an instant, Hallie's lungs grew tight, making a breath hard to come by, and ice started spreading through her veins. "What do you mean, she's gone?"

Shay came around the counter. "She called Brady about a half hour ago, then had a piece of cake and talked to the Harris twins. Right after they left—probably…ten minutes ago—she said, 'There's my ride,' thanked me and went outside. I haven't seen her since. I just assumed— Oh, my God, Hallie!"

For a moment Hallie stood there, too numb to think or move. "You didn't see who she got in the car with or what kind of car it was?"

Shay shook her head. "I was waiting on some customers. I just told her goodbye, then went into the kitchen."

"Were these people here?"

Without looking at the customers, Shay nodded.

"I'd better tell Brady. I'm sure he'll have some questions."

"I'm so sorry, Hallie," Shay murmured.

"It's not your fault," she said quietly as she turned toward the door.

It was *their* fault.

Brady's...and hers.

Chapter 13

Canyon County had never been a hotbed of criminal activity. They had plenty of small stuff to keep the sheriff's department busy—burglaries, barroom brawls, assaults, domestic disputes—but for the most part they didn't see a lot of major crimes. There had been only four homicides in the past nine years, and to the best of Brady's knowledge, there had never been a kidnapping.

Why did the first have to be Lexy?

He'd known the instant Hallie walked out of the café that something was wrong. He'd met her on the sidewalk, and in a shocked, numbed tone she'd told him Lexy was gone. He'd called the dispatcher and damn near every deputy on the payroll had shown up, whether they were on duty or not. While waiting for them, he'd questioned everyone in the café, but learned nothing. A few diners had seen Lexy leave, but no one had paid attention to where she'd gone.

Without a description of the vehicle, they couldn't even look for her, short of putting up roadblocks on every single road leaving the county, and they didn't have the manpower for that. Besides, the bastard—or bastards—already had a good head start. They could be halfway to Tulsa by now.

Still, most of the deputies were out looking for her. A purple-haired kid would be hard to miss, Mitch had remarked, and for the first time Brady had been damned grateful that she didn't look like every other teenager out there.

Ryan Sandoval came to stand beside him at the door. "Lexy knows these guys have been after her. Why would she leave with them or anyone else without kicking up a fuss?"

Staring sightlessly outside, Brady shook his head. "I don't know."

"She told Shay, 'There's my ride.' You're driving your patrol unit, aren't you? And she knew that?"

Brady nodded.

"Which would suggest it was...a deputy?" Ryan shook his head. "It just doesn't make sense. She couldn't mistake any other vehicle for a black-and-white SUV with a light bar."

No, Brady silently agreed. But maybe she'd seen a deputy approaching and had gone outside, thinking it was him and Hallie, and the guys had grabbed her then. Or maybe...maybe...

Damn it, he hated this! He hated being on the other side of a police investigation, hated the sick feeling in his gut and the fear that intensified with every beat of his heart. He hated not knowing where his daughter was, and he hated like hell that he hadn't protected her. He shouldn't have let her help out Shay. He never should have left her alone unless she was safely behind bars in the courthouse basement.

"Does she have a cell phone?" Ryan asked.

Brady shook his head. Of course she did, she'd mentioned once—everyone at Marshall High had them—but she hadn't brought it with her. There wasn't anyone in Texas she wanted to call, she'd said with a dismissive shrug.

He should have gotten her one. Should have come straight back here after Hallie checked out Neely's house. Damn well shouldn't have gone all the way back to Buffalo Plains and shown Hallie the hill or made love to her. God help him, he'd gotten close to Hallie when they were standing on top of that hill, and he'd forgotten all about Lexy.

After Ryan walked away to talk with Lucy and a state trooper who'd stopped in, Brady looked over his shoulder at Hallie. She was sitting on the nearest bar stool, legs crossed, looking cool and elegant. Anyone who didn't know her could be forgiven for thinking she seemed unconcerned, but he knew better. He could see how tightly her jaw was clenched, and the shadows in her hazel eyes, and the nervous movement of her foot.

He should go to her, put his arms around her, reassure her, but he didn't have any assurances to give. He didn't know if everything would be all right, didn't know if they would get Lexy back safe and unharmed, or at all. Those two bastards had been damned determined to grab her. It wasn't likely they'd give her back easily.

When he turned his gaze outside again, he saw a couple approaching. Automatically he opened the door for them, then stepped back.

"Hey," Ethan James greeted him as he followed his wife, Grace, inside. He glanced at the other deputies and the somber faces, then asked, "What's up? Has something happened?"

"My daughter, Lexy, was kidnapped here this afternoon," Brady said, his jaw clamped so tight he could barely force the words out.

"Oh, my God!" That came from Grace, holding her baby, Annie Grace, in her arms. "I'm so sorry!"

"Did you happen to see anything between four and four-thirty?"

Grace shook her head, then readjusted her glasses on her nose when she looked at Ethan. "No," he agreed. "Nothing suspicious. But—"

"But?"

James's forehead wrinkled in a frown. "A guy came in earlier, maybe three or three-thirty—a stranger. He bought a roll of duct tape."

The muscles in Brady's stomach clenched. If he were a kidnapper, duct tape would be his restraint method of choice. It worked for binding wrists and ankles, as well as a gag. It was quick to apply and, for removal, didn't require a key like handcuffs, a knife like rope or special scissors like Flex-cuffs.

But not all the advantages went to the crook. It was also a terrific source for fingerprints. If they found the tape. And Lexy.

"You sure you'd never seen this guy before?" Ryan asked.

Ethan shook his head. "He's not the sort I'd forget."

"Why do you say that?"

A faint tinge of red appeared high on James's cheeks. "In the old life, I would've considered him a mark."

In "the old life," Brady knew, Ethan James had been a thief, a gambler and a con artist. He'd spent so much time in the Canyon County Jail when he was younger that they'd practically put his name on the cell. He'd drifted from town to town, state to state, looking for the easy money, until one day, he'd decided to straighten himself out. And he'd done it. Grace and the baby she'd been carrying had played a part in his transformation, but Ethan had done all the hard work. Brady admired him for being able to pull it off.

"What would have made him a mark?" Lucy asked from her place beside Ryan.

Ethan shrugged. "He was dressed well, wearing a couple of nice diamond rings and an expensive watch, had a Gucci wallet with a wad of cash in it, along with a couple gold cards and a couple platinum. Oh, and he was driving a Mercedes. A convertible. Pretty."

The stool squeaked as Hallie slowly swiveled around to face them. "Blue?" she asked.

Ethan thought about it a moment, then nodded. "Yeah. Kind of a silver-blue."

Brady went to Hallie as she slid to the floor. "You think someone stole your car and Lexy thought it was you?"

Slowly she shook her head. "The first day she was in town, when I took her with me after lunch, she said, 'Nice car. Adam has one just like it.'"

Brady stepped aside so the Jameses could get past, staring at Hallie all the while. After the tall guy had tried to grab Lexy off the street, he'd made a mental note to check into Adam Napier's background the next day. But first thing Monday morning, there had been the aftermath of Sunday's shooting to deal with, then the break-in at his house, the argument with Hallie, the second break-in, the fire, the broken wrist.... Damn it, he'd forgotten all about Napier.

"Who is Adam?" Ryan asked.

Brady's gaze remained locked with Hallie's. In addition to the shadows there earlier, there was also now fear. "Adam Napier," he replied. "He's my ex-wife's current husband. Lives in Marshall City, Texas. Get a tag number and put it out on the radio. Have the dispatcher run him through NCIC and see if he's got a record." When he'd asked Lexy what Napier did, her answer hadn't been the one he'd wanted to hear. *I don't know. But he makes a lot of money and has a lot of creepy guys working for him.* Sounded like someone who just might generate a hit or two with the FBI's National Crime Information Center computer.

While one of the deputies went to do as he'd ordered, Ryan asked, "Why would Lexy's stepfather kidnap her?"

"Unless...he didn't actually kidnap her," Lucy suggested. "Maybe her mother didn't send her here for a visit. Maybe she ran away, and her stepfather found her and is taking her home. Did you talk to her mother when she showed up?"

Brady shook his head.

"Do you think it's possible she might have lied about it?"

This time both Brady and Hallie nodded.

Lucy shrugged. "It makes sense. I mean, her stepfather drives a forty-thousand-dollar Mercedes, and she shows up in town on the bus? With no return ticket?"

Brady leaned against the counter. "It's possible Lexy lied. It's also possible that her mother put her on the bus. Sandra's not particularly maternal, and her judgment is usually flawed."

Beside him, Hallie was shaking her head. "Even if Lexy did run away and that's why Adam is here, and he thinks he's just taking her home.... Lexy would tell him she was staying with her father. She would want to pick up her things, and she absolutely would not leave without saying goodbye to Brady."

"And there's no legitimate reason for Napier to refuse," Lucy conceded. "So back to the question—why would her stepfather kidnap her?"

There was a moment of heavy silence before Ryan cleared his throat. "Maybe...I'm sorry," he said to Brady. "But maybe something's going on at home that he doesn't want her to tell anyone about."

The ice that had frozen in Brady's chest when Hallie had told him that Lexy was missing started to spread. If Adam Napier had molested Lexy, if he'd laid so much as a hand on her, Brady would kill him and take great pleasure in it. And he'd kill Sandra, too, for allowing it to happen.

"Maybe he didn't do anything to her," Lucy said. "Maybe she saw him do something to someone else. Maybe she witnessed some shady deal and doesn't even realize what she saw."

"Or maybe he doesn't want her at all," Hallie murmured.

Brady looked sharply at her. "Those bastards tried to grab her *three* times."

Again she shook her head. "That night at the dance, they followed her for three blocks, but they never got close or did anything. When the guy tried to force her into his car…he didn't have hold of *her*. He had her backpack. And when we got mugged outside the courthouse, from what I understand, they didn't drag her away. They struggled over the backpack, and when the strap broke and they got hold of it, they ran. The first time they broke into your house, she wasn't even there, but they searched it anyway…and didn't take a thing. They certainly didn't empty your kitchen cabinets because they thought she might be hiding inside. They were looking for something, Brady."

"Something they thought might be in the backpack," he muttered thoughtfully.

"They didn't find it in your house, so they took the backpack. They didn't find it there, so they took…Lexy."

"And if she doesn't have whatever it is…." Grabbing her hand, he started toward the door. "It would most likely be at your house."

He'd never made the trip from Heartbreak to Buffalo Plains in so little time. With the emergency lights flashing, he used the siren only when traffic made it necessary. Just outside town, he screeched almost to a stop, then turned into Hallie's driveway.

The minimal furniture in the house made searching an easy prospect. Presumably, Lexy didn't have a clue what the men wanted, so she wouldn't have deliberately hidden it. But a search of the guest-room closet and the two drawers in the night table turned up nothing that shouldn't have been there. They took the bed apart and checked between the mattress and springs, and he looked through her makeup bag while Hallie patted through the pockets of every garment in the closet, then dragged in a chair so she could see the shelf above the clothes.

They found nothing.

Silently they remade the bed, then sat down on it. "What if this guy calls and says he'll trade Lexy for whatever it is he wants," Hallie asked softly, "only we don't have it?"

He needed to think about that—to come up with some kind of plan—but he couldn't. There were too many possible outcomes to the situation, most of them not good. He just couldn't face them at the moment.

After a time, she leaned across to hug him. "She'll be all right, Brady. She's smart and tough, like her father. She'll be fine."

The only response he could make at the moment was to slide his arm around her waist. Maybe whatever the men wanted had been destroyed in the fire, and once Lexy persuaded Napier of that, he would release her. Yeah, sure, and face kidnapping charges and twenty-plus years in prison? Not likely. Unless he'd underestimated her and thought no one could possibly believe her over him.

Abruptly he got to his feet. "Let me have your keys. I want to check your car."

"They're on the table by the front door." Hallie watched him go, then slowly followed. She stopped on the porch, hugging herself tightly, and watched as he searched her car. The Mercedes was small, so it went quickly. Next he repeated the action in his truck, checking under seats, in the glove compartment and console, flipping the sun visors down. Finally he searched his sheriff's department vehicle. When he turned away after slamming the rear doors, he looked so dejected that she could hardly bear to look at him.

He'd just reached the top step when another black-and-white vehicle pulled into the driveway. It was Ryan Sandoval. The deputy was about Brady's age, Hallie estimated, though a few inches shorter and a few pounds thinner, and he wore a troubled expression that she suspected had little to do with the case he found himself investigating. All was not well in Deputy Sandoval's life, and she sincerely hoped it didn't affect his job performance. They needed all the help they could get.

He came to the top of the steps, nodded politely to Hallie, then turned his attention to Brady. "Looks like Lucy might have been at least partly on the right track earlier, when she'd suggested that Lexy might have witnessed a shady deal between Napier and someone else. I called a buddy of mine at the FBI. Napier's currently under investigation by the bureau, the DEA and the IRS for drugs and racketeering. They know he's dirty. They just haven't been able to make a case yet."

Though they weren't in physical contact, Hallie could feel Brady go stiff and cold at the news. She laid her hand on his arm as she asked, "What is the IRS's interest in drugs and racketeering?"

"Taxes," Ryan replied. "He's making a hell of a lot of money on his illegal activities, and he's not declaring it as income or paying taxes on it."

She stared. "They expect you to pay taxes on ill-gotten gains?"

"Income is income," the deputy said with a shrug. "Actually, it's sometimes easier to get these guys on tax evasion than on the drug charges. Either way, they go to prison, which is what you want."

"So my ex-wife moved my daughter into a house with a drug dealer." Brady's voice was low and menacing. "Does she *know* she married a drug dealer?"

"My friend didn't know," Ryan replied.

"A damned drug dealer." Muttering curses, Brady went inside the house and slammed the door behind him.

Hallie smiled tautly at the deputy. "Thanks for finding out...."

"Sorry it wasn't better news."

"Yeah, me, too." She waited until he'd made it halfway to his truck, then she went in, too, leaning against the door after she closed it. Brady was methodically searching the couch—removing the cushions, shoving his hand into the crevices, tilting it back so he could see underneath. He did the same with the two armchairs, then began rummaging through the end-table drawers.

Finally he straightened and faced her. "The last eleven months we were married, she wouldn't let me touch her because she was so repulsed by my scars," he said, then his voice grew louder and angrier with each word. "But she has no problem going to bed every night with a damned *drug dealer?*"

"Maybe she doesn't know," Hallie said softly.

"And maybe she does, and she just doesn't give a—" He broke off and drew a shaky breath. "I should have checked…. I should have taken the threat more seriously. Hell, what I really should have done is sent you both away. I didn't want you here, disrupting my life. I should have put her on the next bus out of here, and I should have told you to stay the hell away from me. I knew you were both trouble, and I didn't want you making trouble for me. I didn't want…" Taking a look around the room, he gave a forlorn shake of his head and finished bitterly. "Damn it, I didn't want either of you."

As he left the room, something inside Hallie shriveled and died. Her hope, her dreams, her future, her family. She didn't feel any pain—though she knew from experience that would change. All she felt was a great emptiness inside where the best parts of her had lived. Emptiness and disappointment and anger.

She'd *known* better than to get involved with Brady. Hadn't Max taught her anything? She'd warned herself over and over, but she'd gone and fallen in love with him anyway, and for what? Another broken heart. The one she'd said she couldn't survive.

Numbly she replaced the sofa's cushions and pillows, then the chairs'. She closed the end-table drawer he'd left partly open and straightened the afghan on the back of the chair. When she heard his footsteps coming down the hall, she wanted desperately to dash into the kitchen, but forced herself to remain where she was. She wouldn't hide from him, not in her own house.

He had changed into his uniform. His gun was in its holster, and he was carrying one of his rifles. He didn't look at her. Didn't speak to her. He simply walked out.

She heard the door close. His footsteps cross the porch. The SUV's engine start, then a moment later, fade into the distance. And still she stood there, wondering how such a wonderful afternoon had turned into the evening from hell.

She didn't know how much time had passed when a sob shuddered through her. Unwilling to cry just yet, she sniffled and headed for the bedroom, turning on lights along the way. She hauled her suitcases from the closet, laid them open on the bed and began methodically packing. Her impulse was to throw everything into the bags in a tangled heap, slam them shut and get the hell out, the way he wanted, but she forced herself to do the job neatly. She would not fall apart. She was leaving here with dignity and self-respect, even if no one else saw it.

Tonight, alone in a motel bed somewhere, she would fall apart.

Working on autopilot, she managed to get almost everything into her bags. As usual, she'd made a few purchases on her and Lexy's shopping trips, so the shoes that had come out of the largest bag wouldn't fit back in. Not a problem. She had shopping bags in the pantry. Granted, a Wal-Mart bag wasn't quite as elegant as Louis Vuitton, but it was functional, and that was all she cared about.

She carried the tote bag that contained her toiletries and the largest suitcase into the living room and left them on a patch of bare floor, then returned for the medium-sized case and her camera bag. Then she circled around to the pantry, flipped on the light switch and reached for a bag on the bottom shelf. When she lifted it, something slender and black slithered over the edge of the shelf. Her first thought was a snake, and she shrieked and jerked back, then realized it was a cord—the cord to Lexy's headphones. She pulled them out, then the CD player, then the CDs.

Hands trembling, she carried it all to the dining table. She'd completely forgotten about confiscating them on Thursday. When they'd left the house that day for lunch and grocery shopping, Lexy hadn't even noticed that they were missing from her backpack, and after the mugging...

After the mugging, she'd thought they'd been stolen.

Could this be what Adam Napier was after?

Hallie slid into a chair and examined the headphones and the player. She was no expert, but they appeared normal to her. Next she spread out the dozen cases. She was familiar with most of the artists by name only. Her tastes in music were vastly different from Lexy's…except for one.

She wasn't a big jazz fan, but Max had been, so she was more than familiar with Ella Fitzgerald. She couldn't imagine that Lexy had ever even heard of her, but that was Ella's face smiling up from the case. Hallie picked it up, turned it over and scanned the song titles, then opened it.

She didn't realize she was holding her breath until a burn started in her lungs. As she exhaled, she carefully removed the disc from the case, balancing it on one fingertip, and looked at it. It was bright, shiny silver, unblemished, and looked like about half the packaged CDs she'd seen before except for one detail—there was no label affixed to it. Nothing to identify that disc as having Ella's music on it.

Maybe Adam Napier had burned the disc himself and hadn't bothered to label it because he was the compulsive sort who returned a CD to its case the instant he was finished listening to it.

Or maybe it didn't hold Ella's music at all.

She put it in the CD player, slid the headphones into place and pressed the play button. Nothing happened. Oh, the lights came on in the display and the whirring sound indicated that the disc was spinning, but that was all. She checked the volume, pressed the skip button, stopped it, then started it again. Nothing.

After putting another CD in the player, she hit Play and music blared out. Once more she tried the unmarked CD, and once more nothing happened.

Why would a disc not play? she wondered as she returned it to its case. Given that the CD player and headphones were working just fine, she could think of only two reasons: because it had nothing recorded on it…or because it held data rather than music.

Data such as business records. Illicit business records.

That could explain going to so much trouble to steal a kid's backpack, then kidnapping the same kid.

She went to the phone just inside the kitchen door, dialed the first three digits of Brady's cell phone number, then stopped. She wasn't being petty, truly she wasn't, but she didn't want to talk to him, not yet. If she gave the disc to him, who knew what he might do next—what danger he might put himself in to save his daughter? And even though he was Lexy's father and the acting sheriff, Ryan Sandoval seemed to be in charge of the case.

She disconnected, then dialed the non-emergency number for the sheriff's department. The call was answered by a man with a scratchy voice who sounded as if he had an awful cold or had spent fifty years too many smoking. "This is Hallie Madison," she said calmly, coolly. "I need to get in touch with Deputy Sandoval right away about Lexy Marshall's kidnapping. It's urgent."

The man put her on hold, and she waited impatiently. She would tell Ryan what she'd found, make arrangements to deliver all the CDs to him, and then go from there to…wherever she decided to go. Tulsa seemed a good bet. She could hole up in a motel, but still be reachable by Dane Watson if anything came up regarding Neely's house, and be close enough to make a couple of trips. Then, once Neely got home next Saturday, she would give her a hug and a kiss and get the hell out of Oklahoma.

Even if the mere thought of it made her want to weep.

After what seemed like forever, Ryan came on the line, and she told him what she'd found. "I'll be there in five minutes to pick it up," he said, but she quickly spoke up.

"No. I've got to go out anyway. I'll bring it to the courthouse. I'll be there in a few minutes."

"We'll be waiting."

She stuffed the CDs and player in the shopping bag she'd gotten, then took another from the pantry and threw her shoes inside. Her arms filled with bags, she managed to get the door open, then froze.

There at the foot of the steps were Lexy, the two punks who'd burned down Brady's house and a third man.

I knew you were both trouble, Brady had said. If he were there, she would beg to differ with him. She knew trouble when she saw it, and right now it was standing on her steps.

In the form of Adam Napier.

Chapter 14

Acting on instinct, Hallie slammed and locked the door, dropped all the bags except the one with the CDs and made a mad dash for the back of the house. As the sounds of splintering wood filtered back to her, she pulled out the Ella CD, tossed the bag through her open bedroom door, then skidded into the kitchen. A small lip edged the top of the cabinets all the way around. She threw the disc up there, made certain it wasn't visible, then turned to the back door. Just as she reached it, it swung in and the tall, unremarkable man stepped inside, made oh, so much more memorable by the gun he was pointing at her. A moment later his shorter companion came racing down the hall.

"You should have better manners than to run out on your company before you even get introduced," the tall man said. "Let's go back with the others."

Her heart pounding, Hallie walked back down the hall ahead of them. When she reached the living room, Lexy flung herself into her arms. "Oh, Hallie, I was so afraid! I thought you'd come to get me, only it was *him* and he took me to this awful place way out in the country and—"

"It's okay, sweetie," Hallie murmured, patting her gently for a moment before holding her at arm's length for a quick look. The skin around the girl's wrists and her mouth was red and irritated—from duct tape, Hallie would bet—and her eyes were red, too, from a few tears. But there wasn't any sign that she'd been mistreated, beyond being bound and gagged.

Pulling her close again, Hallie hugged her hard. "I promise you, Lexy, it's going to be okay."

"Aren't you going to introduce us, Alessandra?" Napier asked.

Hallie gave him a scornful look. He was exactly as Ethan James had described him, though Ethan had left out handsome, with a smile as phony as a three-dollar bill. "I believe that can wait until the day I see you arraigned in court for kidnapping and breaking and entering."

"That isn't going to happen. But suit yourself." He gestured with his weapon. "Alessandra."

Lexy turned her fearful gaze on Hallie. "He wants my CDs. I told him they were in my backpack when those goobers stole it, but he says they weren't. Do you have them?"

"As a matter of fact, I do. I got tired of seeing you with headphones growing out of your ears. They're in my bedroom." She gently freed herself from Lexy's embrace and took two steps before finding both goobers' guns pointed her way. "Fine," she said with a shrug. "You find them."

"Go on, Jeff," Napier said. "While we wait, why don't you two sit down over there on the couch?"

Hallie pulled Lexy to the sofa, and they sat side by side on the third farthest from him. She was pleased that Lexy seemed to feel she offered some protection, but she had to nudge the girl to move over a few inches and give her room to breathe.

"Where's my dad?" Lexy whispered tearfully.

"He's out."

"Looking for me?"

"Yeah."

Lexy rubbed her nose with the back of her hand. "I sure wish he would come home."

Hallie didn't tell her that he probably would in the next few minutes—if not him, then Deputy Sandoval—looking for the same CD Napier wanted. She just hoped whoever came was observant enough to notice there were two Mercedes out there instead of one. But dusk had already fallen, and her car was parked in front of Brady's truck. Anyone could be forgiven for overlooking it.

"There's nothin' in here but clothes!" Jeff yelled from down the hall.

Hallie coolly looked at Napier. "He's in the wrong room."

Napier grimaced impatiently. "Aw, jeez, take him to the right room, Bud. This house isn't big enough to have more than two bedrooms. How difficult can it be?"

Bud disappeared, and a moment later came the sounds of dresser drawers opening and closing. Only a few minutes later, both men returned. "There's nothin' in that room at all," Jeff said. "The closet and the drawers are all empty."

Hallie gave Lexy a wide-eyed how-stupid-can-they-be look. "Did you look under the bed?" She'd given the bag a hard enough fling at a low enough angle that it should have slid right under the edge of the bed. "You know, Mr. Napier, if this is an example of the kind of help you hire, it's a wonder you can stay in business."

"I'm sorry to say you have a point, Ms. Madison." Then he gave her an oily smile. "See? We didn't need introductions after all. Our Alessandra likes to talk, doesn't she? She told me all about you, and apparently she's mentioned me to you."

"A time or two." Hallie glanced at her watch. She could have reached the courthouse by now if she'd been bunny-hopping on one foot. Surely Ryan was wondering what had happened to her.

Mutt and Jeff—er, Bud and Jeff came back carrying the bag. "Here it is," Jeff said, handing it over to his boss. "We found it."

"Found it?" Napier repeated. "Hell, she told you exactly where it was, and you still needed help." He dumped the bag out in the nearest easy chair, then sorted through the CDs.

In spite of her marriage to Max and rubbing elbows with the film community for years, Hallie had never had the slightest interest in acting. At that moment, though, she was praying to discover just a smidgen of talent somewhere deep inside, because any second now, Napier was going to discover that his CD was missing, and her and Lexy's lives might depend on how convincing her denial was.

"Where is it?" Napier came around the coffee table and jerked Hallie to her feet. "Where is the Ella Fitzgerald CD?"

"You're asking the wrong person. I don't listen to Ella." Though his fingers were biting into her arm, she pretended it didn't hurt and glanced at Lexy. "Do you listen to Ella?" She tried to sound surprised while at the same time just slightly shaking her head.

"I—I do," Lexy said, "but—but I don't have it w-with me. I didn't take any of your CDs."

"You lying brat. How do you explain the coincidence of my CD disappearing the same night you did? Who would you have me believe took it? Your mother? She wouldn't know good music if you piped it directly into her brain."

"I *didn't* take any of your CDs," Lexy repeated, a bit more agitated. "Why would I? I don't like that stuff you listen to!"

"It's just a CD," Hallie added. "They sell them everywhere. If Ella is that important to you, tell me which one it is, and I'll drive to Tulsa tonight and find another copy."

Napier's gaze settled on her face. His eyes were light brown, with enough hint of yellow in them to give them an unholy look. "This one has information on it, not music—information a lot of people would very much like to have. But I suspect you already know that, don't you?"

A chill went through Hallie. She didn't know much about being a hostage, but it seemed to her that the crook confessing anything to his hostage was a bad sign—like maybe he intended to kill them. Was Napier so evil that he could kill his own wife's daughter? Was he that desperate to protect his illegal activities and his freedom?

"I'm sorry to disappoint you, Mr. Napier, but we can't give you something we don't have."

"Oh, but you do have it."

"Lexy told you—"

"Alessandra is lying."

"I am not!" Lexy cried, sounding so sincere and distressed

that Hallie would have believed her if she hadn't known better. Unfortunately, Adam Napier seemed predisposed not to believe her.

"I'm not a foolish woman, Mr. Napier," Hallie said, her voice trembling. "I don't like being assaulted, and I really don't like being held at gunpoint in my own home. If I had what you're looking for, don't you think I would give it to you? Do you really think I'm stupid enough to stand here and *lie* to three armed men?"

He gave her a shove back onto the couch. Taking a seat on the arm of the easy chair, he studied them both, then slowly smiled. It reminded Hallie of a snake that had located its prey. After a time, he spoke to his thugs. "Get the girl."

Lexy clung to Hallie, but they were no match for the two men. Kicking the coffee table out of the way, they dragged her, struggling and cursing, into the center of the room. Once she was secured in the men's hold, Napier walked over, extended his arm and held his pistol mere inches from her forehead. "I don't think you're stupid at all, Ms. Madison. I think you're beginning to understand the lengths I would go to to retrieve my property."

"Hallie!" Lexy whispered as tears ran down her cheeks.

Hallie was horrified. "You would kill your own stepdaughter?"

"She's been nothing but a nuisance from the time I met her. Her mother and I will both be happier without her. In fact, it's probably fair to say that you're the only person who might miss her...provided you're alive to miss anyone."

What was it about Madisons and Marshalls? Only a few months earlier, Eddie Forbes had put a gun to Brady's head in order to persuade Neely to come out of Reese's safe room. Now it was Lexy's life on the line, and Hallie's decision to make.

But Neely had had a gun hidden in her pocket, and the cavalry, in the form of Jace Barnett, had been right outside the door. Hallie didn't have a weapon, wouldn't know how to use it if she did, and had no clue where the cavalry was.

She stood up, fingers laced tightly in front of her to keep them from shaking. "Okay. I'll make a deal with you."

"I'm not interested in deals. I've got the gun, the accomplices and the hostages."

"And I've got the CD."

For one interminable moment, the room was utterly still. Other than Lexy's sniffles and her own heart thudding double time, there was no other sound. Then, very slowly, Napier lowered the gun. "What's your deal?"

"You let Lexy go, and I'll give it to you."

"I have a better idea. You give it to me now, and I won't kill Alessandra."

"You just said you didn't think I was stupid, yet you expect me to believe that you'll let her walk out of here alive after you've got the CD?" Hallie shook her head. "She leaves first, and we watch her go. When she reaches the first intersection unharmed, I'll give you your property."

Napier considered it a moment, but he clearly wasn't wild about the idea. "What if we just go ahead and shoot her?"

Hallie's chest tightened until she could barely breathe. "Then you'll have to kill me, too."

"We can do that."

"Yes, but you'll never see the disc again, and I swear to God, her father will track you down and kill you."

"Aw, hell." Napier pulled Lexy away from the two men, then pushed her toward the door.

Lexy stumbled and caught herself, then turned toward Hallie. "I can't just leave you here!" she cried. "Please, Hallie, you can't…!"

Hallie smiled in spite of the tears burning her own eyes. "It's okay, sweetie. Go to the courthouse, all right?"

Lexy started toward her, no doubt for a hug, but Napier blocked her way. "Go on, get out of here, brat."

With Mutt and Jeff leading the way and Napier bringing up the rear, they moved as a group onto the porch. Hallie watched Lexy haltingly walk to the end of the driveway, where she looked back and lifted one hand in a forlorn wave. When she started toward town, she picked up her pace until she was running.

When she reached the intersection with Cedar, Hallie drew a

calming breath. Walking back into that house, knowing they would probably kill her, was the hardest thing she'd ever faced. But at least Lexy was safe, or would be in a few more minutes. And who knew? Maybe she would bring back Brady and his deputies in time to rescue Hallie, or heck, maybe she would find a way to rescue herself.

Unfortunately, she was fresh out of unarmed-untrained-heroine-saves-herself ideas.

But she'd saved Lexy. That was the most important thing.

Napier shepherded them back into the living room, then gave Hallie an expectant look. "I fulfilled my end of the bargain. Where's my disk?"

She remained motionless for a moment, then slowly led the way into the kitchen. "It's on top of the cabinets."

"Which one?"

"I don't know. I threw it. It's up there somewhere." She gestured toward the cabinets on the wrong side of the sink.

"Jeff, get the CD," Napier said sharply. "Bud, get my laptop."

As the tall one climbed onto the base cabinet, Bud returned to the living room. He came back with a black leather carrying case that Napier had obviously brought with him. Hallie hadn't even noticed it. But then, she'd been preoccupied with a few other things.

Napier removed the laptop from its case and booted it up while Jeff crabbed his way across the sink to the corner, then around so he could reach the disc. When he got it, he jumped to the floor with a loud thump and triumphantly handed it to his boss.

While she waited, Hallie strained to hear even the faintest hint of powerful engines, squealing tires, blaring sirens, but there was nothing. She wondered if she could get out the back door before one of them caught her, but she would have to get past Bud, and besides, how fast could she run in heels?

If this was one of Max's movies, supper would be cooking on the stove and she could throw a pot of boiling water on the men, wield a butcher knife against them and crack someone's skull with an iron skillet. But her countertops and stove were empty of weapons.

Napier was smiling when he removed the CD from the drive and shut down the computer. "Well, Ms. Madison, now you've lived up to your end of the bargain."

"And now you plan to kill me."

"Me? Oh, no. I don't do that sort of thing." He zipped the carrying case, then slid the strap over one shoulder. "I pay people to do it for me." As he started toward the hall door, he made a gesture to the men that she assumed meant, *Take care of her.* Both Bud and Jeff began closing in, the taller man wearing that slick grin again. He had just taken hold of her upper arm when she made one last desperate attempt to stall.

"Mr. Napier, what about another deal?"

He turned in the doorway. "What could you possibly have to offer? I've got my disc."

Hallie smiled as if she hadn't a care in the world. "How about the copy I made?"

"Something's wrong. She should have been here by now." Brady headed out the door of the sheriff's department and cut through the courthouse lobby to the rear entrance, with two deputies right behind him. "Come with me, Ryan," he commanded as he unlocked his SUV. "Mitch, follow us."

He never should have left Hallie alone at the house, but he couldn't have stayed there one more minute. He'd had to *do* something, to feel as if he were somehow helping in the search for Lexy. But he should have brought her with him, or taken her someplace safe. He shouldn't have left her alone.

Turning on the emergency lights, he accelerated out of the parking lot, then screeched to a halt when a slight figure darted out in front of him. "Lexy!" He jumped out of the truck, and she collapsed into his arms, sobbing. "Thank God you're all right! I've been so worried—"

She grabbed his shirt with both hands. "They've got Hallie, and they're gonna kill her! She made 'em let me go before she'd give 'em the CD, but when she gives it to 'em, they'll kill her! You have to stop them, Daddy, you have to save her!"

For one awful moment Brady couldn't think, couldn't speak, couldn't do anything but panic—and panic was one sure way to get Hallie killed. Then the moment passed and an icy, angry calm came over him, chilling him from the inside out. "How many men are there, Lex?"

"Th-three. Adam and th-those guys who set our house on fire."

"Are they all armed?"

She bobbed her head.

"Ryan, get on the radio. Have everyone meet us at the old Tucker place—no lights, no sirens. Mitch, take Lex inside and tell Harvey to take care of her, then come on down to the Tuckers'."

"I want to come with you!" Lexy wailed, clinging to him.

"It'll be okay, babe," he promised as he uncurled her fingers and Mitch pulled her away. "When we come back, we'll have Hallie with us." *Please, God!*

He climbed into the truck and pulled out of the parking lot. He was more grateful than he could put into words that Lexy was safe, but damn it, why did they have to drag Hallie into it? She didn't deserve to die, and God help him, he couldn't bear it if she did. There were so many things he hadn't told her, so many things they hadn't done. If he lost her now....

"What are we going to do?" Ryan asked when he got off the radio.

"Damned if I know." He dragged his fingers through his hair as the Tucker house came into sight. He switched off the emergency lights and slowed to a stop on the side of the road. "First we need to close the highway."

"I've already taken care of that."

Brady smiled mirthlessly. "Of course you have." Ryan was nothing if not efficient.

He rolled down the windows, then studied the house. It looked as if every light in the place was on, as well as the lone light outside by the driveway. There were two Mercedes in the drive, his own pickup and a fourth car, an older-model sedan. Three men, three guns.

He and Ryan had five between them. Unfortunately, he would

be shooting with his off hand, thanks to the cast, but he practiced for that. He was almost as good as with his right hand.

But was *almost* good enough when Hallie's life was at stake?

Mitch pulled in behind him, followed by Lucy, and, after Brady reached in back for his rifle, he and Ryan got out to meet them. "Lucy, let's see if we can find out what's going on inside."

"I'll go, Brady," Mitch volunteered.

Brady rested his hand on the deputy's shoulder. "I know you would...."

"But I'm a better shot than you are," Lucy finished for him.

Lucy's marksmanship was a large part of his decision, Brady admitted as they crossed the highway. But she was also older and more experienced. She'd never killed anyone before, but if she had to, he figured she could deal with it better than Mitch. He was a good deputy, but he was just twenty-one. Too young to deal with taking someone's life, no matter how necessary it was.

As they made their way through shadows to the property, Brady explained the layout of the house to Lucy. To minimize the risk of being seen from the living-room windows, they both went down the north side of the house. She lagged behind, meticulously checking each room. He went ahead, anxious to reach the south-facing living-room windows. Instinct told him that was where Napier and his thugs were holding Hallie.

He stumbled over a chunk of sandstone sticking up out of the ground and bumped one shoulder against the house. For one endless moment he remained frozen, but when no response came from inside, he continued toward the front of the house, ducking underneath the dining-room windows that spilled out yellow light, then easing up to the first living-room window.

Hallie sat on the edge of the chair seat, her fingers knotted together. She was pale and unsteady, and faint tremors shivered through her. Other than that, though, she appeared all right. They hadn't done anything to her...yet.

The bastard he'd caught in his house was standing a few feet behind her, a .9 mm pistol in his right hand, and the one who'd broken Brady's wrist was off to his side. He had a .45.

And then there was Adam Napier. In Brady's entire life, he'd only truly, violently hated two people—his parents. Now he could add Napier to the list. He stood near the front door, and on the table beside him was a laptop case, as well as a small handgun.

"Brady." Lucy whispered his name from a few feet away. With one last glance at Hallie, he moved back to meet her.

"The back door's open a few inches," she murmured in his ear. "If we could get a couple people inside...."

"Napier would see them," he whispered. "Unless..."

Abruptly he gestured for her to go back the way they'd come, and he followed. They moved swiftly and quietly back to the highway, where he outlined his plan for the officers gathered. Accompanied by Mitch and two other deputies, they returned to the house.

Brady stood in the shadow of an oak and watched as they moved silently to the back of the house. When the last deputy turned the corner, he crossed the yard to the steps, avoiding the creaky places, stopping in front of the door. After drawing a deep breath, he waited a few beats for Ryan to let Lucy know via radio that he was going in, then he opened the door and stepped inside. "Hey, darlin', I'm—"

Napier spun around so fast he almost fell, and the other two men immediately pointed their guns his way. Brady looked at each of the three men before letting his gaze settle on Hallie. "Looks like we have company," he said softly.

Napier snatched up the gun from the table and waved it. "Come in, Sheriff...or is it Deputy? Come in and join us. We were just debating the best way to determine whether Ms. Madison is being truthful with us. Jeff just wants to kill her and be done with it. Bud, though, has a taste for inflicting pain. I understand that's his handiwork." He gestured to the cast, then went on. "He insists if he had just a few minutes alone with her, he could find out. I understand you're quite the expert on torture. What do you think?"

From the corner of his eye, Brady saw Lucy and Mitch moving stealthily through the dining room. That meant the other two deputies were coming down the hall. He smiled coolly at Napier. "I think you'll be lucky to leave here alive."

"Really? There are three of us and only one of you, and we have your woman. You do have a weapon, but—oh, by the way, I'll take that now. Carefully."

Brady undid the thumb-snap strap that secured his pistol in the holster, then eased the gun out and handed it over. That was the deputies' signal to come into the room. They advanced quickly and had the two punks covered an instant before Napier noticed them.

Though he smiled, he couldn't hide the panic that flared in his eyes. "Well, this is interesting."

"Drop your weapons," Lucy ordered.

No one obeyed. No one even twitched a muscle.

"You see, they've got Bud and Jeff covered, but I've got *you* covered," Napier went on, centering his aim on Brady's chest. "Frankly, I couldn't care less what you do to Bud and Jeff. They're expendable. But I'd bet a million bucks that every one of those deputies cares a great deal about what happens to you, Sheriff. And you are, unfortunately, unarmed."

Brady slid his left hand behind his back and pulled out the .38 he'd borrowed from Ryan earlier. "Not necessarily," he murmured as he brought the muzzle up dead center on Napier's chest.

The bastard's panic flared again, and his Adam's apple bobbed as he swallowed convulsively. He managed another smile, though not nearly so smarmy or confident. "I believe this is what's called a standoff. If we don't shoot you, you won't shoot us."

Brady let his gaze slip to Hallie for one second. He thought of the terror these bastards had put her and Lexy through, of how carelessly they intended to destroy their lives—*his* life— and then he looked at Napier again. "I'm not sure that's exactly how it works," he said agreeably, then lowered his aim to about midthigh on the man and pulled the trigger.

Napier went down with a howl of pain, screaming curses as his pistol clattered to the floor, and Brady shifted his aim to the shorter of the two punks. "You want to be next?"

Apparently not, particularly after that *expendable* comment. They sullenly surrendered their weapons, and the deputies took them into custody.

Looking shaken and teary, Hallie stood up, took a few halting steps, then flew into his arms. Brady hugged her tightly, murmuring, "It's okay, darlin', it's okay," over and over.

When the trembling eased and her breathing returned to something close to normal, she raised her head. "Lexy?"

"She's safe."

"Thank God." Then she shuddered once more. "They were going to kill me."

"I know."

"You saved my life. Thank you." Rising onto her toes, she pressed a kiss to his jaw, then pulled out of his arms, waited for several deputies to enter, then walked out the door.

Bewildered by her behavior, Brady started to follow her, but Ryan caught his arm. "We need you in here. She's not going anywhere."

Grimly Brady nodded. But when he turned to follow the deputy into the dining room, his gaze fell on the luggage near the door. Hallie's luggage. She'd been packed and ready to leave before Napier had shown up. Where had she planned to go? When had she planned to tell him? And damn it, *why?*

He wanted to go outside and shake her until she told him— to kiss her senseless and make her change her mind. He wanted to hear her say it wasn't so, that she would *never* leave him.

But deep inside he already knew why. She hadn't wanted anything more than a fling. No relationship, no involvement, no risk of a broken heart. Just a temporary affair to help her get over her last divorce. And that was what she'd gotten.

He was the one with the broken heart.

Brady was in his office early Sunday morning—easy to do since he hadn't gone to bed the night before. It had been hours before the investigation at Hallie's house was wrapped up, and long before that, one of the deputies had delivered a message to him that Hallie was taking Lexy to the motel and getting a room. She hadn't bothered to tell him herself, hadn't said, Come over when you're done, or even Call me when you're done. Once everyone had cleared out, he'd spent the rest of the night sitting on the porch steps, wondering what the hell he could have possibly done to deserve losing her. Maybe this life was payback for the truly despicable person he'd been in a previous life—or five or six previous lives. Maybe God hated him. Or maybe he was just the damned unluckiest man in the world.

He'd been getting phone calls all morning—from the feds, newspapers both local and in Texas, and various other interested parties. A handful of feds were coming up from Texas and wanted to talk to Lexy and Hallie, and Brady wanted Ryan to interview them first. He'd started to call Hallie at the motel and ask her to come over, but the fear that that wouldn't be the question coming out of his mouth stopped him. He had little doubt if he heard her voice on the phone that his first words would be, "Why are you leaving me?"

Instead, he had the dispatcher call. They were due any minute…and no way was he ready to face her. So he was staying in his office, the door closed. Lexy was welcome to come back and see him, but right now he'd rather face anyone else in the world than Hallie.

The intercom buzzed, then the dispatcher said, "Someone here to see you, Brady."

"Is it Lex?"

"Uh, no." Wilda picked up the phone. "This is your…uh…her name is Napier. Mrs. Napier. Should I send her back?"

Sandra. Well, hell, she'd just proven him a liar. He'd much rather see Hallie than her. "No. I'll come up."

The walk from his office at the back to the lobby at the front seemed endless. By the time he got there, the muscles in his stomach were knotted and, he swore, he was about to break out in a cold sweat. Stopping at the front desk, he rested his hands on the countertop and faced her. "Sandra."

She turned from the window she'd been staring out, and he blinked. Funny. He'd always remembered her as being beautiful, but truth was, she didn't qualify as anything more than average.

Maybe it was the years; they didn't appear to have been kind. Or maybe it was just her true nature showing through.

Maybe he'd finally found out what true beauty was.

She came to the counter and laid her bag there. "Where is she?" Her words were clipped, cold and filled with anger. "Where's that incredibly stupid daughter of mine? I cannot believe the trouble she's caused this time. You know, we're going to sue you for assault and excessive force and kidnapping and anything else our lawyers can think of, and *she's* going to a school for troubled children. I won't have her living in Adam's home again after this mess she's made."

Brady stared at her. He shouldn't be surprised—God knows, he was well aware how petty and selfish she could be—but he couldn't help it. She didn't show the slightest concern for her daughter, less than the total strangers who'd helped search for her. He couldn't believe it.

"Well? Where is she?"

"Lexy will be here soon."

"Lexy." Sandra snorted. "Another stupid nickname. Hell, she can call herself Moron for all I care. She doesn't deserve my name, anyway."

"You do know your husband kidnapped your daughter yesterday and was going to kill her?"

"More of her lies," Sandra said, waving her hand in the air. "Alessan— She doesn't like Adam, and she's constantly causing trouble for him."

"There were witnesses, Sandra. One will be here soon, and two are locked up in jail."

"Liars, all of them. You know, she didn't have permission to come here. She stole money and Adam's business records, and she ran away. It took his investigators nearly a week to find her."

And then the trouble had started. "If she hadn't stolen the records, would he have bothered to send someone looking for her?"

"Probably not."

"Would you?"

"Probably not."

Her answer, and the callous way she said it, made Brady sick inside. "She's your daughter, Sandra. How can you not care that she was missing? That your husband was going to kill her?"

"What do you care? She's not *your* daughter."

"What do you mean?"

He swallowed a groan as he shifted his gaze from Sandra to the partially opened door. Lexy was standing there, wide-eyed and pale, staring from her mother to him then back again. Right behind her, Hallie looked as if she'd rather be anyplace else but here.

Lexy came into the room, circled wide around her mother and stopped near Brady. "What do you mean, I'm not his daughter? Of course I am. I'm a Marshall. His name is on my birth certificate. I have pictures. How could I not be his daughter?"

"Oh, for God's sake, shut up!" Sandra snapped. "I have more important things to deal with at the moment."

"No!" Lexy snapped back. "You brought it up, you deal with it! How could I not be his daughter?"

Sandra looked bored as she rolled her eyes, then heaved a sigh. "There's a chance," she said at last. "Not a very good one, but...a chance."

For a time everything was silent. Not even the radio made a sound. Then Lexy turned toward him, the tears welling up making her eyes look twice their size. "And you knew that all along, didn't you?" she whispered.

He nodded.

"That's why you left me with her. Why you never wrote or called or asked me to visit." She turned to Hallie. "Did you know, too?"

Finally Hallie came inside and let the door close. "Yes, sweetie. I'm sorry no one told you."

Lexy swiped at the tears dripping down her face. "Well, I guess that settles that," she said in a sad little voice. "I was gonna ask if maybe I could stay with you, but I wasn't sure you'd let me when I thought you were my dad, and now that I know you aren't—"

"You don't know that, babe," Brady said. Taking hold of her thin shoulder, he pulled her through the swinging gate and wrapped his arm around her. "Look, *I* was going to ask if you wanted to stay with me. You can go to school here and help me with the new house and do your room however you want...."

"But if you're not my dad—" Abruptly she looked up, her eyes brightening. "We could take a blood test or a DNA test and prove it—"

"Lexy, I don't need a test to prove it. You're my daughter, and no test is going to change that."

Her lower lip started trembling. "Really? You don't wanna know for sure?"

"It wouldn't change the way I feel." Brady swallowed hard, tried to forget that they had an audience and forced out words he hadn't said in fourteen years. Oddly enough—or maybe it was fitting—the last time he'd said them had been to the same person. "I love you, Lexy, and I want you here with me."

Grinning through her tears, Lexy hugged him tightly. "That is so cool! I love you, too, and I'd love to live here—just you, me and Hallie. That's so cool!"

"And it's not going to happen," Sandra said coldly. "You're not her father. You have no legal claim to her."

Brady's muscles clenched at Lexy's assumption that Hallie was going to stick around, but he ignored it as he faced his ex-wife. "Your husband is a drug dealer who's going to prison soon for a very long time. He kidnapped your daughter and threatened to kill her. He would have killed Hallie if we hadn't stopped him. On top of that, as Lexy just mentioned, my name is on her birth certificate, and I've paid child support for fourteen years. *And,* seeing that she is fourteen, any judge in the country is going to ask *her* where she wants to live."

"And I'll tell him with my dad," Lexy added triumphantly.

"How stupid can you be, Alessan—whatever?" Sandra spat out. "Do you think he really wants you? Do you think *anyone* really wants you?"

Hurt flared in Lexy's eyes for a moment, then disappeared. "Yep," she said smugly. "My dad does. And Hallie adores me."

Hallie smiled at her and gave her a wink, then looked away before her gaze reached Brady. He wondered what it would take to make her look at him, and how much more it would take to make her stay with him.

Sandra swore. ''You'll stay here over my dead body.''

Hallie couldn't stand it anymore. She was already edgy enough, because she'd come here with the intention of confronting Brady about their relationship—starting with telling him she loved him whether he wanted her to or not—and finding his ex-wife there hadn't helped any. Still, she'd stayed as quiet as she could, but enough was enough. ''That can be arranged,'' she said quietly.

''And who the hell are you?''

''The woman who's going to smack you if you say one more unkind thing to or about that child.''

''And I'll have you arrested for assault!''

''Try it,'' Hallie replied, smiling sweetly. ''The sheriff in this county is my brother-in-law. I sleep with the undersheriff, and I know a number of the deputies. Let's see who they're more interested in protecting—you or me.''

Sandra looked at each of them with venom in her eyes. ''You people are going to be so damn sorry when I get finished with you. I'll be back tomorrow with my attorneys to pick up my daughter.'' Grabbing her bag from the counter, she swept out of the room, and Hallie would have sworn that suddenly the air was lighter and smelled sweeter.

''I'll be right back,'' she said, then ducked out after Sandra. She still had plenty to say to Brady, but it would wait while she took care of this one detail. Catching up with Sandra halfway to the curb, she spoke her name.

''What do you want?''

''To make a deal. Your husband's going to prison, probably for the rest of his life, and the government is going to seize every asset he's got. That means you'll be left alone with *nothing*.''

Fear darkened the woman's eyes. So she could worry about being penniless, but not about her own child's safety. How in the world had Brady ever fallen in love with such a heartless witch?

''So what's your deal?''

"If Brady sues for custody of Lexy, you and I both know he'll get it. He's respected and admired, he holds a position of authority, and he clearly loves Lexy and is happy to have her, while you'll never convince anyone you're a loving mother or that you've provided your daughter with a healthy home environment. And with Adam going to prison, you're going to be getting a divorce and looking for husband number six. You won't have time for Lexy."

"So…?"

"How much support does Brady pay?"

"Five hundred a month."

"Six thousand a year. And that stops when Lexy turns eighteen?"

Sandra nodded.

"Four more years—that would be twenty-four thousand dollars." Hallie hesitated a moment, then flatly went on. "I'll give you double that—make it an even fifty grand—if you'll terminate your parental rights and let Brady have her, free and clear."

"Why would you do that?" Sandra asked suspiciously.

Because she loved them both and was hoping—praying—that after she talked to him this morning, she would have at least a chance at living the rest of her life with them. Of course she couldn't give that answer to his ex-wife, of all people. "Because they're family, and people like you shouldn't be allowed to screw up families like theirs. It's your choice. You can go through a court battle, lose Lexy anyway and have nothing to show for it, or you can relinquish your rights and walk away with fifty thousand dollars in your pocket."

The woman stared off into the distance for a long moment, then curtly asked, "Where can I reach you?"

Hallie pulled a pen and a scrap of paper from her purse and wrote Neely's cell phone number on it. "Don't take too long. I might decide I'd rather use that money to hire the best damn lawyers in the country to take you on."

Sandra tucked the paper in her purse and stalked off to her car.

Tilting her face to the sky, Hallie closed her eyes and let the sun's heat seep into her. She'd been so very cold ever since

Lexy had disappeared, and she wasn't sure she would ever get completely warm again. But when she turned to go back inside and saw Brady standing on the steps, watching her, suddenly she felt much too warm. She covered the distance between them, stopping a few feet away.

His first question echoed Sandra's. "Why would you do that?"

"I have to do something with Max's money." She gazed at him, getting lost in his incredible blue eyes, before she realized he was waiting for her to go on. She drew a deep breath of air so hot it could sear her lungs, then blew it out. "I've come to the conclusion that I'm good for something, after all."

"I can think of a number of things you're very good for," he said, then one corner of his mouth quirked up. "What's your conclusion?"

"Negotiating. I made a deal with Napier last night that set Lexy free, and I made another that delayed his killing me long enough for you to get there. And Sandra's going to accept my offer. There's no way she won't."

"Feeling pretty confident this morning, huh?"

"Hey, Lexy and I are alive and well, and her future's looking pretty good. I'm Superwoman. So now I want to make a deal with you." She'd lain awake all last night, listening to the air conditioner and Lexy's snoring and wondering why the powers that be had named her Queen of Broken Hearts. All she wanted was someone to love who loved her back, a family, a home, a cherished husband to grow old with. Other women had them. Why couldn't she?

Instead, she kept falling for men who found it so easy to make the switch from wanting her to not wanting her. When Brady had said that *he* didn't want her, it had broken her heart. But about five o'clock this morning, she'd realized something important—he hadn't said, I *don't* want you. As in present tense, now, *get out of my life.*

He'd said, I *didn't* want you. In the past. And that was no secret. He'd been satisfied with his quiet life before she and Lexy had come along. He'd been up-front about the fact that he didn't want any relationships. He'd just found himself in the position of not having much say in the matter. Lexy was forced on him, and her presence in his life required Hallie's. He hadn't wanted either of them there, but he'd been stuck with them, and they'd grown on him.

Hey, love at first sight was a wonderfully romantic thing, but she'd settle for it any way she could get it.

"All right," Brady said, his words quiet, his gaze intent. "I'll give you anything you want. Just…please…don't leave me."

The intensity of his plea boosted her confidence about a hundred percent. She closed the distance between them, and he backed away until the stone wall stopped him. She didn't stop until there was no place else to go, until she'd thoroughly invaded his personal space. Funny. He didn't seem to mind at all. "Don't agree to the deal until you hear my terms."

"I don't care about the terms. The answer's yes."

"I'm warning you—this will be an iron-clad agreement. The only way out of it will be death."

He touched her for the first time in too long, brushing a strand of hair behind her ear. "Sounds like what I'm looking for."

"I have expectations," she murmured, leaning so close that her lips brushed his jaw.

"I told you weeks ago you should." He slid his arms around her waist, then kissed her gently, sweetly—nothing too passionate. Just a little encouragement to go on.

Hallie got serious. "I want to stay in Buffalo Plains. I want to be a part of your life and Lexy's life. I want strings, a commitment, a future. I know it wasn't supposed to turn out like this. I know it was supposed to be temporary, and I tried to keep my emotions in check, but—"

He was smiling so tenderly at her that she lost her train of thought. "What?" she prompted.

"Do you have any idea how much I love you?"

The air rushed from Hallie's lungs, and her stomach gave a funny lurch. "I think almost as much as I love you."

"So back to the deal…." He brushed a kiss across her jaw, then nuzzled her hair back from her ear. "I have a few terms of my own."

"All right. Anything you want."

"Don't you want to hear them?"

"Do they involve you, me and Lexy living happily ever after?"

"Absolutely."

"Then that's all I need to know." Rising onto her toes, she kissed him possessively, greedily, and he kissed her back the same way. When they were both breathless, aroused and weak, they ended the kiss and for one sweet moment, he simply held her. In his arms was the best place in the world to be.

"Hey, Brady," she murmured after a while. "You know all those labels my family hangs on me? The ditzy one, the flighty one, the one who could never do anything right?"

"Stupid labels."

"And wrong. You know which sister I really am?"

He gave her another of those tender smiles that warmed her all the way to her toes. "Besides the beautiful one? The one Lexy and I love? The one who gives my life life?"

"Besides all those." She grinned with delight. "I'm the *lucky* one. I have you."

And that made her the luckiest woman in the world.

Epilogue

On a sunny September afternoon, Lexy walked out of the courthouse with Brady and Hallie, just as she'd done a dozen times before, but this time was different. Oh, not on the outside—nothing obvious—but inside…inside she felt like a whole new person.

Brady had always been her legal father—whether he really was or not, having his name on her birth certificate made it so. But as of fifteen minutes ago, Sandra was no longer her mother. Now she was the legal child of Hallie Madison Marshall. Now she had two parents who loved her and worried about her, when only three months ago she hadn't had any. That was too cool for words.

She wasn't supposed to know that Hallie had paid Sandra a bunch of money so Lexy could live with Brady. She guessed they thought it would hurt her feelings to know her mother had basically sold her, but she'd been so happy to be with her dad and Hallie she hadn't cared *how* they managed it. Then when Hallie had said she wanted to adopt her…. Too cool.

She loved living in Buffalo Plains. She liked the school, and she'd made some good friends, and she even got along with her teachers. And she liked watching her dad and Hallie together. They were really sappy sometimes—grown adults laughing and making out all the time like kids. Her friends giggled and said stuff like, How embarrassing, but Lexy knew better. Someday some guy was going to fall in love with her, and they were going to laugh and neck all the time, too. They were going to be happy, and she was living with the happiest people she'd ever seen, so she would know a lot about it by the time she got married.

"You're falling behind, Lex," her dad called, and she hurried to catch up with them. They had asked her what she wanted to do to celebrate the adoption, and she'd had one answer—get a family portrait. She had pictures of her and Brady when she was a baby, and Hallie took tons of pictures of both of them, but since she was taking them, she wasn't *in* them. Lexy wanted a portrait of the three of them on the day they officially, legally became an honest-to-God family.

The photographer's studio was across the street from the SteakOut, where they were going for dinner tonight. Lots of people were coming—Neely and Reese, Lucy, Deputy Mitch, Deputy Sandoval, her friends from school. Even Hallie's sister, Bailey, was flying in from Memphis. She'd wanted to be there for the granting of the petition, but work had made her change her flight. Lexy was really looking forward to seeing her, because Bailey was in the business of finding lost people, and now that Lexy had all these aunts by adoption, there was this uncle by birth that she wanted to find.

When they reached the studio, her dad held the door, then followed them inside. The lady at the desk told them to sit down, so they did, with Hallie in the middle. Digging in her purse, Lexy pulled out a not-too-neatly wrapped box, then twisted sideways on her chair to face Hallie. "I, uh…I wanted to get you… Here."

"Oh, Lexy." Hallie hugged her, then tore off the paper, opened the box and laughed.

Lexy's face turned pink and a lump rose in her throat. "You—you don't have to wear it."

"Oh, no, babe, I love it. It's just—" Holding up one finger

for her to wait, Hallie pulled the same size box wrapped in beautiful blue paper from her purse and handed it to her.

Inside Lexy found the same pendant—an outline in sterling silver of a mother and daughter that formed a heart where they joined. Sniffling, she ducked her head, swiped at her eyes, then asked, "Can we wear them for the pictures?"

"I think that would be great. Thank you so much, sweetie."

Hallie put Lexy's on while Brady put Hallie's on. They'd just finished when the photographer came to take them back. He moved them around, tugged at their clothes, told them where to look and when to smile. Keeping her smile pasted in place, Lexy said through clenched teeth, "Hallie, can I call you Mom?"

The flash went off, then Hallie tearfully said, "I would like that very much."

Still smiling, Lexy asked, "Hey, Dad, if I ran away, would you come after me?"

"With handcuffs and leg irons, darlin'," he replied as the flash went off again.

"Good. I just wanted to be sure."

The next question came from Hallie. "Do you think this might be a good time to tell you guys I'm pregnant?"

The flash blinded Lexy, but she managed to hug both her parents before the photographer moved them around again. That was so cool—she had her dad, who loved her even if maybe he wasn't really her dad; a new mom who loved her like her old mom never had; and sometime next year she would have a new brother or sister.

She was the luckiest kid in the whole world.

But these pictures were going to suck.

* * * * *

CODE NAME: DANGER

The action continues with the men—and women—of the Omega Agency in Merline Lovelace's *Code Name: Danger* series.

This August, in TEXAS HERO (IM #1165) a renegade is assigned to guard his former love, a historian whose controversial theories are making her sorely in need of protection. But who's going to protect *him*—from her? A couple struggles with their past as they hope for a future....

And coming soon, more *Code Name: Danger* stories from Merline Lovelace....

Code Name: Danger Because love is a risky business...

 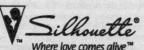

 Silhouette®

COMING NEXT MONTH

INTIMATE MOMENTS

#1165 TEXAS HERO—Merline Lovelace
Code Name: Danger

When forensic historian Elena Maria Alazar was called in to examine the remains discovered outside San Antonio, she dug up more than Texas history. Ellie uncovered a murder plot—and she was the next target. Then ex-marine—and ex-lover—Jack Carstairs became her bodyguard, and Ellie realized her heart might be in as much danger as her life!

#1166 SECRETS OF A PREGNANT PRINCESS—Carla Cassidy
Romancing the Crown

Princess Samira Kamal thought she'd found true love when she became pregnant after her first royal affair. But when Samira shared the news, her nobleman wasn't so noble after all. Fortunately, Farid Nasir, Samira's loyal bodyguard, offered to marry her to protect the family name. Samira didn't want to give up on love, but judging by the possessive look in her new husband's eyes, maybe she wouldn't have to....

#1167 M.D. MOST WANTED—Marie Ferrarella
The Bachelors of Blair Memorial

All London Merriweather wanted was a few minutes away from the bodyguard hired to protect her from a stalker. What she got was a stay in the hospital under the watchful eyes of handsome Dr. Reese Bendenetti. As emotions grew, London's stalker moved ever closer. Would the devoted doctor be able to cure London's dangerous situation?

#1168 LOVE UNDER FIRE—Frances Housden

An unusual arson case brought ex-cop Rowan McQuaid back home to Nicks Landing and reunited him with his former partner, Jo Jellic. As the arson case turned into a murder investigation with ties to a satanic cult, Jo and Rowan's professional relationship turned personal. Jo had once cost Rowan his career. Now would she cost him his heart, as well?

#1169 SHADOWING SHAHNA—Laurey Bright

Kier Reminton was on a mission to find Shahna Reeves, the woman he had loved and lost. After nearly two years he finally found her...and her eleven-month-old son. Unwilling to lose Shahna again, Kier was determined to marry her and claim his son. But there was something Kier didn't know, and Shahna feared what would happen once he learned the truth.

#1170 WHEN NIGHT FALLS—Jenna Mills

Since his wife's murder, Liam Armstrong had lived under a cloud of suspicion. When his daughter, Emily, suddenly vanished, Liam was forced to turn to detective Jessica Clark, daughter of the officer who had tried to ruin him. Jessica was fiercely attracted to this mysterious man, but unless she kept her mind on work, a little girl's life could be the price.

SIMCNM0702